THE RUNAWAY OFFERING

ALYTHIA CONNER

For my papou, Nicias—the
voyager, the questioner, the
cloth from which I was cut.
You should know I kept my
promise: I still look for you in
the eastern stars.

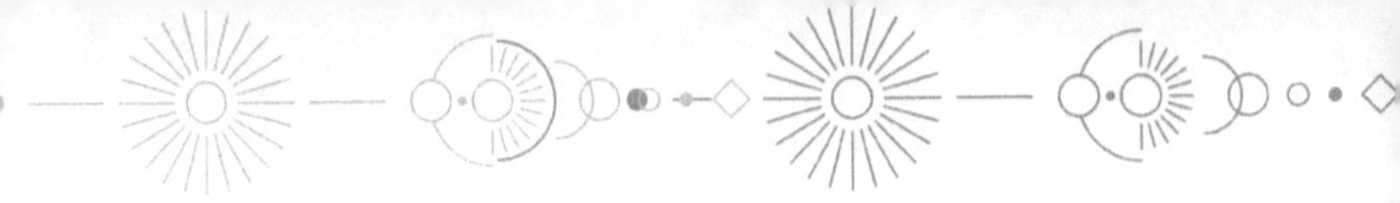

Chapter One

Honoring the Sun God

I danced barefoot in the village square with the other maidens, waving a palm leaf over my head as red sand flicked into the hot air and bells jingled around my ankles.

There was much to celebrate. My best friend, Lileena, was to be sacrificed—a quick death on a stone altar before she would rise to live as a demi-goddess beside Waikenu, the sun god.

My body knew the ceremonial steps by heart, but deep inside, I wanted to scream and cry and curse the day and everything it was sure to bring.

Sunset approached in the desert. Buttery orange and pink shot across an endless blue sky as every villager from Bahmisi gathered to place their personal offering at the base of Moruka Temple. They piled bountiful portions of nuts, dried meat and fruit, and palm leaves to pay homage.

Sacrifice was an honor given to only the most worthy, and the women had spent days preparing every inch of Lileena's body for the transformation. Every time I saw her, she could barely keep from grinning.

As for me, I hadn't spoken since I heard the news. I wasn't sure why. My dearest friend would ascend to the highest rank in the afterlife and become a demi-goddess. Her mother would be treated as nobility and want for nothing ever again. When we were little, we'd taken turns as the make-believe offering, and everyone in the village had grown up knowing that to die was to live forever.

But for the last five nights, I'd wept bitterly into my pillow.

I didn't dare tell a soul about my sadness. They would think it unholy and wicked, and High Priest Vikton would have me punished and sent away like that one man who once refused to surrender his son for sacrifice. No one heard from either of them ever again.

At first, Lileena and I had quarreled. She thought I was jealous. And at first, I thought I was, too. Now that the day had arrived, all I felt was a rock in the pit of my stomach. I didn't envy her as I had so many other offerings who were sacrificed yearly during the spring equinox.

I spotted Kea glaring at me from the corner of my eye as we danced with the other girls our age. "Akedia, you're going to mess everyone up! You're barely dragging your palm around on the ground."

Kea was one of the tallest girls in the village, which made the matchmakers go on and on about her *childbearing abilities*, but I'd punched her in the throat the last time she tested me, and I wasn't afraid to do it again. I was about to throw the stupid leaf at her and tell her to do it herself if her one undying talent was to wave things back and forth in the air when I caught a glimpse of Lileena and the group of handmaidens and holymen who would accompany her to the altar walking between buildings in the village. They were leading her to a private chamber where she could pray alone for the last time.

I had to see her.

"I'll be right back," I said to Kea over the noise of the wailing instruments and pounding drums, before shoving my palm leaf into her arms and darting away.

She snarled something nasty at me but didn't follow, and I scurried around the side of our community's mud-brick Moruka Temple. The structure's base consumed a great portion of Bahmisi's soil and towered toward the gods with a set of stairs etched into its side. Some of the village's finest artists had carved pictures in the walls depicting the spring sacrifices, along with Waikenu's might, fury, and mercy.

I slipped into an open back door with long curtains to find Lileena inside, pampering her skin with loose powder as she sat before a looking glass. She gasped and stood when I entered. I could only stare at her in astonishment. Someone had painted intricate cactus lilies around her temples and lined her green eyes in black kohl. They had lathered her olive skin with something that shimmered gold in the candlelight. Her black hair gleamed with rich perfumed oils, and a string of fire opals set in gold hung from her neck. She looked like the demi-goddess she hoped to become.

At first, we let discomfort capture the moment and render it useless with silence. Our fight lingered in the air between us—almost threatening to push me back out the door—but our sisterhood smothered it. Fresh tears pool into my eyes. I rushed to her and wrapped my arms around her waist.

"Oh, Akedia," she said with surprise, stroking my hair. "What's gotten into you?" I shook my head, afraid to look her in the eyes. "Is it our fight?" Her gentle hand paused, and she lifted my chin. "I'm sorry. I am. I know you're not jealous of me. You've loved me as only a sister can."

Tears blurred my vision, and I dragged them away from my cheeks with the back of my hand. "It's not that, Lileena. I'm going to miss you so much."

"Miss me? How could you possibly miss me when I'm going to watch over you from the heavens?" She pulled me by the hand to take a seat on a finely woven vanity chair.

"Because what if..."

What if we snuck out the back door instead?

What if my heart never heals from losing you this way if we don't?

What if... What if this... is all wrong?

The kohl around Lileena's green eyes creased when she smiled at me, and I knew then—seeing her beam with joy on the day of her sacrifice—that I couldn't shatter that and send her to death with fear. Fire churned in my gut, like a serpent rearing its head from the earth before disappearing again. How could any child of good faith entertain such thoughts?

I smiled weakly. "What if I can't remember the prayer you taught me?"

"There you go, thinking again," she said, laughing. "I wrote it down for you, remember?"

Of course, I had remembered. And I felt bad for lying to my best friend on her last day breathing air as a mortal, but I couldn't share my true thoughts. There was no changing her mind, and even if I could, there was no changing her fate.

The curtains flew open, and a man filled the door frame with billowing deep-purple robes, a jewel-studded black head cloth, and an all-consuming presence. High Priest Vikton. His short black beard was flecked with gray hairs and came to a point at the end, a sharp angle to match the other sharp features of his face.

"Your Eminence!" Lileena exclaimed, dropping to the floor to bow before him.

I followed her lead, though probably a half second too late. When we stood, the high priest shot me a fierce look with amber eyes lined with thick black lashes and kohl.

"Lileena, you are to become a demi-goddess, my dear child," he said, cooing to her. "You no longer need to bow before such a lowly priest as myself."

However, Akedia, you may keep groveling, I thought bitterly, catching myself off guard with my own cynicism. Maybe I was a *little* jealous of Lileena's new status.

The high priest lifted a jar from the vanity and powdered his skin with the contents as he spoke. "You're going to be a little nervous, of course. Just try to stay calm and think only of the transition into the afterlife." He resealed the powder lid and looked between us both, only glimpsing at me as if I were some statue in the room. Ever since I could remember, this man never acknowledged my existence unless I had done something wrong. Even then, he never seemed to remember my name.

His thin lips formed a smile that didn't seem natural on his sharp face, especially since his amber eyes remained trained on Lileena the way the desert fox watches the rabbit. "Finish up and meet me outside the door. I will take you up the stairwell to the top of the offering tower."

Lileena took a deep breath, nodded and smiled, clutching my hand as he left the room. This time I pulled her into a hug that felt different than any other hug I'd ever given her. I was saying goodbye, because it was goodbye, regardless of what she believed.

What I should believe, I thought.

"I love you, dear sister," I told her when I pulled away to look in her eyes. Then I dug for something from a hidden pocket on my chiton. It was a bracelet I'd made by spinning goat hair into a thin length of cord, dyeing the fiber a variety of colors, and then tying tiny knots into a pattern. I secured it around her left wrist. "I know you shouldn't be wearing this to the offering table, but I wanted you to have something from me on your last day... as a mortal."

Still giddy with excitement, she pulled me into the hug once more and squeezed my neck a little too hard. "It's beautiful, Akedia. I will love you always."

After she finally pulled away and waved before she left the room, I watched her follow the high priest up the passageway that would lead them to the top of Moruka Temple, where the light first touches our village each morning. The offerings were sacrificed over a circular stone with engravings at the top. I was supposed to go back to waving my palm leaf around in celebration with the other maidens. Instead, I ran out the back door and away from the massive festival.

Lileena was going to lose her head. It was said that her body would dissipate and ascend on high to serve the sun god. But when I heard a sickening thwack in the distance,

Chapter Two

The Next Offering

N early two full moons had passed since Lileena had willingly climbed the altar to her death, and I had to make up a host of reasons to explain my sour mood. Everyone in the village celebrated for weeks after a new sacrifice, because we had pleased the sun god and ensured He would part the sky for our crops to grow. This tradition had become necessary in the past twenty rains as the sun god ordains—as time is calculated in Bahmisi along with the yearly storms. It was when High Priest Vikton saved our village from famine by helping us see the error in our interpretation of holy scripture. The sun god required human blood. And so the sacrifices began just a year before my birth.

During the celebratory weeks, people would say, *Blessings on your home* and the return reply was, *Blessings on your harvest.* But I could scarcely force a smile, and I didn't understand it myself. She had gone on to become a demi-goddess, a dream come true for any girl.

My mother made generous comments about my womanly wave of temperament rearing its head more than usual in those two months as I went from one menial household task to another with a scowl, but I couldn't pretend that was the issue. I had hung my menses cloths on the line to dry two weeks ago and not again since. That time had clearly passed, and the lie only worked for so long.

Finally, it was my father who brought me into his study chambers and kissed my brow.

"My girl, what troubles you?" he asked, stroking the long salt and pepper beard that framed his rugged face. His matching hair, still thick despite his years, protruded from the sides of the evening cap he wore at home.

I draped my long black locks over one shoulder and twirled the ends like I always did when I was nervous. He knew this habit of mine well, so I flung my hair into its usual place, cascading down my back.

"I think, it's just..." I searched the room for a distraction, but everything fell flat. B'Ba watched me with a strange twinkle in his black eyes. Could I take a chance? The last time I'd shown defiance, the high priest ordered his right-hand man, Nevario, to place me in the *box of learning*, a small punishment prison with barely enough room to sit upright. I'd received two full days once for asking why we didn't eat grains before temple days. But this was my father. I trusted him with my whole self. "I didn't feel right before they killed—*offered*—Lileena to Waikenu. I don't know why, but I just didn't feel right."

B'Ba nodded and paced in his slow methodical way, before turning back to me. "It is hard to believe in something that we do not see," he said. "When we can't see the loved ones who have moved on to serve the sun god, it's difficult for us simple mortals to understand they are still here. This is a natural concern, sweet one. It will pass."

His light brown skin crinkled as he smiled at me, and for the first time since I'd parted with the friend who was more like a sister, I felt a jolt of warmth paired with the deepest melancholy I'd ever known.

"B'Ba... I..." I cleared my throat, hoping I wouldn't sob, hoping he wouldn't notice I was on the verge.

He was my father. He knew me like only the gods who had stitched me together piece by piece.

"The goats need bringing in." He patted my hand and adjusted the tunic cloth draped over his shoulder before winking at me. "You'll be needing that fresh air."

I grinned, grabbed my satchel, and flew out the door before screeching to a halt to turn and kiss B'Ba's cheek. He never let me tend the goats, since it was considered a boy's work, and my parents had already employed Mikah, a young shepherd, to tend our herd while he watched his family's own. But B'Ba knew how much I loved to run free in the canyon, splashing in the river where the animals drank. And I loved our goats like pets, even though some people thought it was silly.

They are meat and milk, Akedia, M'Ma had said more than once, but she never quite understood me. She was a perfect desert flower bride, as some would say—dark, beautiful, charming, long and lean, not one to challenge the way things were. She did not change, she did not grow. She simply maintained her home and cared for her husband and side-eyed me often.

I grabbed my satchel that hung on a peg on our clay walls and scurried out the door before M'Ma could intervene and task me with a chore meant to sharpen my future wife and motherhood skills.

The endless sky was a brilliant blue hovering over our village of orange clay homes with reed-thatched roofs. It was said the founders of Bahmisi had discovered this little oasis in the desert over four hundred rains ago, in a time when writers who compiled spellbooks frequently noted methods to keep the long-fanged big cats from killing their livestock. The nearby river gave life to palms and cacti that gave us nutrients when harvest was scarce. Beyond our little commune, there was nothing but a sea of burning sands. At least, as far as we could see.

High Priest Vikton had once claimed there was no other life beyond our own, until travelers—travelers who spoke of other people in far-off lands—came to town and disproved the statement. He then said he had meant it in a *figurative* sense, but come to think of it, we never encountered visitors again. Perhaps it had something to do with the men on horseback posted atop the highest dunes, equipped with large swords, bows, and arrows. They were also the ones who kept people from leaving... It was for our own safety, though. Out in the tireless sun, there is only sin and burning fire. That is what I was told. It must be so.

I made my way down the goat trail that led out of town. Plumes of tall grass that grew wild in patches of sand waved in the breeze on either side of the path, which zigzagged down the side of a cliff. At the very top, I took a moment to breathe in the scenery. Behind me were the clusters of mud and sand homes packed together to form a village in the middle of nowhere, and before me, a sparkling river snaked through a canyon where the water had given life to a belt of green plants. I spotted dots of color in the vegetation along the riverbank and immediately recognized our pure black buck charging another male with his long, curved horns.

Tik. He was a grumpy old thing.

The herd was fifty heads strong this year, and since the offering season took place in the spring, the single death was paired with many births. I trotted down the hillside until I was level with the grazing animals. Our herd alone had twenty new kids, running around and bleating like human babes. The sight of them swarming around me with wagging tails as I neared made me laugh.

Cool wind from the river fanned my face. It was a shame this was the job of a young boy. Girls had the same needs—to escape the daily chitchat of the village and find companionship with animals and a bit of fresh air. I was certain, too, that some boys desired indoor time to craft the artwork that many simply called blankets or baskets. The rigidity of our roles left much to be desired.

Mikah approached and leaned on his staff. His large curls were still soft like a baby's. Soon they would become the tight ringlets I'd seen on his father's head.

"Do your parents have a message for me?" he asked. It was always so uncomfortable with Mikah. He was twelve—too young to speak frankly with, yet too old to coddle—and our age difference was altogether too large and small all at once.

"You are relieved of your duties to our family for today. Thank you," I said, wondering if I needed to be more professional or casual.

He didn't mind one way or the other, it seemed, as he shrugged and walked away, back to his herd and probably relieved that he could separate the fighting bucks.

Tik trotted over to me and bumped the side of his body against my legs, nearly knocking me over. His musky male scent was almost too much to bear, but I loved him enough to not care.

"Hey!" I said, laughing. Then I scratched his rump, which I knew was what he wanted all along. "You are a silly beast."

I gave the goats gathered around me scratches behind their ears and grazed my hand over their backs to check for ticks. We gave them a homemade remedy each season—a concoction that called for a pinch of magic and a hefty serving of garlic—but sometimes the little pests were immune. The spells weren't as strong as the garlic, and the garlic wasn't strong enough anymore.

As I searched for ticks on a brown goat, I heard a nanny wail in dismay. It was one of the nursing mothers, and her kid was nowhere to be seen.

"It's going to be alright, girl," I said, taking her by the head before I ran two soothing hands down her back.

If it calmed her at all, it only took the edge off her anxiety, because she paced through the herd, searching for her lost one and bumping other goats who turned their heads with irritation before returning to nibble their patch of grass. I couldn't bear to watch her frantic eyes searching for her baby. Mikah was a good distance away with his herd, but I knew if I shouted, my voice would echo to his ears.

"Mikah!" I hollered, and when his head looked around, I waved my arms to get his attention. "Will you watch the herd? I have to find a lost kid!"

He nodded and issued his signature whistle, the one only the goats who were meant to follow him would heed. Honing a distinct whistle made it easier for the boys to separate their herds after a day of grazing.

My goats ran off, though the nanny lingered behind, torn. Her kid had wandered off somewhere around here, and she wasn't keen to leave without her. Once again, I clutched her face and gazed into her eyes.

"I will find her," I whispered. And when Mikah whistled again, the nanny followed the departing herd.

The only problem was I liked to play at being a goat herder, but I knew I wasn't one. With the animals in Mikah's care, I was too afraid to admit I didn't have the faintest clue where to begin my search. I had no plans to ask *him* for advice, either.

I held two fingers to my temple and closed my eyes, trying to tap into the sense the way the village mage, Matka, had tried to show me. Magic was a holy tie that honored Waikenu. In magic, Matka had often said, your soul is lifted higher to where the gods dwell. Thinking only of the lost kid, a flicker of sight pooled into my vision, and I saw it, prancing from rock to rock downstream. I couldn't hold the image for long—fear that I would mess up and lose it was enough to make it fizzle.

But I'd seen the kid. Was she... outside Bahmisi?

No one went outside Bahmisi.

Spinning around to search for the high priest's men, I scanned the towering dunes and cliffs where they usually stood watch. They were probably on break, and my location beside the river was hard to spot. It wasn't as though I planned to go far. Barely even beyond the border. The holy scripture *did* command us to care for our animals, as they gave us life in a land of death. I was obeying the goddess of fertility, Tikinti, by caring for my family's herd—especially the kids. I was sure the high priest would understand if one of his men stumbled upon me too far downstream.

I walked along the river, away from the herds and Mikah and the one bleating nanny goat who watched me leave. B'Ba always said animals know *intent*, and I saw that trusting look in her eyes.

I had always known the river cut through a gorge that ran beside Bahmisi and away into the world unknown. I just didn't know the world became rougher, the gorge walls taller, and the water whiter with fury the farther I stepped from my home. I tripped and scraped the side of my ankle on a boulder, sending a terrified lizard darting for its life. I tried to view the kid's whereabouts again, but heat and fatigue had set in, and I was never very good with my magical skills. The mage always looked at me like a disappointment whenever I completed my time with her. Many people in the village didn't practice at all—some couldn't conjure anything—so the trace abilities I'd shown as a child had given Matka hope. She once thought I would become a temple magician—a priestess—performing sacred rituals to honor the highest on high. But she had been wrong.

Perhaps my image had been wrong too.

I slumped beneath a tree, though its sparse shade was hardly a break from the blazing heat, and opened my satchel to retrieve a waterskin. Heat waves danced in the distance. Abandoning my forethought to keep my clothes dry to avoid a lecture from M'Ma, I waded into the cool water and eventually bent my legs so that I was in up to my neck. Dropping my temperature helped me to refocus. I could find the lost one. I could.

My black hair waved in the water like underwater plants dancing in the current. I stood and wrung the length of it out, twisting it into a knot on top of my head before dragging myself from the water. The long chiton I wore felt wonderful against my skin, and I only regretted that it didn't have sleeves to keep me protected from the sun's rays.

Just as I stepped from the water, ready to continue my search for the kid, I caught sight of the little animal, standing on a rock and staring at me with those bizarre horizontal pupils.

"There you are!" I said, sighing with relief. After hearing the desperation in the mama's call, I truly didn't want to return empty-handed. "Come along now."

I stepped forward, but she darted away playfully, which made me growl under my breath. Wringing the excess water from the hem of my dress, I followed her, clicking my tongue in hopes of coaxing the kid toward me. I rounded a wall in the gorge and spotted a cave.

Nice try.

I stepped into the darkness of the cave, and the first thing that hit me was a heavy wall of moisture and a noxious scent of something rancid and metallic. The hairs on my neck rose. At first, all I could see was blackness tainted with the awful stench. *Just get the kid and leave. It's simple,*

Akedia, I told myself. Slowly, my vision adjusted, and I stalked deeper inside.

"Come on, little one," I whispered. When I tripped on another stone, I dug for the piece of flint and the bit of bark I always kept in my satchel. The sparks flew in the darkness when I struck the flint, and I sighed with relief when they latched onto the torch and a small flame gnawed at its fibers. My relief quickly turned to horror when it lit up the inside of the cave.

That rock I thought I'd tripped on was a bone. And it was one of very many. A gasp caught in my throat. I wanted to scream and run from the place, but I was paralyzed with horror. Human carcasses—some merely the white bones of someone long gone, others still decaying—lay scattered in careless piles. The strangest of all was that none of them had connected skulls.

Beheaded.

I was ready to dart from the cave when something stopped me in my tracks. The bracelet I'd made for Lileena was tied around the left wrist of one partially decayed corpse.

Panic made my heart race, and my chest heaved up and down. If this corpse wore my bracelet, then this corpse was... Lileena? But that couldn't be. It wasn't possible! The sun god consumed the offerings upon their deaths, using each fiber of their being for His own glorification, as was written in the holy books and tablets. Lileena was supposed to be a demi-goddess in the afterlife. There were not to be any remains.

Had all of these beheaded bodies been *offerings*? It looked like wild animals had been feeding on my Lileena. The world around me spun. I could hear every sacrificial song wailed by the village singers, every drumbeat, every thwack of the machete blade that I'd heard throughout my nineteen rains pounding in my ears. It grew louder and louder until I couldn't take it anymore.

I covered my ears, as though the noise existed not in my own mind but around me and ran from the cave, spotting the goat on the way out. She didn't try to run this time, so I grabbed her. I had to get far away from this horrible place. When I rounded the gorge wall to find the river's edge and follow it to the village, a shadowy figure appeared, making me yelp with surprise. The sun made the figure impossible to see, but when the person moved to the side and pulled down the black linen head cloth, I saw the kohl-lined amber eyes of High Priest Vikton.

"Akedia," he said. "Why have you come out this far? You know better than to wander away from the village."

At the sight of another human in his whole form, relief flushed through me. "Oh, High Priest! I'm so glad I've bumped into you. I was just searching for this lost k—"

I nodded at the goat in my arms and looked up in just enough time to catch him staring at the cave mouth. Then he glared down at me, taking a step forward to stand a bit too close.

A shiver rippled through my body.

"I-I've found my lost kid, but I was hoping for directions back home. I'm afraid I've lost my way," I said.

His head turned to the side as he looked down at me. "Your goat wandered this far without its mother?"

"She's an especially mischievous one, High Priest. I just found her down there," I lied, pointing at the edge of the river—anywhere but to the cave of bodies.

His harsh scowl morphed with irritation as he waved impatiently upstream. "Simply follow the river back upstream, girl. It's not that difficult."

I bowed and nodded, eyes cast downward. "Yes, of course. Thank you, High Priest."

With that, I ran. I ran so hard the kid in my arms didn't dare fight me as I darted over rocks and brush along the way back to the herd. It probably felt the beating of my terrified heart and took it as a cue to cooperate. We made it back to the herd in record time.

"Are you alright?" Mikah asked when he saw me gleaming with sweat and gasping for air.

I nodded my head but didn't answer him. Instead, I let the kid slip from my grasp to greet his bleating mother and headed home. I had to talk to my father. He was the only one who would hear me out and the only one who would let me ask questions without reporting me.

I ran up the hillside that overlooked the river, panting as I rounded the top, and headed toward the village. Our little home was three rows up on the stack of clay-brick houses that lined a hillside, and I climbed the steps, ignoring my burning legs.

But when I got inside, my chest burned with horror. M'Ma served tea and bread to a guest at the table.

High Priest Vikton.

As he sipped his tea, he watched my every move, as though after nineteen rains, he finally noticed my existence and didn't care for it. A knot of anxiety formed in the pit of my belly and grew, working its way up my chest and constricting my breath.

Was he here to dole out a punishment for leaving the boundary line?

"Oh, Akedia!" M'Ma exclaimed with a smile, rushing to my side to pull me into her slender arms. "His Eminence has graced us with his presence today to bring us the most joyous news. *You* will be the next offering."

CHAPTER THREE

SADNESS IS SIN

B'Ba sat beside the window, gazing outside with distant eyes. I kept looking to him for some kind of reaction, but he didn't so much as glance my way. High Priest Vikton missed nothing. He, too, turned his attention to my father.

"You seem quiet, Brother Armedes." The high priest reached for my mother's kettle—his hands studded with rings of fire opals laced with veins of purple and orange—and poured himself more tea. Then he doused a heaping spoonful of our finest honey into the steaming brew. The golden contents of the jar gleamed in the splash of sun that poured through the window, illuminating the miniscule air bubbles trapped within. My mouth watered just thinking about its sweet flavor. M'ma shoved a cork in the top before I could grab one of the clean spoons. I was only allowed to taste that sweet flavor on holy days.

B'Ba looked up and smiled. It was forced, and I knew it. Something wasn't right. Every home in the village looked forward to the day one of their own would be selected for sacrifice, but my father's face was far from jubilant. That smile triggered a wisp of a memory I'd forgotten, as though I had buried it until that very moment.

I was four, maybe five, rains as the sun god ordains, wearing a pretty dress and preparing to walk into the temple for worship with my parents. Upset about being late, M'Ma had already rushed inside to find us seats, but B'Ba, patient as ever, held me on his hip and helped me take a long white candle from a basket by the door. We approached an icon of Waikenu glowing in the dim temple entryway where the many flames from candles placed by those who arrived before us danced in the darkness. With B'Ba still holding me, we each lit our own candles and buried their ends in the sand among the others. I kissed the heel of my palm, touched it to my forehead, and lifted it to the sky, just as I'd been trained.

But the most striking thing about this memory—probably why it took up space in my mind after all these years—was that B'Ba did not. I looked up to him inquisitively and saw tears glistening in his eyes as he stared at the icon, an image of Waikenu with open arms hovering in the sky above a harvest scene. My tiny hands cupped either side of his face. *What's wrong, B'Ba?* I had asked. And he had smiled a smile that aimed to cover his feelings for my sake. Then he brushed away his tears and said simply, *I miss Waikenu.* Looking back, it's strange to recall how quickly I'd accepted this answer, how I never asked why, how I never thought of it again until now.

"I am most pleased and humbled with your choice, High Priest," B'Ba replied, rising from his seat to stand beside me and wrap a comforting arm around my shoulder.

"Splendid." High Priest Vikton stood as well, squaring his broad shoulders. "Your brother was also an honorable offering. He brought your parents much pride. I'm sure young Akedia will do the very same for your family."

I could have sworn my father's fingers tightened on my shoulder when the high priest said the word *brother*.

"When will the offering take place, High Priest?" M'Ma asked, bustling in to remove the tea service.

"Two days."

I could feel B'Ba go stiff beside me. "Your Grace… But we've just had an offering. Won't Akedia become the offering next spring? We are still celebrating Lileena's sacrifice… If I may, why so soon?"

"Why, Brother Armedes, I should think you'd be happy to see the process pushed forward nearly a full year." The high priest's amber eyes narrowed for a half second. Flecks of black kohl floated on their glossy surface where some of the dark pencil had gone astray. "The truth is, Waikenu has made it known to me that He is having a difficult time parting our sky. Our great sun god requires more blood for His sake."

"It is an honor to bestow upon Him this sacrifice." If I didn't know any better, the common saying fell flat on my father's lips.

"Rightly so." The high priest issued a curt nod, studying both my father and me before my mother interrupted with a basket of sweets. "Sister Tiana, you are always forthcoming with the most delicious treats. Thank you for your hospitality."

My mother's olive-brown cheeks flushed with a delicate shade of pink at the compliment, and she quickly tucked a stray clump of black curls back into a loose bun. She beamed with joy as the high priest left, but my father and I exchanged a glance before heading into separate rooms.

I slumped down on my bed of woven reeds with a bamboo frame. It was suspended knee-high above the ground to discourage the crawly things from wiggling into my mattress at night.

Maybe even yesterday, I might have found joy in this *honor*. Excitement that I had been chosen from among countless youths in the village to serve the sun god might have overshadowed the doubt I'd felt before Lileena's sacrifice. My parents would be treated as nobility, and I would go on to watch over them in paradise as a demi-goddess, commanding whatever realm best suited my taste. I once thought I'd ask Waikenu and the goddess Tikinti for command over the fertility of Bahmisi's goat herds, deciding when to give and when to take away, should I become an offering.

Yet, the little knot of tension hadn't fizzled. It sat in the pit of my stomach, and my mind flashed to that cave where my best friend's carcass had been thrown carelessly into a heap. There had to be an explanation. Someone, somewhere would be able to explain it. Maybe the sun god could not consume the bracelet and it was cast onto another maiden, who later saw a horrid fate.

But the offerings had their heads removed before they disappeared into a cloud of smoke at the altar...

I stood and paced my bedroom, tripping more than once over the rug M'Ma and I had braided one summer from rags. I had one small window, a square of wooden slats with a thin papyrus screen to keep the bugs from wandering in—well most of them, anyway. I pushed it outward to allow the breeze to waft inside.

Two days. I was to die in two days.

No, Akedia, you're to live—an extraordinary life awaits you!

A small smile formed on my lips as I turned to examine my reflection in the looking glass that hung on my wall, imagining my tan skin shimmering with the same golden sparkles they'd lathered on Lileena. M'Ma's mother used to tell me that my eyes were too light for my face. She'd say their hazel color was unnatural, too piercing, always hinting that, had I taken more after her side of the family, I'd have a lovely shade of warm brown or black. The comments had made me avoid looking at my eyes for many years, but in that moment, I looked straight into them as would a fearless demi-goddess.

But then a wave of tingling darkness swept into my chest, making me look away from myself and feel like a foolish child caught up in her own make-believe game.

There must have been an explanation for the cave that I couldn't understand. All I wanted was to take comfort in the knowledge that I was to become a demi-goddess.

No more thinking for now. Just rest, I told myself. Sleep had the magic of making mountains look like sandhills only hours later.

I crawled into bed, ready to blow out the flame that flicked from the spout of an oil lamp, but right before I did, I caught sight of the little rock my uncle had given to me the night before his sacrifice in the year of my fifth rain. He knew I loved to collect pretty stones back then and brought it just for me. I picked it up and remembered his words exactly:

"There is love, there is life, there is everything in be-tween..."

I smiled, thinking of him, my Uncle Peko, and thinking of the last thing he said to me before he kissed my forehead and left this world. I liked to think I felt him often, watching over me as the demi-god he was now. But sometimes, all I felt was pure sadness for missing his laughter and the way he'd throw me on his shoulders like I weighed nothing. It was the same sadness that Lileena had left in my heart. I just hadn't recognized it before.

To feel sad is to sin. We must not mourn for the sacrificed, as they are in a better place, I had been told many times.

Even still, I felt it, and I could tell no one.

Chapter Four
DOUBT CREEPS IN

I forced myself to think of goats passing through a cool stream of water and the mother and babe I'd reunited before falling into a restless, conflicted sleep.

Dreams of headless creatures walking after me haunted my sleeping hours, making me gasp awake throughout the night. Sweat drenched my skin each time I saw them, shuffling after me from the cave. Even the corpse with Lileena's bracelet trudged among the undead skeletons and those who were still decomposing. Partially *eaten*.

Finally, after tearing at my bedclothes for about the fifth time, I sat upright and screamed into my wool-stuffed pillow. Hot tears rolled down my cheeks and dripped onto my bare legs as I cradled my knees to my chest and tried to gasp for air as quietly as possible.

Sleep was doing nothing for me. I hadn't wanted to admit that headless body was Lileena's before, but what if it had been her? And if it was, why was it in that cave with piles of other bodies—presumably sacrifices? Why hadn't the sun god consumed them? Who or what was keeping them there?

Again that tiny, venomous thought whispered in the back of my mind: *What if we had been utterly wrong about the sacrifices?*

A chill crept over my body, and I looked up to the moon as it shone through my window, just like I'd done as a child to pray to the nightkeeper goddess for blessing our evenings with cool breezes. What if Evanya, too, was not what we believed Her to be?

I spotted a cloud in the night sky and wondered if our understanding of Shaiku, the god of rainfall, was also misplaced.

What if we had been wrong about... *everything*?

Another rush of tears poured down my face, my body shaking with the rhythm of a broken heart. *Waikenu, strike me down for thinking such things!* I was an abomination to my family and my home. My parents. How would the sun god receive me after I'd toyed with these blasphemous thoughts? I would have no place in this desert or the hereafter for ruining my life with doubt and question.

A shuffle outside my bedroom made me hold my breath. I wanted only to be comforted when I wept alone, but now the presence of company seemed horrifying. The flap of curtain that separated my room from the rest of the home ruffled, and B'Ba's face poked through.

"My girl," he whispered. "What troubles you?"

I considered lying and telling him I was fine, but his soft face, wrinkled with wisdom, and his voice, deep and melodic, undid the adult I was trying to become. Suddenly, I was just a little girl who needed her father. "Oh, B'Ba."

Pulling the curtain back, he stepped into the room and joined me on the bed. "What is it, dear? Overwhelmed with excitement?"

How to answer such a question?

"No." I didn't blink for fear of missing his expression. "B'Ba, I think something is very wrong with me."

"Wrong with you?" he asked, clasping my hand to comfort me. His calloused skin was smooth as tanned leather.

"I've been thinking about some things..." I lowered my voice even more. *Here it goes...* I had to tell him what I saw. I had to.

He looked over me softly and peeled away the hair that sweat had pasted to my shoulder. "You mustn't worry about not being worthy. You are the greatest gift any god could want."

The breath I'd gathered to tell him everything rushed from my lungs, but the words remained sealed in my mouth. The doubt I had detected on my father's face in the presence of the high priest was a huge misconception on my end and nothing more. He was a devout servant, as he always had been. And I loved him too much to rattle him with the shame that perhaps I no longer was.

I rose with the sun the next morning to watch its light shoot bright pink across the ridgeline of the distant dunes and feel the morning coolness kiss my skin. Atop the highest hill overlooking the village, the river, sky, and sand, I inhaled life in the quiet early solitude.

Tomorrow would be my last morning, and even though I'd only slept for a few hours, I had to soak up every moment I had left of my home where the people gathered water from a crisp blue river and the most beautiful animals came to drink, to live and survive. I had to breathe it all in, every last minute, because my magical home would be mine no more. Where I would end up after my death would be the same regardless of what I did or did not believe, which was all the more reason to savor every last hawk screeching—every breeze caressing my long black hair. The afterlife didn't matter at that moment. Only that very moment did. My fate was to either die for the sun god and become an immortal demi-goddess or die for my parents, who would be shamed greatly if I didn't.

A single dot of deep purple garments flickering behind a person in a hurry caught my eye. The shepherds and farmers were up already to make the most of the hours before the sun's rays licked everything with a thin layer of fire. They were in the fields, however, and I couldn't see them. Merchants would soon be out with their handcarts, but for the most part, Bahmisi was supposed to be sleeping.

Who was the figure moving quickly through the streets? Something about the way it moved made me pull the wool shawl M'Ma had woven for me tighter around my shoulders.

Descending the hillside, my feet slipped over the hard-packed dirt brushed with a sheet of sand from the windy dunes, and I made it to the bottom, sliding a few times on my woven papyrus sandals. I didn't want the person to see me, but my curiosity was the demon on my shoulder, prodding me to investigate.

Once among the houses stacked like little mud balls with windows and thatched roofs, I slithered into the shadows. Already they offered a break from the heat that was sure to blaze my skin well before midday. I removed the shawl and carried it in the crook of my arm. The camel-tan linens I wore draped off my bare shoulders and trailed behind me, the light fabric sailing on the wind in a land where the sun dictated everything we did—how we worked, how we dressed, how we ate. How we died.

Despite the growing warmth, a chill seeped into my blood when I caught another flicker of deep purple whip around a corner. There were murmurs of life in the house-holds, but out in the streets and the walkways between craggy boulders and houses where humans and goats had to pass in a single-file line, there was only the quiet sizzle of sand skittering across stone and clay.

I followed behind, poking my head around a corner of one house to see who was up with me at this hour and saw *him*. His Eminence.

He was headed for the river, and I watched him from my hiding place, wondering if he would turn left to head downstream where I had looked for the goat. Then he did. Back to the place where the bodies were kept...

"What are you doing, Keidy?"

I nearly jumped to the sun god a day early when the voice broke the silence behind me. Even though I knew who it was, it didn't keep my heart from hammering.

"Athalo!" I screeched, slapping his arm a little harder than I meant to.

"Ow! What was that for?" Athalo, Lileena's brother, rubbed his arm as he looked down at me, though his expression remained playful. He had tied his tight curls—a shade of brown lighter than his skin—in a low knot at the nape of his neck, showing off the squared jaw and dark green eyes that usually hid behind a curtain of his locks.

"Sorry. You frightened me." I looked away. It never used to be hard to think of things to say to him, but ever since Lileena's sacrifice, I didn't know how to look into those eyes that looked so much like hers without feeling a sting—a sting made worse knowing it shouldn't be felt.

Athalo never seemed to notice. Or if he did, he was gracious enough to ignore the awkward pauses and brush-offs. "I hear you're going to become an offering. Many blessings to you."

"Um, thanks." *It is an honor to bestow upon Him this sacrifice?* But that part didn't come out. It was clogged up by the thoughts running rampant in my mind.

Athalo nodded and turned to leave, but before he did, he paused and looked me straight in the eyes with something I couldn't quite decipher. "My sister would have been excited for you."

She would have—it was something we'd played at all the time, and he'd teased us for when we were growing up. But Lileena's big brother had said something that sparked another wave of doubt and question in my mind.

He didn't say she *is* excited for you. *Is*—as in, the present moment. Athalo spoke of her as though she were in the past. Dead. Which possibly meant I wasn't the only one doubting this religion of the sun god.

CHAPTER FIVE

THE DECISION

The oil was low in my lamp that evening, so I went to my parents' room to collect some from the reserves M'Ma kept in a jar beside her wash basin. I found her there, sewing the final beads onto a gown that would become my offering garment, while B'Ba finished patching a hole on our home's exterior wall. She had rushed the job, given the last-minute notice, but everyone in Bahmisi said she had the finest stitching in the village. Even though the garment looked amazing, I heard her sigh.

"If only I'd had proper time, my darling," she said, staring hopelessly at the dress. When she looked up, I saw a tear glistening in her eye before it fell. I sat beside her on her bed and waited in silence as she wiped her cheek. Then she reached for my hand.

"M'Ma?" I didn't know what to say. My mother never cried, and she certainly was never affectionate.

"You're my daughter. I wanted to give you a special gown for this occasion," she said, before reciting a common saying. "You will breathe life into this land with your gift."

"It *is* special, M'Ma. It looks beautiful." I didn't bother to mention that my blood was sure to soak the white linen—that it couldn't possibly matter how many colorful beads were sewn onto the collar. It would all be red once my head was removed...

More tears filled her black eyes. "I know I never say it, Akedia, but I love you."

Never, indeed. My mother was rigid and aloof and sent me away to perform chores if I ever leaned in to give her a hug as a child, so I learned not to touch her. I imagined it took a great deal of determination (or possibly tainted magic) to get those words out of her.

"I love you, too, M'Ma."

She pulled me into a hug that seemed to last forever, her tight curls like a pillow of soft wool against my cheek. Perhaps she had been saving hugs for the day before my death.

I retrieved the oil for my lamp and retreated to my room as something blackened my heart with a deep sadness. My mother loved me—the only child she'd been given before the goddess Tikinti put a stop to her fertility—and now that I knew it for certain, I had no more time to spend with her. It was over.

The flap of fabric that covered the entrance to my room slithered over my back as I entered without touching it for fear of spilling the oil. Once I got to my bed, I set the oil lamp ablaze to chase away the encroaching darkness. The flame danced from the end of the spout, casting shadows across my ceiling. They used to frighten me as a child, and M'Ma would come in to tell them to be nice to me to make me giggle. A smile spread over my face at the memory. I suppose I always knew she loved me, in her own way.

Why had she decided to tell me as though I wouldn't know it as a demi-goddess?

That same sickness flared in my gut.

Why had B'Ba seemed so stiff about the entire arrangement—his brother? Why had Athalo spoken of his sister in the past tense?

The more I thought about the way people close to me were acting, the more I dissected every little thing they'd said or done until my head was spinning and I couldn't possibly sleep.

I was going to die tomorrow. This was my last night. I should have made peace with it. I should've listened to my wiser self who said it was either for the good of my parents or the good of the people, if not both.

But I couldn't just sit there in my bed, waiting to sleep so I could spend the next day waiting to die at sunset. A little voice I had only ignored in the past came to the surface, and its whisper became clearer, louder.

This isn't right. Why are we killing people?

How many more must die before the sun god is pleased?

That did it. I bolted upright, heart pounding. A breeze rippled into my bedroom, and in the distance a coyote pack howled in tragic harmony.

I was about to do something incredibly stupid, selfish, irrational, and no doubt poorly planned.

I quietly pulled a chair to a tall bookshelf and grabbed a traveling bag I kept hidden on top inside a large clay vase. When I was little, Uncle Peko had given me the beautiful leather item stitched with the finest sinew threading, and M'Ma had made a comment about it being a useless gift. *What good is a traveling bag for a girl who will never go anywhere?* she had asked. I remembered frowning when she said that, as though I one day intended to prove her wrong. Once travel beyond the village became strictly forbidden, I knew that if I wanted to keep the bag, I would need to hide the item that was designed for leaving.

Or escaping.

Being careful not to scrape the legs across the tile floor, I put the chair back against the wall and began to pack.

To run away from sacrificial duties was to accept a public torture (if they caught you) and an eternity of punishment in Kakaura. While I knew this, I couldn't help but think I knew nothing. That the *village* knew nothing. What raced through my head as I hastily packed garments, oil, food, and water for the road were questions of how we could stop it all. If I left and found a world different than what we'd been told, maybe the deaths could end. If nothing else, I could begin a new life.

I kicked myself for not running away when I heard Lileena was next. What if I could have stopped it? I tried to push away the thought that would only torment me now that she was gone. I hadn't questioned enough by then. I hadn't found the cave. Wherever I was going, it certainly wouldn't be into that dark place that smelled of rot and blood.

With my bag packed, I grabbed my shoes and held them in my hands to head for the door. The dry scrape of papyrus sandals over rogue sand that always managed to find its way into our home was sure to make more noise than the warm pads of my bare feet.

Just then, someone flung open my fabric door, and a shadow standing in the threshold made me gasp.

"What are you doing?" B'Ba asked, his tone grave.

"B'Ba!" I cried, still surprised that he'd heard me packing when I had been impossibly quiet. A father's sense was nothing to underestimate.

Quickly, he stepped into my room and clutched my shoulders. "Why do you have that bag?"

Why did he whisper if only M'Ma was in the house to hear? They never kept secrets from each other. If I ever caused trouble, both always knew, so together they could plan a punishment. But tonight, my father's whisper was secretive and laced with something I had never heard in his words before. Fear.

I spoke quickly. "B'Ba, I found something. Something that may change everything we've ever believed about the sun god."

The moonlight was a brilliant blue in my room, and it shone on his features like a watery spotlight. "Go on."

The secret that haunted me and twisted my dreams made my ears ring with the overwhelming voice in the back of my mind as it challenged my entire belief system—a thunderous pandemonium that demanded its freedom. At first, I could only stutter a few words before sentences formed as I began to tell him about the lost kid and the day I'd spent following my weak vision down the river. Once I'd made a small fracture in my silence, however, the floodwaters forced through and shattered my resolve to keep it to myself. I explained how I found the cave filled with headless remains.

"The one body wore the bracelet I had given Lileena before she was sacrificed," I said. "I *know* it was her, B'Ba."

He was quiet, thoughtful. Furrowed.

I kept going. "I don't think it's the will of the sun god to take another sacrifice. I ran into High Priest Vikton just outside the cave—he knows I know—and now he wants to silence me."

B'Ba's hand lifted to his face and rubbed his temples. I had disappointed him. I was the worst daughter he could have hoped for, made worse by the fact that I was his only child.

"B'Ba... please say something."

Anything.

He walked to the table beside my bed and picked up the rock Uncle Peko had given me, turning around to place it in my palm. "*There is love, there is life, there is everything in between,*" he recited. Then he looked at me with melancholy in his eyes. "You will need this reminder of love when you leave."

I threw my arms around his neck and buried my nose in his tunic. The scent of frankincense and lye and a bit of musky sweat from laboring in the fields was forever woven into the fibers of his clothing. I inhaled that smell as though I would never know it again.

He pulled me from the hug and held me by the shoulders. "You must follow the river away from here. The sentinels will not be able to see you properly. Then get as far from this place as you can. I will make excuses for you in the morning to buy you time. Take a camel from the stalls."

I nodded eagerly, heart racing with his hurried commands. He was nervous, too.

"B'Ba?"

He kissed my forehead for a long moment and then looked back at me. "Yes, child?"

"Why are you helping me? Aren't you afraid the sun god and High Priest Vikton will punish our family? What will happen to you and M'Ma?"

A small smirk played on his dry lips. "Daughter, I haven't been afraid of the sun god for a long time. It's people who worship Him I fear. Nevertheless, you don't worry about us. We will make do while you make distance. Until you are a safe stretch from Bahmisi, *run*, Akedia. Run like the demons of Kakaura are chasing you every step you take. When the time is right, M'Ma and I will find you."

"But M'Ma... will she...?"

"I will tell her you're in danger." He took a ragged breath and let it out again. "She will need to get away from this place before she can open her mind to other truths, and only then will I tell her more. There is much about your mother that you don't understand. Do not worry about that right now. Akedia, listen to me. This life is your own;

you will cross the deserts and mountains far from our home, but may your saddlebags never be too heavy to carry the only truth I've ever known with my whole heart—" At this, he fiercely clutched my face and kissed my forehead, and I could hear his voice crack with the tears that threatened to dissolve everything that kept him together in that moment. "—You are loved, you are loved, you are loved."

"Oh, B'Ba," I sobbed, falling into his arms.

"Sh, sh, sh, my girl. Don't cry," he whispered and stroked my hair.

But how could I hold myself together when my heart was breaking into the tiniest pieces of sand that floated on the desert wind? I placed my uncle's stone in my pocket and kissed my father on the cheek. If I had been right about his doubt, how many more lived with unasked questions under the law set into place by High Priest Vikton?

"I love you far beyond any distance I could ever travel in this lifetime, B'Ba."

We embraced one last time, squeezing hard. I felt the devastating completeness of knowing I was loved beyond measure paired with the utter despair of knowing I was leaving it all behind. But I couldn't afford to delay another moment.

The night was hot and stagnant—suffocating—as I darted amongst the shadows to our little stable of livestock. In addition to the goat herd, we owned two llamas and a camel, who snorted as I entered, startled by my sudden appearance in the nighttime hours. After saddling the lone camel—a small female named Coska—I opened the stable door, pulling her by the harness rope. I placed a palm on her face.

"If you ever loved me at all, Coska," I whispered, "you will be the quietest camel who ever lived."

The stars overhead twinkled in the infinite blackness. Who would I ask for guidance this night as I planned to flee from everything? I craned my neck and lifted my head toward the sky, letting my arms fall open to the side. *Where will I go?* I asked no one in particular. Tears streamed down my cheeks as I tutted at the animal to pick up the pace.

I was going to abandon my sacrificial duties and everything I'd ever known or loved to search for answers. By morning, once they realized I was gone, I would become a fugitive offering.

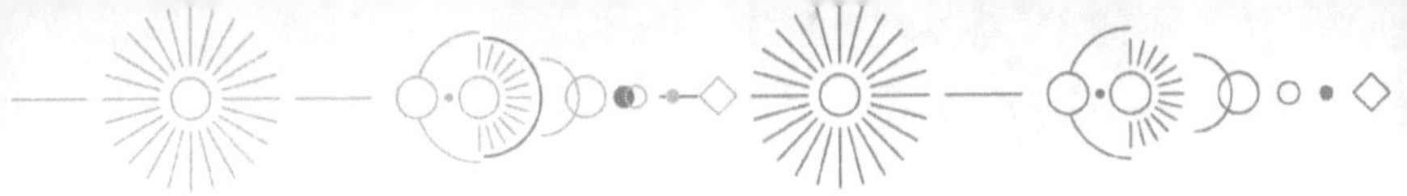

CHAPTER SIX

THE STRANGER

On any other night, Evanya, the nightkeeper god-dess, blessed us with the soft light of the moon to guide our paths when the sun had left. On that night, however, I was sure she meant to curse me with its garish brightness. I was a flurry of rippling chiton fabrics on display for all to see as I scurried through abandoned streets and walkways with Coska in tow. The soft huff of her breath made me fear the window shutters. Who would look out and see the offering escaping into the night and know my father told lies in the morning?

I couldn't worry about that now. I had to focus.

I scanned the dunes and spotted Nevario and the other lookouts. When they paced to places out of sight, I crossed open stretches of land. Once beyond the houses and along the little path that led to the river, again I cursed Evanya for illuminating us, if it was even Her fault at all.

I kept forgetting that if I no longer followed the religion of the sun god, I couldn't exactly pick and choose the pieces I wanted to believe... Was this an all or nothing situation? My heart felt heavy with the possibility. I had fostered a deep love for many gods and goddesses in my life. To lose them all with this shaking of my faith was like watching the sun god butcher more friends whose bodies would go on to rot in a cave.

Coyotes sang their love songs to the nightkeeper goddess as Coska and I made it down to the river, though the animals were no concern of mine. They hunted rabbits and mice, all while making beautiful music for the stars. They were my friends even if they didn't know it, but their howls made Coska flinch and stumble on her wide feet.

"Come on, my friend," I whispered to her. "We will cross the river and get away. The beasts won't harm you."

B'Ba had told me to follow the river, but I worried it would be the first place the high priest and his sentinels looked once they discovered my absence on the day meant for pampering. Water is life, and only a fool would venture away from it on a journey. A fool or a fugitive. I had to take the risk for now.

I took two waterskins from my supplies and forced them beneath the chilly water, watching them bubble as liquid pushed away the air inside. When I looked up, a large creature on the opposite bank made me gasp and drop the waterskins. The shadowy being rose to its full form, striking me with paralytic terror before it was sure to slash through me with its claws. As my vision focused on the moving thing, I realized it was not a hunter of the night. It was a human. The fear changed.

Immediately, I thought of a variety of excuses. I was still close enough to Bahmisi to pretend I wasn't trying to escape.

"Who goes there?" I called across the water, but to my horror, he—it was definitely a he—didn't reply and instead entered the river to approach me. "Who are you?!" I tripped over the hem of my chiton and crashed to the rocky bank, landing hard on my wrist. A sting radiated on my skin, and I felt the wetness of blood. Still the person approached. "Stop right there!"

He didn't stop. He rushed forward and grabbed me by the throat, lifting me as if I were nothing.

"Who sent you?" His voice was a deep growl, and as the moon shone on his face, I could see he kept a short beard. The man was young—about my age—with dark shimmering eyes, long black curly hair tied into a low knot, and skin a few shades browner than my own. The most shocking part of his appearance was that it was not familiar. I knew everyone in Bahmisi. This was the first time in my entire life I was standing so close to a—what was the word? A *stranger*?

"W-What?!" I managed a choked and husky shout.

The man released my throat and looked me up and down, eyeing me with suspicion. "You don't know me?"

"Why would I know you, fool?" I snapped, straightening my chiton and rubbing my throat as I retrieved my dropped waterskins. "Do *you* know *me*?"

He shook his head warily. "Of course not." Then, as though trying to convince me, he added, "We don't know each other."

I cocked my head to the side and placed a hand on my hip. If my own father never thought to grab me in such a way for all the times I probably deserved it, this idiot had no right to touch me. Then I looked at his dark, shifty eyes and realized he might have been one of those cast out from

his village for possessing a sickness of the mind. "Are you…
ill?"

I'd meant it to sound a little more sympathetic, but he
scowled. "No! I'm just—"

The clatter of horse tack rattling and hooves clopping
approached, and we exchanged a glance before I grabbed
Coska by the reins and dragged her into the cover of the
gorge wall. The man followed, pressing himself close to
me, smelling strongly of sweat with a hint of mint and
sage. We waited without moving as the shadows of two
riders danced on the opposite wall. They were at the top.
Lookouts. For what felt like an eternity, the two of us held
our breaths, his firm body pressing mine against our rocky
hiding place.

Their bored voices echoed above as they made the
rounds. When the shadows disappeared, the man released
me, flashing a smile of white teeth.

"Since it's obvious we're both hiding from someone,
let's simply be on our way and never mention this again," I
said, standing upright and ignoring the heat in my cheeks.

He struck like lightning, pressing me back against the
wall, hands moving along my form. "I don't think so."

I couldn't breathe; everything moved so quickly as he reached into my clothing, groping as he held me down with unbelievable strength. When he pulled out a small leather pouch and looked inside, I realized it wasn't my first fear, but my second. He planned to rob me.

"You have no coin on you?" he said, tossing my bag aside.

"No, you scoundrel!" *Would I need coin to travel the world?* I should have brought coin. I wasn't off to a good start...

His dark eyes narrowed. "And you're sure you've *never* seen my face? Not even in a picture?"

"What are you going on about?" I barked, reaching to pick up my bag. "I have never seen you before in my life! Not in person, not on papyrus. Never."

I made to walk around him—to go to Coska and leave before more sentinels came to watch the river again—but he grabbed my arm and pulled me toward him.

"See, that's the problem," he said, purring into my ear. "I'm a businessman, and I know a good deal when I see one."

"Get off me!" I cried, trying to slap him, but he moved like a viper, seizing my other wrist.

"You're worth something to me. And since I've run low on coin, I'll have to take a different kind of opportunity."

His breath was warm on my neck as he held me, and panic seeped into my gut.

"What do you want with me?" I cried, trying not to sound as scared as I was.

"You're running away from something. I'm sure I could ask for a pretty sum if I brought you back." I squirmed in his grasp, which tightened as he shook me. Then a knife gleamed, catching bits of moonlight on its surface. He held it close to my throat. "In case you couldn't tell, I'm in a desperate situation. And I'm willing to act desperately." When the sound of more horses echoed in the night, he spun me around and held me from behind, clasping a hand over my mouth. "Shhhh... Wouldn't want them finding you before I can make them a deal."

I hated him for holding me captive, but I didn't want the high priest's men finding me at all. So I obeyed. I stayed quiet. We watched the riders' shadows move farther upstream before he grabbed my wrist and Coska's reins to drag me away toward a place where a large black stallion waited beside the river. I fought him, digging my feet into the ground. I had to think quickly.

"I'm worth nothing to you!" An idea hit. "*Unless...* we're working together."

At that, he dropped my wrist and spun around, his face looming over mine. "No tricks, girl. I have no time for games."

"Nothing of the sort, *boy*. Just listen. If you go into the village with me, they will just take me away from you and give you nothing. But if you take me far from here, you can pretend you stole me and tell them to leave the money in a disclosed area. You get the money, and I get away. We both win."

"A false ransom?"

I nodded, hoping he couldn't see my eyes flit to the ground when I realized I didn't know what a *ransom* was. "Sure."

The plan had just popped into my mind, but it meant I could send Coska home and travel on that giant steed, which was sure to be faster and more surefooted. Camels can venture long distances in the desert without water, but if the man had traveled here on horse, it meant either the river stretched farther or the nearest watering hole was closer than Bahmisi villagers had been told. Not to mention my camel's disappearance would raise questions earlier in the day back home, sending sentinels out to find me that much sooner...

He weighed my offer, looking as though he still thought it would be in his best interest to take me by force, but the longer he took to decide, the more I knew I'd won. A frown scrunched his brow. "How would I prove that I had you?"

"I would give you something only my father would know was mine. I-It would serve as proof. You ship it to him with a note, and he will tell the rest of my village." My palms became clammy. If I was right about the high priest trying to get rid of me, would he care enough to pay the price of bringing me home?

"What proof?" He stepped closer as though he could simply rip it away from me.

I held up a hand. "Ah, ah, ah! I won't be telling you that until you hold up your end of the deal—take me away from this place as fast as possible on your horse, and I will give you the thing." A hawk screeched overhead, and voices in the far-off distance made us both flinch. I cocked an eyebrow and smiled wickedly at him. "You know, the more I think about it, the less likely it seems you would even *want* to walk into my village. Are you some kind of wanted criminal? Maybe I *should* allow you to take me back there. I wonder if I'd be the one to end up with some kind of reward..."

"Just get on the horse and don't fidget," he growled at me, sheathing the knife.

That did it. I gave Coska a kiss on the snout.

"Go home to B'Ba," I whispered to the beast who was both my family's means of transportation and my sweet pet. My throat tightened when she pressed her large face against my cheek, as though she knew we were saying goodbye. I draped the reins back over her head, so they wouldn't drag near her feet when she ran. Then swallowing hard, I slapped her rump and watched her leave before climbing onto the high-handed steed.

The slim saddle had a high horn that rose above a colorful woven blanket, but it didn't have a cantle to frame my seat, which would make it easy to share the mount. The man climbed on behind me and wrapped his arms around my waist to clutch the reins. His chest was hard against my back as he squeezed our bodies together and kicked the horse's sides.

I was just congratulating myself for being quite the stealthy negotiator, when he whispered in my ear.

"Who's the fool? You've just sent away your only ride and climbed onto a stranger's horse," he said, his voice rippling with a sinister edge as his fingers dug into my stomach and his thick arms tightened around me. "You're mine now."

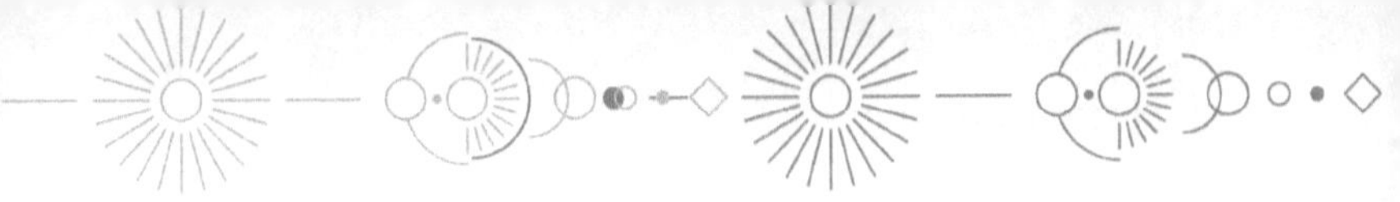

CHAPTER SEVEN

THREE FAVORS

I didn't dare struggle on the horse as it raced at a speed I had never felt before in my life. The animal's rhythm was a tyrant over my lungs as I worked to hold on. In addition to being kidnapped by a criminal, I couldn't forget the giabden monsters that were said to lurk in the sand. One false move...

You are stronger than you've ever needed to know, B'Ba had once said when teaching me that fear constricts our magical abilities. *One day, you will need to know how strong you are, and you will amaze even yourself.*

I desperately wished in that moment that I could amaze myself.

When we'd run the horse hard and for a great distance, the man slowed the beast to a stop and pulled me from the saddle. The criminal mistook my unease on the stallion for submissiveness, not knowing the demons roared within me for revenge, so when I kneed him in the groin, he collapsed, cursing more gods than I even knew existed. I tried to run, but he was faster, pulling me to the ground by my ankle and pinning me in place by both wrists.

"Don't you know the desert code?" he asked, fighting me with little effort as I thrashed.

"Get off me!" I tried to spit in his face, but he grabbed me in such a fierce way, I froze on the spot.

"When a traveler is caught off his—in your case, *her*—guard, without a ride, without funds, and in need of a favor, they are bound to fulfill three favors to the one who assists or captures them," he explained, ignoring my plea. He muttered something unintelligible as his hand waved in the air and a ball of blue light filled his palm. With his other hand, he pinned my shoulders down while the hand with the glowing blue light pressed it into my heart. "You are now bound to me to fulfill three favors before you are released."

Whatever he had done—whatever magic he knew how to harness—it was powerful as it wrapped around my lungs like a cobra and squeezed and squeezed. I tried to cry out, but the words wouldn't come. I had been raised in the shadow of Moruka Temple, where the priestesses conjured spells to honor the gods and goddesses, but I had never before seen anything of this nature. Black magic? A flash of doubt burned my resolve. If this man was an example of the world that awaited me beyond Bahmisi, perhaps I truly had been safer to follow tradition. He stood and brushed the sand from his robes, before slipping the outer layer of his attire from one brown shoulder that rippled with muscles. I shrank away, wary of the first favor, but when he saw my face, he rolled his dark eyes.

"I wouldn't need to bind you magically for *that*." He unfolded a mat and lay down on his side, winking at me. *The snake*. "You'd do that on your own free will, I'm sure."

Either the magic he'd pressed into my heart had settled or the outrage rising in my gut overpowered it, because I found my voice. "I would never with the likes of you! You're a rotten coward—an accident child, whose mother wouldn't bother to name!" The insult was pretty generic, but it held great weight in Bahmisi, given the heavy significance we put into naming ceremonies for new babes. But this devil laughed.

"I promise you she named me, thanks. You can call me *Master Tanu*."

This time I spat and managed to make my mark on his cheek. He lunged at me, holding my face between the tightening fingers of his right hand as I flailed. "Don't *ever* do that again."

My voice was broken and sounded on the verge of tears, but I yelled at him anyway. "I will never call you master! And you're a beast for tricking me even when we could have worked together."

He shrugged and settled on his mat once more. "There are no partnerships out here. Only debts. I needed you to help me with more than one deal, but I didn't have much to barter with. I do what I have to do when I have to."

I looked up to the velvet black sky studded with brilliant diamonds. Was this my punishment for disbelieving? "What are the favors, then?"

He turned his head toward me, his beard thick and dark in the moonlight. "You will give me the item for your father to perform the ransom—"

"But I already said I would!"

"You will pretend to be my wife. One visit in particular is of great importance for it to be believable; you must be very convincing. And the third favor will be issued when I feel like telling you." He was quiet for a moment as I soaked it in, but I didn't even want to give him the satisfaction of a reply. "In the meantime, you must tell me your name."

"You can call me Leena."

"Your *real* name."

"But—" He held up his hand and acted as though he clutched something in the air, and in that moment, I felt powerless, unable to lie. Matka could have only dreamed of this power, and yet I wondered if it was just scraping the surface of magic found in the places beyond Bahmisi. Yet my pride kept me from asking more about his craft.

"Akedia," I whispered.

"Much better." The horse snorted between gulps it took from a large livestock waterskin, and Tanu put his hands behind his head. "We will leave soon."

I couldn't believe it. We'd been riding for hours, and he didn't want to sleep? Only minutes passed before Tanu sat upright and rolled his mat to tie onto his horse's pack. He looked at me sitting in the sand and nodded.

"Onward we go," he said.

Even though Tanu had allowed me to use the stirrups, my thighs burned from holding onto the horse for dear life, and I waddled to its side, unsure of how he expected me to continue riding.

"We can't stay still for long," he said, probably a reaction to my grimace. "We should make it to Manitu by sunrise. Trust me, you don't want to be out here during the day."

I snorted. As though I hadn't grown up in the desert, shuttering windows by midday and lathering my skin with rice bran to protect it from the sting of the sun?

But just as I was about to lift my foot to hook it into the stirrup, a shadow flickered in the corner of my eye, making me scream and bump into Tanu. *Giabdens.*

"It's the flurries of sand," he said, grasping my shoulders and turning me around. "The moon casts shadows on the sheets of sand that kick up. Honestly, I'm not sure how you planned to cross the desert dunes. It's not like life by the river."

I looked again and saw the sand swirling in the wind just as Tanu had described it, and shook my head. No giabden monsters, though I wouldn't know what they looked like if I saw them. The wind was fiercer away from the river that ran beside Bahmisi—I'd never seen it make the sand appear so monstrous.

Do not allow fear to constrict your heart and the little magic you have, I reminded myself.

The temperature in the open sand dropped drastically, and I pulled the loose tails of my garments closer around me. I had never felt this kind of cold before. Tanu placed a hand on the small of my back and pushed me toward the horse. When I mounted and he climbed on behind me, I was a little grateful for his body heat, if not his overall presence. He pressed his heels into the horse, and we carried on.

I couldn't say how far we'd traveled, because I'd fallen asleep from pure exhaustion sometime along the journey. When my eyes flickered open, they were crusted with sand, and my sore body bobbed between both of Tanu's arms as he held the reins. The sun's rays cast a soft veil of pink along the horizon of dunes.

I gasped when I saw it and couldn't tear my eyes away.

In the distance, clusters of homes stood nestled together to form a small community. I stared, mouth wide open, at the sight I once believed couldn't exist: another village beyond Bahmisi. Another lie. Tanu's existence alone had supported my doubts, but it wasn't hard to think of excuses the holy men might concoct to explain him—he was once of Bahmisi, but he was sent on a spiritual journey to test his faith in the desert; he was created from thin air as a messenger to encourage women to speak less and clean more.

But as I saw an entire community, living and thriving, drying their garments in the scorching heat, selling their wares in the market that, if I had to guess, was buzzing with gossip and flies from the butcher's stand—a place not unlike my own—I knew it couldn't be that Bahmisi stood alone in the world as the chosen kingdom of Waikenu.

Another truth I thought I knew fell and shattered beneath the stallion's hooves, which trod over the remnants until they were fine dust swirling among the sands behind us. How many more pieces of me would crumble away on this journey far from home?

"Will we stop here to rest?" I asked, my voice cracking.

"Yes, but keep quiet. Let me do the talking."

He dismounted and took the horse by the reins to lead while I rode. We walked into the small cluster of houses built along flat land. They were made of brick that was washed with white paint. When a man crossed our path,

Tanu wrapped most of his head in the fabric he had floating around his body, and his voice became overly friendly.

"Excuse me, sir." He bowed to the man and waved his hand in my direction. "My wife is with child, and we have traveled from afar. Does your village offer accommodations?"

I didn't listen to the mumbled conversation that followed, because all I could think about was the fact that he'd called me *with child*. My chiton flowed loosely around my body, but it gathered at the waist, and I was clearly *not* with child. The very idea.

Tanu turned and winked at me once the man had left. "Come along, dear. Wouldn't want you overexerting yourself."

"Mark my words, I will end you," I hissed. "You better not fall asleep on my watch, because I swear—"

I stopped short when Tanu held up a long metal key and grinned. "The man felt so sorry for you, he agreed to let us stay in his spare cottage." I crossed my arms and turned my head away from him as he led the horse to this supposed cottage. "You're welcome."

"Does that count as one of my favors?" I asked, feeling a little lighter with hope.

"No. *You* didn't do anything. As I said before, *you* will need to convince someone you are my wife. I can lie about who you are all I want."

Tanu led the steed down a little dirt path lined with trees and tied him near a watering trough. Then he tried to help me down, but I swatted his hand away.

"You're supposed to be my pregnant wife, remember?" he whispered into my ear once I'd pulled my foot from the stirrup. "You'll be wanting to keep up this charade as much as me. You easily forget I'm not the only one on the run."

I nodded tautly and pulled some of my loose linens over my head to conceal my hair. Would High Priest Vikton recognize me by the waves that rippled at the crown of my head if he were looking from behind?

Tanu walked to the front door and turned the key, only to open the door to an empty shack of a building with a few scattered piles of hay.

"Yes, I can see he took great pity on your *pregnant wife*," I said, rolling my eyes.

Tanu shrugged, unfazed. He walked into the cottage, shut the door behind us, and locked the bolt. "All I care about is that the shutters work. Build yourself a bed and look out for rats. When we've rested enough, you will fulfill the first favor."

Something compressed in my chest, as though the mention of the favors I still owed to Tanu weighed heavy—the symptoms of his spell's possession over me. The simple magic my family honed for medicinal and practical purposes had a warm, bright feeling. It was the rosy orange of the sands as the sun set. It was all of the senses as much as it was none of them. In training for a possible priestesshood with Matka, I had felt glimpses of green before it fizzled, along with my hope to secure that role. I could rarely *feel* the colors like an aspiring priestess should. Tanu's magic, however, was a brittle, acidic blue of a stranger squeaking out an existence on the run. It was as cold as it was fierce, and that blueness seeped into my core illuminating my pure exhaustion from the road. With a flick of his wrist, he pulled it away from me as though he were calling off a dog. I tried to contain the gasp when he released me, but I couldn't, and I hated that smirk on his face.

Perhaps I owed Tanu my life for taking me away from my home. Looking back, I wouldn't have escaped and crossed the desert on little Coska in the same amount of time. I probably would have been caught. He didn't exactly deserve a wax-sealed envelope with a heartfelt note for binding me the way he did, though, so I kept quiet as we lay down in the hay to rest. Had I not been so tired, it would have been awkward, and I didn't even realize I'd fallen asleep until a hand clamped over my mouth a few hours later.

I writhed under the pressure and squirmed until I realized it was Tanu. He pressed a finger to his lips, motioning me to keep quiet as he mouthed the words, *Someone's outside.*

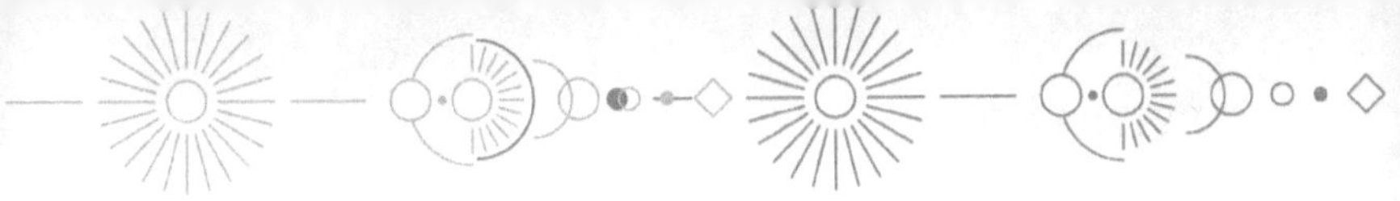

Chapter Eight

ANOTHER SACRIFICE

As he hovered over me, Tanu's scent was mostly that of an unwashed man mixed with mint and sage—especially strong since he didn't wear a tunic and the exposed skin on his chest was close to mine. He slowly released my mouth and waved me over to the wall to hide beneath the tiny window as the sound of heavy footsteps stomped around outside.

Katika, goddess of mercy, please let us not be found by High Priest Vikton's sentinels. Nevario always took a little too much pleasure in punishing those who disobeyed.

Tanu clutched my wrist and peeked through the window, loosening his grip and sighing when he looked back at me.

"We're fine," he said with a sigh. "It's just the man's wife."

He pulled a long sheet of the white linens he'd worn when I met him from the hay and wrapped the garment around his body in the fashion of men. I looked away as he dressed himself, though I wasn't sure why. He was putting on more clothes than when I'd first woken up to him pressing himself on top of me. But now, with the fear of discovery diminished, the moment seemed more intimate.

He grazed a hand under my chin and spoke in a mocking tone. "Don't worry, wife. Everything you see here is already yours."

I slapped his hand away as he laughed. "You swine. Don't touch me."

Knuckles rapped the wooden door, which gave off a hollow splintering sound from years of drying in the hot sun. Tanu went to answer, and in bustled a short, overweight woman with a wiry black and gray mane and a fine layer of dark hair on her upper lip. She stepped into the cottage with a tray of cups, a briki kettle, and colorless pastries.

"I am Kabon's wife, Orella," she said without waiting for a word from either of us. "I hear you are with child, dear. You'll be needing your coffee."

Tanu looked at me with a lifted brow as though I had him to thank for Orella's hospitality. For once I didn't sneer at him. The sight of the woman, with her plump arms that dimpled at the elbows and her tray of treats and morning brew, put me in too good a mood. Inside the long-handled copper kettle that had suns embossed on the sides, I knew there would be fresh grounds brewed in hot water. If she were a good barista, there would be a fine layer of crema at the top.

"Bless you, Sister Orella," I said, reaching for a pastry, but she pulled the tray away.

"No, no, no, we will feast with the others." She examined my belly. "Must not be far along, then?"

I looked at Tanu, whose dark eyes warned me to play along. "No, ma'am. Not far along at all."

The woman nodded and then told us to follow her before leading us outdoors to a gathering place near a large tree, where two other men and one woman sat tending to a small fire.

"Well, you're quite young to be bearing children," Orella continued. "I have five grown daughters myself, and I made them all wait until their hips were wide enough for the task."

I tried not to roll my eyes. Many were mothers even before reaching nineteen rains as the sun god ordains. She probably thought I was younger based on my height alone. Tanu grabbed my hand and tugged me close.

"She just couldn't wait, I'm afraid," he said, and it took everything in me to keep from slapping him in front of the person who thought we were newlyweds.

Orella pointed at the people around a small morning campfire meant for roasting coffee and small meals.

"There is Bavlo, Kounelli, and Stefan," she said, pointing at each of them as they nodded.

At last, she filled my cup with coffee. The hearty sludge of finely ground beans at the bottom gave me a bit of happiness to chase away the exhaustion. While people in Bahmisi could make their pots of boiled grounds last the entire day, Tanu and I had ridden through the night. We gulped down its rich, bitter flavor like we'd never taste it again.

The other woman, Kounelli, tossed the pastries on a skillet over the flame and toasted them on both sides before dumping them back onto the tray. Now that they were warmed, they smelled of cinnamon and honey with a hint of anise. Kounelli broke the three discs into pieces and passed them out.

"*May we be fed in our hearts and souls, even when the platter's clean,*" she said, and by the way everyone nodded and tucked into the food afterward, I could tell it was some kind of saying or prayer. I took it to mean a request for happiness even when resources are scarce.

I nodded along and sank my teeth into the delicious doughy thing, which dissolved into buttery goodness in my mouth. *Praise Waikenu for this bountiful...* I began the prayer in my mind, but it fell flat on a heavy heart. Loneliness replaced it—the earth-shattering feeling of being completely alone. Tanu bumped my knee with his knee.

"Eat plenty," he whispered to me as the others spoke. "We'll need to leave soon."

I helped myself to another portion left untouched on the platter. His leg didn't move away from mine after it had neared, though, and I wanted to swat it like a fly.

All of our fast-breaking companions were quite old, but the man named Bavlo had the leathery look of a man who had spent his entire life baking in the fields. Deep creases folded his otherwise happy face, and spots from the sun's damage marked him profusely beneath dark brown skin. Yet he smiled and spoke with his hands in a way that made everyone quick to laugh.

Then he said something that sent the blood pounding in my ears.

"Let us honor Waikenu with a sacrifice!"

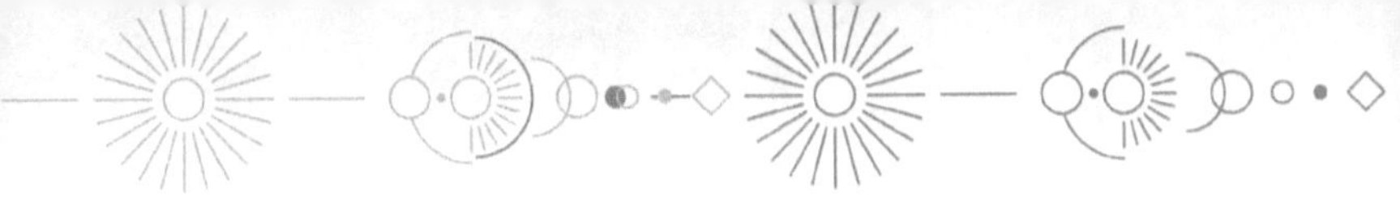

Chapter Nine

THE FIRST FAVOR

The corners of my eyesight darkened as a thin layer of sweat formed on my brow. I wanted to run—or vomit—but fear froze me like a rabbit who had just spotted a falcon's shadow sailing on a sea of grass.

How did they know I was the offering? Would they kill me here without any preparation at all?

Shaking myself from the trance, I finally clambered to my feet, gasping for air as our hosts raised their meal knives above their heads. Before I could scream, however, the weapons came down, and each person punctured their own fingertip. Then they squeezed to draw out red beads of blood, which they dripped into fire where we'd cooked the coffee and treats.

When Kounelli looked up, she frowned at me where I stood and examined my face that must have been pale and shimmering with sweat. "Is everything alright?"

Something acidic burned at the back of my throat. "Y-You're making a... *sacrifice*?" Memories flashed through my mind at the word. The beheadings. The bodies in the cave.

Lileena...

"Yes..." Kounelli's frown deepened, one crooked line creasing between her brows.

Tanu glared at me, nodding his head for me to sit down. "My wife gets rather jumpy around blood, what with her delicate disposition." When I didn't sit, he stood beside me and placed a hand on the small of my back. His touch was warm, and it shot through me, making my cheeks burn. "Come along, dear, you should probably rest." Then, he turned to the others. "It was wonderful meeting each of you. Thank you again for your hospitality."

Once inside the tiny cottage, Tanu whirled around with an angry scowl. "What trick are you trying to play?"

"No trickery. I-I'm sorry, I just..." My thoughts trailed off mid-sentence. Images of home and my family swirled through my mind. My head was light, and my heart wouldn't slow down. I had to sit. No, I needed to lie down. I slowly found a place to rest in the hay and concentrate on breathing through my nose.

"What's going on with you?" Tanu's voice felt far away, even though I heard every word.

"Nothing. I just need a minute. This heat is making me feel ill," I lied.

He busied himself with something as I counted my breaths, like little goats splashing through a cool stream. The next thing I knew, Tanu pressed a wet, cold cloth against my neck. He wrung out another and draped it over my forehead. Our eyes met briefly before I looked away.

This was too much. I was being a foolish girl in a grown woman's body. I tried to sit upright, but the light-headed feeling returned, and he gently pushed me back down.

"You need to tell me what's happening with you. We're going to be traveling together for some time, and I will need to know. Are you diseased?" He dragged the cloth over my skin slowly, and the relief was so great, I didn't bother to push him away. I didn't even mind the bits of straws poking my skin.

"No. I was chosen," I mumbled. "That's why I ran away."

The wet rag stopped moving on my forehead. "What do you mean *chosen*?"

"To be sacrificed. I was going to die for the sun god, but I made my own choice: to run away instead."

"Really? You're from that village that kills humans for Waikenu?" He seemed a little *too* entertained… "I knew to stay in the shadows when I saw the guards on horseback, but I didn't realize I was in such grave danger. Is it true they kill babies and drink the blood of their sacrifices?"

"No! What a ridiculous question. Why would we do that?" Being angry with Tanu helped me feel a little better, and I sat upright, snatching the cloth from his hand. Light poured through the window, illuminating dust motes on its path to the floor. Everything felt brighter than it probably was, so I squeezed my eyelids closed and laid back down.

He shrugged. "Legend has it that only some of your people escaped to tell the truth of what goes on in that place. No outsiders. Death and persecution. Are you saying the legends are lies?"

I sucked in air to counter the ignorant comment and then realized the truth of what happened in Bahmisi wasn't much better. Perhaps that man who had refused to give his son for sacrifice had escaped with his family to start over. "I am certain the *truth* has been distorted a few times over the years. We offer a new sacrifice once a year. Only rarely is it more than that. They're never younger than fourteen rains, and of course, we don't *drink the blood*. What kind of foolish idea is that?"

"Forgive me, but killing someone once a year is still the work of dangerous people." His point was true. After all, I had run away because somewhere deep down I'd realized what we were doing wasn't right. The dizziness returned, and I had to take more slow breaths. Black flashed through my vision, making me wish for a soft pillow of linen stuffed with the cashmere wool from one of my goats. I didn't say anything, but Tanu continued. "So... you were supposed to be sacrificed? And you ran away?"

I nodded. I knew what was coming. I was a sinner, a coward. I was shaming my people for turning my back on them, even if what they believed was barbaric.

He gently removed the rag I'd stolen from my hand, dipped it back in the water, and dragged it across my fore-head. "Not many would be that brave."

The spinning stopped, almost too suddenly. I didn't know what to say or do. It was by far the nicest thing Tanu had said to me.

"I'm not sure that I was," I whispered.

Tanu tossed the rag into the wash bowl and hooked his elbows around his knees. "Do you feel better?"

I nodded, somewhat ashamed that he would think me a wilting maiden, and sat up. This time, my head didn't spin.

"Good. Now you can complete a favor," he said, his voice returning to its commanding baritone.

"The third one? What is it?" I could handle favors one and two, but that third one he'd cryptically refused to tell me gnawed at my curiosity.

His dark eyes rolled. "Nice try. No, the first one. Give me the item that only your father would recognize."

I dug into my pocket and removed the stone Uncle Peko had given me, offering it to Tanu. It was just a stupid rock, but I felt as though I was preparing to surrender my uncle's love, my family, and everything that I once held dear to this person who cared nothing for any of it.

Tanu's palm was smooth and warm, and his fingers slightly closed around mine when he took it from my hand. While his touch was soft, his words were harsh two seconds later.

"Are you tricking me?" He stood, towering over me with a scowl. "You cannot disobey the bind."

"Tanu, that *is* it," I said, scooting away from him, but he held his hand in the air and murmured. That bluish pressure in my chest increased—almost painful as it sucked away my breath. I could feel his power demanding more, but the words I spoke before were the absolute truth. All I could do was shout again.

"That *is* it!"

He lowered his hand, and his eyes fell. "If you wouldn't fight me so much, it would be easier to believe you."

"You *could* just believe me. What reason do I have to lie to you?" I stood and glared up at him with my hands on my hips.

"If you're trying to leave, you have plenty of reasons." His face was stern, but his lips twitched nervously. "You don't get far in the desert with trust."

Tanu looked down at the sandals that wrapped around his feet and ankles, and for a moment, we let the whisper of wind beyond the house fill the silence. Even for the fast-breaking hours, Waikenu's sun was a tyrant over us all, heating even the soil that perfumed the air outside the cottage with the scent of hay and wild grasses as it baked.

I cleared my throat. "I will write the note myself if you'd like."

"Good. That's good. Let's do that," he said, disappearing to go on what I presumed to be a search for papyrus and kohl. "I will be right back. Don't go anywhere."

"Where would I go?" I barked back, but he was already gone.

I took a moment to gaze out the window. The cottage was at the edge of the village, with rolling dunes beyond, and I gasped when a huge wall of sand lashed into the air in the distance before settling. In the darkness, I hadn't realized we'd ridden through that. I wasn't sure I could do it again in broad daylight.

"Here we are." Tanu's voice made me jump.

I whirled around and saw him with the papyrus and a bit of kohl and offered to take the materials before sitting down to write.

I held the kohl poised over the papyrus. "What should I write?"

Tanu paced. "'Dearest Father—'"

"I wouldn't say that."

His pacing slowed. "'Papa, it is I, Akedia...'"

"I most certainly wouldn't say that."

Tanu stopped walking altogether and grinned at me. "'I've been captured by a tall, dark, and devastatingly handsome stranger, and I don't need rescuing.'"

I laughed out loud. "How about this: 'B'Ba, by the will of Waikenu, please send help for me. I was searching for another lost kid when a brute of a man with hair on his knuckles came wandering out of the wilderness and stole me. I think he is part animal, if not by birth, most certainly by smell—'" Tanu probably didn't want me to see him discreetly sniff his own armpit or glance at his hands, but I did.

"I do not stink!"

"Not to other animals, no."

He glanced at the tops of his hands once more, and I smirked realizing I'd chipped away at that towering ego.

"'I fear for my safety,'" I continued. "'I long to return to Bahmisi to sacrifice my mortal body to the sun god, but the revolting beast won't release me until the village has paid dearly for my return.'"

"You'll write what I say and nothing more," he barked. "'B'Ba, I have been captured by a desert rider and am being kept in a remote cave at the edge of the world. He has requested the payment of one hundred gold pieces for my safe return. His men will await your payment in the City of Tigrea. Come alone, and leave it in the drinking well at the western edge of town in five days time or I will be killed.'"

I dug one of my sandals into the sandy floor of the room. "Huh. One hundred gold pieces? I'm not sure the village has even that."

He brushed my long dark hair from my shoulder and grinned. "Don't think you're worth that much?"

"Stop." I pulled away. "I suppose that letter is fine."

I put his words onto the grainy surface of the papyrus scroll. This *ransom*, as he called it, could work out well. Hopefully, my father would use it to convince High Priest Vikton he and M'Ma needed to leave town to deliver the funds, but we would all stay gone. We could all start over...

When Tanu reached to grab the letter, I placed my hand on his wrist to stop him. "Wait!" Once he moved away, I held the kohl over the scroll once more and murmured aloud. "'There is love, there is life, there is everything in between.'"

"What's that?"

I rolled the scroll into its preferred shape after jotting down the words and avoided his gaze, waiting for the burn along the bridge of my nose to fade. "Nothing. Just something we used to say."

CHAPTER TEN
THE MAIL CARRIER'S MISSION

We stepped outside the cottage to saddle the horse and call for something Tanu called a mail carrier. A boy with light brown hair arrived, and Tanu handed him the package then looked at me.

"He will take this to your village," he explained.

The boy almost dashed away when I shouted. "Wait! You will not be allowed in Bahmisi." I flashed an irritated glance at Tanu. "No outsiders, remember?" Then I looked back at the mail carrier. "When you get to Bahmisi, do not directly enter the village—you must sneak in along the river and stay hidden from the horseback riders. There will be a boy about your age, Mikah, tending goats. Give the package to him and tell him it's for Brother Aremedes. Tell him he *must* tell no one about the package or that he ever saw you. Then get away from there as soon as you can."

The boy's dark eyes widened at the instructions, and for a moment he seemed frozen in his place, unsure if he wanted coin or safety. He must have either needed the payment or was up for an adventure laced with danger because he nodded and ran away.

Once the package was on its way to Bahmisi, the pressure in my chest lightened, and a tendril of bright blue steam lifted into the air, like a neon cloud of vapor escaping my heart.

"What was that?" I cried, stumbling as the thing left me.

"You are one-third of the way to fulfilling your favors and earning your freedom." He chuckled, taking a bite of the fruit Orella had given us. "Actually, you couldn't escape me if you wanted to right now." His black eyes bored into mine, crinkling at the edges with something that bordered on a cocky playfulness. "The farther you step, the heavier the weight until it's unbearable. It could kill you if you're not careful."

"That's cruel." I cringed at the thought of his magic weighing down on me until I was crushed by the invisible force.

"That's business."

I realized he could very well become bored of toying with me and leave me to face a magical execution. Maybe that was why he didn't want to tell me the third favor yet. He planned to finish me off once I'd helped him earn the ransom money and trick someone into thinking he was married...

"Tanu, what's the third favor? Please just tell me. I won't object... I think." The pressure in my chest returned, but I had a feeling it was more from my own anxiety than anything he was doing.

"You'll know when I want you to know. Now get on the horse."

I growled under my breath. *The stubborn fool.* No wonder he was out running around the desert with no home or family. No one could love such a beast.

Once in the saddle, he climbed behind me and wrapped his arms around my waist like a cage. I thanked whatever god or goddess would still listen to me for the kindness of strangers as we made away from Manitu with fresh provisions and a thoroughly fed and watered horse.

Tanu's breath was warm on my neck, and a few times his lips grazed my ear on accident. I pretended not to notice, even though my face burned with the closeness.

"What is your horse's name?" I asked, hoping to distract us both with idle conversation.

"Pharaoh."

My grandfather used to tell me about the pharaohs in lands he claimed to have visited. I always thought they were fairy stories. Regardless, I loved hearing the tales. They were like a magical escape from Bahmisi, and I imagined myself riding in a caravan with other travelers through that make-believe world. The adventure I'd pictured was quite a bit different than the reality.

"Why do you run, Tanu?"

His voice rumbled against my back. "Why do you ask so many questions?"

I tried to lean away from him, but his grasp tightened. "I think it's only fair for me to know something about you, since I'm running around, granting you these favors, and you know my story."

His hand loosened, and he exhaled slowly. The sun blazed overhead, but the white linens we wore over our heads helped to cut some of the volatile rays.

"I am wanted for stealing," he said, moving some of my hair out of his face. "Once you're wanted for one crime, it becomes easier to commit more."

"What about your family? Did they not feed you?"

"Listen, I know you were raised shut off from the world, but were you taught to ignore basic social cues? I don't want to talk about it anymore."

Pharaoh marched on in the hot sand, his tail swishing in the air and swatting pesky flies. We passed several cacti with beautiful pink and purple flowers and brightly colored succulents with meaty leaves. I almost pointed them out to Tanu—they were truly a stunning sight—but decided against it. If he didn't want to talk about his past, I would say nothing about our present.

We rode for an hour in the worst part of the day, until the dunes gave way to firm ground and Tanu directed Pharaoh to stop beneath the shade of a large tree before dismounting. I slipped down before he could touch me and watched as he used a knife to slice open a nearby cactus. Pharaoh had probably been through the ordeal before, I realized, as the horse waited patiently for his master to open the plant and expose its water.

I removed some layers I wore to feel the air on my sweat-covered neck. Tanu watched me as though I were a prisoner in need of guarding.

"You forget my invisible shackles." I tied my long hair in a knot and grabbed a wide leaf to fan myself.

His dark eyes were fierce and penetrating as he watched my every move. Finally, he spoke. "We'll leave soon. Tigrea is just over this pass. I wanted to warn you before we entered..." He found a seat next to me. "This is the place where you will be my wife."

I frowned at Tanu. "Am I *with child* this time?"

"There will be feasts with plenty of wine and music. If you don't want my family to send you to bed early, I suggest you *shouldn't* be with child." A small smile played at the edge of his thick lips, which were a pale tan against his light brown skin. "You should probably know the extent of this mission. My great-aunt, Ama Isla, has promised me a sum of money—"

"Then why the ransom?"

"It is not a large sum, and it will only be granted to me upon beginning my new 'family lifestyle.'"

"Ah." I picked up a twig and removed its bark to keep my hands busy.

"I need her to believe we are married long enough to collect on the inheritance and leave."

My hair slipped from its knot when I cocked my head to the side. "If this is your family village, why are you in a hurry to leave? Or does this question trample on your delicate sensibilities about social cues?"

He was quiet for a long time. "This village is home to my aunt and a few cousins, but the rest of my family has moved on."

"I see." Then, standing, I offered a hand to him to pull him to his feet as well. "Let's go get that money, husband. You should know spouses share everything in my village, and I'll expect no less..." When I winked, he laughed, and it was the kind of laugh that made me smile.

"Here I was, beginning to think they sacrificed people for making jokes in Bahmisi."

We decided to say we had wed six months ago, when the moon was full in a perfect temple wedding. My dowry had been seven goats—not too little to make Ama Isla think I'd been a cheap bride, but not too much to make her think our finances were in complete order.

We rode on with Tanu behind me in the saddle. Once we'd made it over a cluster of dunes from the tree where we'd rested, the land became flat and white with bizarre patterns etched into the surface. The wind whipped my hair around my face, and I dragged strands of it from my dry lips as I stared in awe at the place. If the gods were not real, what kind of miracle had occurred to result in this raw, wild beauty?

"Salt flats." Tanu's deep voice rumbled in my ear. Then he pointed at a speck of darkness in the distance. "There lies Tigrea. We'll arrive soon."

We made our descent. On the flats, Pharaoh's hooves made a soft crunch over the salt and the sun glared off the whiteness of the land, forcing me to squint my eyes to a near close. Tanu dismounted and dragged his fingertips along the ground before clutching my hand. I jerked away.

He rolled his eyes and reached for my hand again. "Just try it." After wiping the gritty residue from the earth into my palm, he licked his own finger.

I pressed it to my tongue. Memories of harvest festivals, helping M'Ma in the kitchen, and the payoff of eating the fruits of a year's labor flooded over me. The men of Bahmisi could derive salt from parts of our land, but the yields were small and the mineral was scarce, special. Homesickness seeped into my gut. Feasting was laughter around a dinner table and family and feeling loved, and there I was, alone save for a thief and his horse in a place my dead gods had most likely not created. Was it possible to mourn something you now believed never existed? I felt hopelessly alone as tears brimmed to the edge of my eyelids.

"It's salt—it's not poisonous." The abrupt sound of Tanu's voice instantly drained me of sadness and replaced it with anger.

"I know salt isn't *poisonous*, fool," I snapped.

"Forgive me, *my sweet bride*, I'm still figuring out just how much you know about the world." His frown sent a shiver of guilt through me.

It passed quickly.

We didn't speak for the next half-hour as we rode toward the village that was always just another mile away. Finally, the large cluster of buildings became close enough to decipher it wasn't simply an elaborate mirage.

Pharaoh clopped into town with me on his back and Tanu clutching the reins. The closer we got to Tigrea, the more the thief's shoulders rose toward his ears.

Once in the village, houses upon houses lined the stone streets, and people and carts bustled up and down the main line of vendor tents. It smelled of meat roasted in cinnamon and oregano, and my mouth watered just thinking of the taste. Tanu kept his head low, but every once in a while, he hesitantly greeted someone who knew him by name.

This place was much larger than Bahmisi. I had only heard about cities in folklore, but none of the stories had described the exhilaration that came with the frenzy of a real city. Out in the street were people selling their wares as they did in my village, but there were also some who performed or sold art. A woman danced with a torch before swallowing the flame as the crowd around her cheered. Another woman had a line of children waiting by her stand as she decorated a little boy's face with bright paint. A teenage boy sold various pieces of flat wood that had incredible pictures carved onto the surfaces. One was of a woman nursing her baby as she sat on the ground with her back against a wall. Another was of an old man sitting beside a grave, his head bowed with grief. They were heartbreakingly beautiful, and I regretted not having the funds to buy one. I thought of the time it must have taken to make the carvings and couldn't believe these people lived in a place where one could spend hours sitting down to create instead of tending to the home or land. I also hadn't realized that someone could sell art or a performance for coin and that someone else would buy it.

Immediately, I thought of Lileena and what I would tell her of my grand adventure and the jewelry we could make and sell together here, only to remember that my dear friend was dead. Not a demi-goddess. Just dead. And her body was nothing but a beheaded carcass in a cave. I squeezed my eyes closed and told her anyway. Wherever she was.

Tanu led the horse all the way to a stable and paid the boy inside coin to freshen up Pharaoh and give him a place to rest. Then he grasped my hand and led me down a narrow footpath between crooked clay buildings that towered into the sky.

I was ready to complain of sore feet when he brought me to a high stone wall covered with plants and shaded with large trees. He pawed the top of the wall and removed a key before taking me to a door and unlocking it. Inside, there was a courtyard of fruit trees and water fountains and a row of houses.

"This is the Batla estate—my aunt is the matriarch of this family," he said, eyes darting around. "Just so you know, I hate my cousin, Salah."

"Very well." *Not sure how that helps my acting role, but fine...*

A girl with shiny dark hair contained in one thick braid appeared on one of the balconies and cried Tanu's name with glee. A grin spread across his face as he waved. When she descended a spiral staircase that ran through a hole in the balcony, I could see she was young, maybe nine or ten, but she was taller than me.

"Tanu!" she exclaimed, throwing her arms around him as he twirled her in circles. "They said you would never return! Oh, Tanu! I'm so glad to see you alive!" When he put her down, she looked up to examine him. "You've been out in the desert a lot. You're a whole new color."

Tanu laughed and patted her shoulder, and for the first time, her black eyes fell on me. I waved awkwardly and smiled.

"Pagria, allow me to introduce you to my wife, Akedia," Tanu said, wrapping an arm around the small of my back and gently pushing me forward.

Unsure at first, Pagria eyed me from head to toe. "Wife? But Tanu, you said you would *never* marry."

That rich laughter of his filled the air. "You forget nothing, little cousin. I also said that when you were four."

Then without warning, Pagria placed her hands on my shoulders and pressed her forehead to mine. "From the sea of sands to the sea of waters, I welcome you to my family."

Her sincere welcome warmed my heart with gratitude and a bit of guilt for the lies I would be forced to tell her. If Tanu felt bad, it didn't show.

Then a woman appeared on the same balcony, her white hair worked into a thousand braids and wound into a large bun at the nape of her neck.

"Tanu, grandson of my sister, returns," she declared. "You will come inside and feast and tell me of the places you've been and of this pretty young woman at your side."

Tanu took my hand and led the way to the stairs, pulling me toward the woman I presumed was Ama Isla. I couldn't help but feel like I was just a fly, squirming in the web of lies Tanu was sure to weave around me.

Chapter Eleven

MEETING THE FAMILY

The metal stairs resonated as we worked our way up the spiral steps toward Tanu's aunt. She was a little woman, but her presence was large at the top of the balcony. Glittering gold and blue chiton fabric fluttered on the subtle breeze. Her deep olive skin was fair from a life lived indoors, and her hair had grown out a little since it had last been braided—tiny tufts of curls formed at the roots.

"Tanu Behman returns," she stated, appraising him with green eyes that seemed stern but not unkind. "You have been missed."

Tanu released my hand and kissed his aunt on the cheek, then turned his attention to me. "Ama Isla, allow me to introduce my wife, Akedia."

She looked past him to me, that same examining gaze. "Your *wife*?" Tanu grasped my hand and pulled me closer, and I got the impression that Ama Isla was someone who didn't come to you; you went to her. "My word, Tanu. You fall off the edge of the world only to return with a bride."

Tanu released my hand when Ama Isla took it from him and tugged me closer. Her green eyes swept over me from head to toe, a smile forming at the left corner of her mouth.

"You chose wisely, Tanu," she said. Then she looked at me with a smirk. "Hopefully, you did too."

"We'll find out in good time, I suppose," I replied, making Ama Isla erupt with laughter.

Tanu laughed along, then narrowed his dark eyes at me when his aunt turned her back to us.

"Well, come along," Ama Isla said over her shoulder. "How long will you be staying?"

We followed behind, Tanu brushing against me every so often as we followed down the long, wrap-around balcony to a door that led us inside to a glamorous home filled with vases and lounge chairs. He was trying to play the role of a newlywed, but he didn't need to walk on my heels. I swatted at him to back up, making him hiss *stop it* under his breath until Ama Isla turned around, and we both smiled.

"Ah! Here we are." Ama Isla opened a door made of beautiful black wood like I'd never seen. Behind the door was a room with a plush bedding mat placed directly on the floor, richly woven rugs, gleaming metal wash basins, and a chandelier of sparkling jewels. "Freshen up for supper you two, then we shall properly introduce you to the entire family, my dear."

She smiled and closed the door, and I turned to Tanu once she was gone. "Your family is wealthy beyond all reason, and you're a common thief? How did that happen?"

He went to the wash basin and dipped a cloth inside before ringing it out to dab his face. Then he untied his hair and shook out the curls that were stuck in the shape of the bun before dipping his head in the water. "You won't meet either of my parents here. This is my extended family, and I'm only welcome with conditions." He finished cleaning, then squeezed his hair dry with another towel as he turned. "Listen, I need you to understand something. These people are twisted. You stay close to me, and if you get separated, be aware that they may try to corner you for questioning. Do not forget the facts we established about our marriage details."

"Alright, fine. But what are we going to do about this room?" I glanced around and saw only one bed for sleeping.

"You'll sleep there," he said, nodding at the bed.

"And you? Where will you sleep?"

He frowned and shrugged. "And *I'll* sleep there."

"Um, no."

"We're married, remember?"

"Have you really come to believe your own lie? We're not *really* married. It would be indecent for us to share the bed." I searched the room once more in hopes of finding another sofa or mat.

Tanu stripped away the upper layer of his clothing as though it were nothing to disrobe in front of me, picking up a fresh tunic that someone had left folded on the edge of the bed. I looked away until he was covered again. "The servants come in early in the morning to freshen the wash water and leave a tray of food. They do it without anyone ever seeing them, but they see us—the sleeping family members. And if they see us, you and me, in separate beds, my aunt will know we're not really married. In fact, I can count on the servants coming in to report back to her."

"But—"

"You will act as my wife and sleep in that bed with me," he said sternly, a dark glower morphing his face. "The second favor is not complete until you help me convince them we're married."

I wanted to throw one of those huge, beautiful vases at his insufferable head or smash my fist into a wall or scream at the top of my lungs. But I couldn't do anything, and hot angry tears threatened to pool into my eyes. I turned away from him, so he wouldn't see me cry if it came to that. Fortunately, it didn't.

"I promise to be absolutely respectful," he said, his voice softer.

"You disrespect me already by forcing me to sleep in your bed," I hissed, storming past him. He grabbed my arm.

"We have to go to dinner now." His hand softened and dropped. "I'm..."

If he was about to say *sorry,* I didn't care one bit. I stomped over to the wash basin with every intention of cleaning my face until I saw the murky mess left behind from Tanu.

"When was the last time you bathed?" I snarled, finding the soiled bath water to be an added insult to the injury he inflicted on me with his magical contract.

Someone knocked on the door, before Pagria poked her head inside. Her dark hair was now tied into two separate buns on the top of her head, and her cheeks dimpled when she smiled.

"Am I interrupting?" she asked.

"No, Gria, we're coming." Tanu wrapped an arm around her shoulder and gave her a playful squeeze. "Why have you grown so much?"

The two walked into the hallway, and I hoped he would leave me alone in the room to have a moment by myself or sleep on that fluffy mattress. Alone.

"Aren't you coming, *my darling*?"

Just the sound of his voice made my teeth grind. Five days was five days too much of this nonsense.

You can do it. Five days, and then B'Ba and M'Ma will arrive to start a new life...

I sighed and stuffed down my pride. This situation wasn't *so* terrible—not worse than getting beheaded, right? Maybe. All I had left after this was one more favor.

"Just one more," I whispered.

"What's that, love?" Tanu asked, waiting in the hall for me with Pagria. Once I trudged out, he wrapped his free arm around my waist and dragged me with him.

"I'm just talking to myself, *dearest*," I said through a clenched jaw.

Walking along the corridors and past doorways made me realize the property was a large, gated estate with many living units. They were connected like one big house, which led me to believe the people inside comprised Tanu's extended family and their servants. Flowering vines and plants of various colors and shapes filled every speck of earth between the stone structures and walkways, as though Ama Isla had somehow captured only the most beautiful parts of the jungle and demanded they grow in her palace.

Pagria told us we'd feast outdoors that evening, leading us to a courtyard where a long wooden table laden with food was set, and lanterns with colored glass dangled overhead. People stood all around the table, chattering and laughing. When we neared, a silence stifled the laughter, deadening the words.

Ama Isla rose from her seat at the head of the table and lifted an arm to point at us. "My nephew has returned from the edge of the world, bringing with him a new wife, Akedia. Treat her well."

The crowd chorused a welcome while most took their seats. One person, however, didn't sit. He had long wavy hair and a thick ashy brown beard and olive skin.

It was his piercing blue eyes that took me by surprise, though. They were like orbs of water, fluid and hypnotic—a color I had never seen on a person before. He had a muscular build and stood over a foot taller than me and a few inches taller than Tanu.

"My lady, please have a seat," said the man, pulling out a chair and offering me a place at the table.

"Thank you..."

"My name is Salah." No sooner had he introduced himself did Tanu reach around me to grasp forearms with Salah in greeting.

"Cousin. It is good to see you looking well." Tanu's voice was taut and forced. Then I remembered the name he had mentioned before. Salah was the cousin he hated.

I could see why. There probably wasn't a maiden in the entire village who hadn't fallen for him.

"It is good to see you, too, cousin. I have missed you. Please, sit and break bread with your family," Salah said, sitting at my left as Tanu sat to my right.

Once everyone had found a seat and filled their cups, Ama Isla cleared her throat. "Once again, we praise Waikenu for his gift of life by the light of the sun, and we offer sacrifice in his name."

A quiet gasp caught in my throat, and Tanu's hand reached for mine under the table and squeezed before letting go. He probably couldn't afford for me to pass out in front of his family.

"It's okay," he whispered, leaning close to my ear, his lips brushing my skin, his beard leaving a subtle rawness on my cheek. I couldn't help but notice he scooted me a few inches farther from Salah in the process.

My mouth hung open as I watched the matriarch place a bowl of food on a stone pillar in the courtyard and set it ablaze. Once the flames died down to smoldering ash, the family members dug into their meals, and the noise of dinner conversation grew loud once more. I couldn't quite find my appetite as my mind raced.

The people of Manitu offered a drop of blood each for sacrifice. The people of Tigrea offered food. Across the sands, we had all decided to worship the same being in different ways.

But who was right?

That vivid image of my best friend's corpse rotting away in a cave when she was supposed to have ascended lingered always at the back of my mind. If any of us had it right, it certainly wasn't the people of Bahmisi. But maybe none of us were.

The utter loneliness of that thought haunted me where I sat at a table full of people who believed. I missed the comfort of loving my gods, yet I could no longer go back to where I'd been.

"I'd love to know what you're thinking about over there," said Salah.

Glancing at Tanu, who was deep in conversation with someone on his right, I decided it didn't hurt to be a friendly fake in-law.

"I suppose I was wondering if it is better to be happy and ignorant or smart and miserable."

He chuckled and took a sip of wine. "I can honestly say I was not expecting that response. Which one do you think you are?"

My eyes flickered to the smoldering pile of food, before smiling at him and picking up my own wine goblet. "I suppose I'm still deciding."

We clinked goblets, and he offered a toast. "May we live."

I felt Tanu's hand on my bare shoulder. Salah's gaze shifted behind me at his cousin, and I looked down, feeling my heart flutter with unease.

"You have not only a beautiful wife, Tanu, but one with a deep soul." Salah smiled, making my cheeks flush with warm blood.

When I glanced beyond him, I couldn't help but notice Ama Isla studying me. So I turned to Tanu and slipped my hand into his, placing the other on top of his forearm coated with a layer of black hairs.

"My Tanu is handsome and wise, more than I could hope to be." It made me want to vomit, and even Tanu flashed a suspicious glare at me like I'd possibly poisoned his goblet, but if Salah was testing me in any way, I needed to resist looking into those bright blue eyes. "Should we go to bed, darling?"

Once we said goodnight to everyone at the table and kissed Ama Isla on the cheek, we excused ourselves from the dinner party and escaped to the room.

With the door shut, Tanu cocked his head to the side. "Couldn't wait to get me to bed, huh?"

"Ugh, please. I couldn't wait to get out of there. Your aunt was... *watching* me." I untied my hair and massaged my scalp.

"I told you they would." A line between his brows creased slightly. "Did you have a good conversation with my cousin?"

"There wasn't much to it, but I suppose."

Tanu unwrapped himself from the tunic he wore and crawled onto the giant floor mat that served as our bed. I stared at the thing that looked like an overgrown pillow with tassels on each corner, anxiety clouding my mind.

"Just lie down, Akedia. We won't even touch each other with all this room. It's no different than that hay where we slept near one another in Manitu." He sighed. "I promise I won't bite... unless you *want* me to."

Ignoring his comment, I kept my clothes on and slowly crawled onto the bed beside him. When my body hit the feather-stuffed surface, I couldn't believe how amazing it felt.

"This is luxury! I feel like I'm floating on a cloud," I said, my hand rippling over the velvety surface.

Tanu chuckled and turned on his side to face me. "Such blasphemy to think the gods would let you sit upon their clouds!" he teased, flashing a playful smile. "You really have been sheltered. It's amusing to watch you see things for the first time. You're like an infant."

"Well, I'm glad I amuse you, thief," I said, but I grinned and he laughed, and for a minute I forgot we were lying on the bed together.

My mind was my own worst enemy, I realized, as more thoughts seeped into me, tainting any light-heartedness I'd enjoyed with melancholy. A knot gathered in my throat, and my only escape was to turn away from him and gaze out the open balcony doors to the stars hanging overhead.

Were they the same stars as the ones Evanya tended like a shepherd of the night? I squeezed my eyelids closed and took a deep breath. Beyond granting Tanu his favors and hopefully reuniting with my parents again, what was left for me? I was either entirely wrong to doubt my own faith, with an afterlife of torture to face, or... I was right. Or maybe I was right in some way I didn't truly understand yet.

I was thinking too much, and it made my heart race with worry when there was nothing to be done. I counted while taking slow, even breaths through my nose. Goats jumping over a stream.

Tanu's voice, though soft, made me jump when it broke the silence. "What will you do once the favors are complete?"

Without thinking, I blurted out an answer, which may have been the answer I needed all along. "I will find a way to prove to my people that the sun god does not require our deaths. And when I have that, I will return to Bahmisi."

Tanu chuckled. "One girl will change the minds and traditions of old people?"

"And why not?"

"You are arrogant to think you can simply show up and explain to these people why what they believe is wrong."

I frowned and tried to keep my nostrils from flaring. "You are condescending and rude if you believe my people are too simple to listen to me when I have solid proof."

What I didn't say, though, was that he was probably right. How many people would ignore evidence to continue believing what made them feel comfortable? I'd wager most of them. And what kind of proof could I provide?

Still, a small yet earth-moving voice whispered in the back of my mind:

Do it anyway.

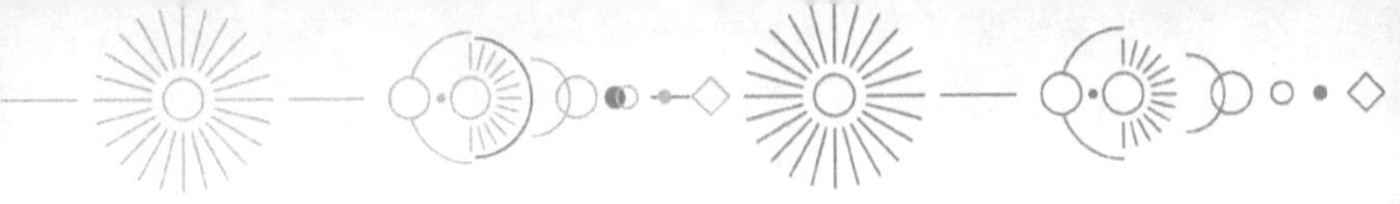

Chapter Twelve

Life on the Road

Tanu took me for a walk through the family's estate the next morning, and we must have looked the part of a couple craving intimacy, because everyone gave us space as we strolled through rows of plants and shrubs hand in hand. Between bouts of shifting his eyes from balcony to balcony, he'd lean close and whisper something in my ear.

"Pretend to giggle," he said, so I did. "Good. Now, about our ransom. I want to collect on both by the time our five days are up. You're doing great so far…"

"Why do I feel like you're going to add a 'but' to that?"

He pulled his hand free from mine and wrapped it around my waist. "Well, because I am. *But* keep your distance from Salah."

"He seems harmless—"

"That's the problem."

Birds darted about, one dropping a seed in our path. When Tanu's foot stepped on the edge of it, the beady thing pinged into the bushes. There were quite a few birds of many different colors in this place. I looked at the trees and saw multiple feeders on the boughs. The estate was truly beautiful. I couldn't imagine ever wanting to leave it for a life in the desert dunes.

"Fine. As your fake wife, I will respect your wishes."

My tone was facetious, but I admittedly meant it. I wanted to get this favor over and done with. Then he stopped walking and clutched my face with two tender hands.

"Someone's watching us from the balcony," he explained, but he kept holding my face, rubbing smooth warm thumbs over my cheeks. "I hope you mean that, about Salah. I really need you to stay away from him."

"I don't understand why you won't let this rest." In the sunlight, Tanu's dark eyes glistened as they stared into mine. I felt my face flush in his grasp and that acidic blue pressure returned to my chest. I wanted to pull away, but I couldn't. Finally it became too great, and I whimpered under his control. "*Fine.* Fine. I will stay away from him. But please, just tell me, what is the third favor?"

He leaned forward and kissed me tenderly on the face before releasing his hold. At least the pretend Tanu could be gentle and sweet, even if the real one was gruff and rude.

"Are you ready to hear this?" he began, taking my hand again.

I nodded eagerly, so he leaned close to my ear. His breath sent shivers down my spine. Maybe I'd finally earned enough of his trust for him to tell me the favor.

"I'll tell you when I feel like it," he whispered.

I swatted him in the chest, which made him laugh and made me hit him again. "You're driving me to insanity with this game! I just want to know."

Pagria came skipping out to greet us. She held two wreaths made of succulents and cacti flowers.

"Akedia! I made something for you," she said, holding up the beautiful ring of flowers woven together with palm fibers.

The gesture took me by surprise at first, and my tongue stayed tied in its knot while she placed the creation on my head. Tanu nodded with approval.

"Pagria, I—" I pulled her in for a hug, grateful for the genuine show of hospitality. "Thank you so much. It's absolutely beautiful."

"You're welcome!" she said, practically chirping like one of the colorful birds that flitted about the Batla estate. "Grandmother said to invite you to a ladies tea time this afternoon."

Tanu nodded when I glanced at him, so I agreed, though I couldn't help but feel like I was being lured into some kind of trap.

Food, honey, and porcelain cups and saucers trimmed with gold and black paint covered the courtyard table, which was surrounded by the females of Tanu's extended family. While servants stood to the side and fanned us with giant palm leaves, I sipped the brownish green water, pretending to be pleased with its exotic flowery flavor, when really I yearned for the familiar taste of bitter coffee grounds swirling at the bottom of a briki pot.

Pagria had initially tried to sit beside me, but Ama Isla insisted I sit at her side to *get acquainted*. More like examined. She ran through a list of questions—some in regard to my nuptials but mostly about me and my family. We hadn't talked about who I was supposed to be other than his wife, so when she asked what my parents were like, I froze. My throat tightened as I remembered the way B'Ba's eyes crinkled at the edges when he laughed and how M'Ma always kept fresh flowers in my room. I could feel the others staring, but I felt pinned down by the weight of my own longing.

"They are... they're more than I could have ever hoped for," I finally replied when Ama Isla gently touched my arm.

For once, her eyes left that somewhat calculating gaze they'd had for me and softened.

"Being away from home is hard, my dear." She gave my hand a gentle squeeze. "But young brides eventually feel less like they've left a home and more like they're making a new one."

I smiled in a way I hoped came across as appreciative. If only it was a simple matter of a new bride feeling homesick for her parents' hut.

When a servant came to take away the cups, I glanced at the room balcony, and Ama Isla caught it. "Go back to your husband," she said, taking a final sip from her cup before handing it to a young servant girl. I stood to leave, grateful for the dismissal, but then she clutched my wrist. "How many months ago did you and Tanu wed?"

"Six."

Her eyes narrowed slightly. "And you're not with child yet?"

Damn it.

Damn, damn, damn. Why hadn't we thought of that? I should've been showing signs of a new pregnancy. Young brides in Bahmisi delivered babes mere months shy of a full harvest cycle.

"I've been a little..." I lowered my head to avoid her gaze and feign an emotional struggle. "I've been somewhat ill. But I'm on the mend now."

"What were you sick with?" she asked.

"The medicine man was unsure. He said I was mostly under duress from moving and life on the road." That sense of desire to return to my room morphed into urgency. I needed to get to Tanu before anyone else did to tell him of my lie.

The other women at the table were silent, shifting slightly in their seats, but Ama Isla's gaze didn't navigate away from me. "Tomorrow, you will have my medicine woman examine you. Perhaps it is time Tanu provides a stable life for you here in Tigrea."

"Yes, ma'am." Somehow I managed to remain calm while I was screaming inside. She wanted her medicine woman to examine me. Tomorrow.

When Ama Isla finally dismissed the ladies, I stormed up to the room and shouted Tanu's name, but he didn't answer. A voice called to me from the hallway.

"Tanu is in the bath house. He should return soon," Salah said, holding a basket of fruit. "But while I'm here, take this for later. I've picked too many."

It was an enchanting problem, to pick too many. Fruit in Bahmisi was scarce on the trees. We had to wait for days between pickings so more could ripen once the bigger ones were out of the way and no longer sucking up all the sun god's life-giving rays.

"These are beautiful," I said, running a hand over the soft pink and orange hues on the large fruit in his basket.

"A Batla family crop. We've cross pollinated the supplies for years to create these particular mangos." He handed one to me then cocked his head to the side. "You know, you could always just go get Tanu. He's your husband after all."

Another subtle test from the family? Tanu must have given them a reason to be suspicious.

"I will wait for his return. Thank you for the lovely—"

Tanu walked in just at that moment with a towel wrapped around his waist and beads of water clinging to his bare chest. "The lovely what?"

"Tanu! Hello, darling." I hastily picked up the large, oddly shaped thing Salah had called a mango and held it up. "Your cousin has brought us some fruit. Wasn't that nice?"

The two looked at each other for a dark moment as Tanu inched closer, his presence hovering over me from behind even though we didn't touch.

"Yes, thank you, Salah." Tanu then walked toward his cousin and clutched the door. "If you'll excuse us, I'd like to be alone with my wife."

Salah stepped into the hallway and nodded. "Of course." His brilliant blue eyes shot to me and then away. "I'm sorry to be a bother."

Once Tanu had slammed the door, he whirled around and glared at me. "You bring him here, in our room?"

"He walked right in; what did you want me to do? Attack your cousin? I can't imagine that would go over well with your family," I replied with a huff. "And will you please put on some clothes?"

Tanu rolled his eyes and disappeared behind a screen in the room. It had feathers woven onto its surface with threads of gleaming golds and muted pinks and browns. They were colors of the desert—dry and brilliant all at once. I plopped down on the bed.

"You don't understand my family," he said, his voice bouncing slightly, as though he had stumbled in his effort to get dressed behind the screen. "I told you they are strange people."

"Then tell me *more*. How can I help if I don't know how?" *How can I complete this favor if we don't get this over with?* But I kept that part to myself.

Tanu reappeared, wearing a camel-tan tunic and loose brown pants. He sighed and sat next to me on the bed, tucking a loose strand of dark curls behind his ear.

"My grandmother decided to marry someone my great-grandparents did not approve of, and even though she would have become the matriarch of the Batla family, she was cast out. Her younger sister, Ama Isla, became the matriarch and inherited the entire fortune," he said, shrugging. "It's all ridiculous if you ask me. The only reason they didn't like my grandfather was because he wasn't from *a good family*. In other words, poor."

I quietly huffed a response. He went on to explain that Ama Isla and his grandmother had eventually mended the tear between them, but the relationship was forever strained.

"Any hostility there might have been didn't quite extend to me, though. I guess Ama Isla always liked me," he said. "She's suggested I come to live here on more than one occasion, especially after my parents died and my grandmother took me and my brother in. But I couldn't do it. In a strange way, it still feels like they're trying to isolate my grandmother."

His eyes softened as he stared at his feet.

"I'm sorry," I said, placing a hand on his arm, but he brushed it away and stood. When he did, that cloud of indiscernible distance pooled back around him.

"There's nothing to be sorry for. It simply is." He walked toward the balcony and pulled the curtain aside to let in the light. It was too warm still, so he let the fabric fall back into place. "I'll tell you one thing, though. This *marriage* is going to get me through for a while."

His sinister smile made my gut turn. Even if his family had turned away his grandmother, it was still hard to think he'd want to con them.

"You're a thief and a liar. How does this sit right with you?" I stood, keeping my chin high. "How do you ever expect to become a man if you live this life of lies and crime?"

He chuckled. "There is no law of nature that says you must be *good* to grow into a man. It merely happens."

I hated the way he laughed. As though I knew nothing and he had seen the world ten times over. But his own arrogance was an ignorance he had yet to contend with.

"You may grow hair on your chest, while the hair on your head grows gray, but if you are still a swine of a human being, you are no man to me," I snarled then stormed into the curtained vanity area where a large looking glass hung from the wall beside a bronze table and chair.

That fool had no idea what it meant to be a man. The thought of my father, who was more of a man than anyone I knew, made me hurt for home. That festering wound ached when poked. Everywhere I turned and everything I thought about reminded me that I could never return. The anger I felt for Tanu and the pain in my heart for home consumed me that evening, and I couldn't escape the gnawing feeling that I had completely forgotten about something.

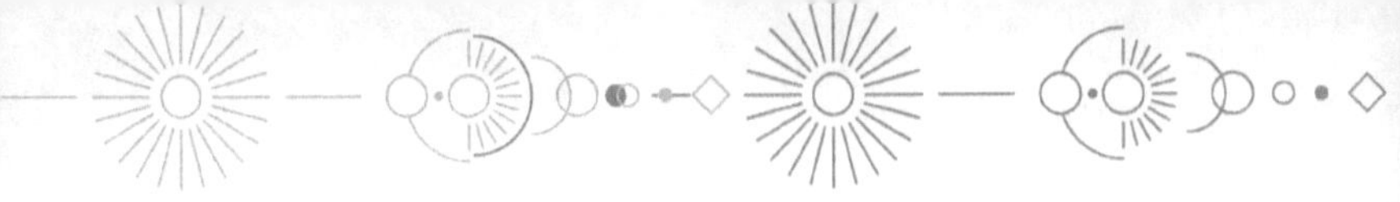

CHAPTER THIRTEEN

THE WOLF

The morning sun poured into our room every time the silk curtains fluttered in the breeze, and I rolled to my side on the bed. Tanu and I had fought about our sleeping arrangements yet again, and yet again he won since I was desperate to cross another favor off my list. That, and I was magically bound to obey.

He had been right about the servants. Refreshments and clean wash water magically appeared in the morning, and I could only assume they'd brought it in earlier than the sun itself. The people with that kind of access to the sleeping family members of the Batla estate clearly had earned a high level of trust.

I poured myself a cup of coffee and took a sip, allowing the bitter warmness to fuel my spirit with happiness. The strong black brew filled every inch of me. If there were a god to thank that it wasn't a pot of mild flowery tea, I would be willing to make prayer in their name.

The morning was quiet as Tanu slept, so I took the coffee to the balcony to watch the sun rise. Beautiful colors shot across the sky, and utter stillness filled the air, as though the world had been made just for me. As though Waikenu still swept the blackness from above, even for a wretched nonbeliever. At least that squeeze of anxiety in my chest was familiar in this foreign land. I'd carried it since before leaving Bahmisi, so in a way it held a piece of home.

I took small comfort in the fake ransom that would hopefully bring my parents to Tigrea. B'Ba and I had said our goodbyes hastily. I prayed he would understand my plan or, if nothing more, believe I had actually been kidnapped and make his own plans to find me. Terrible thoughts darkened my hope. Would B'Ba be able to sneak away at his age without getting caught? What if the high priest's men found the mail carrier and forced him to tell the truth about who sent him with the package? Immediately, I regretted being present when we shipped the note and rock. I clearly hadn't been tied up like the hostage depicted in the letter.

Too many thoughts. I breathed slowly through my nose.

"The sun rises and falls each day, yet we continue to watch as though something different will happen." Tanu's voice made me jump as he emerged from the curtains and walked onto the balcony. He leaned elbows on the banister beside me to join me in staring.

"It's a majestic sight." I shrugged, then looked down at my fingernails. "But in truth, the sight of it makes me incredibly…"

When I hesitated, he bumped my arm with his elbow. "Incredibly?"

"Heartbroken." The sun was buttery warm on everything it touched as more light pooled into the city of clay buildings. It was light I didn't deserve, even if the people around me did. Why would Waikenu still part the darkness to bring light to a place where someone who had defiantly walked away from Him roamed? "I am not worthy of the sun god's light. I have turned my back on my faith, my people, my family." Then, in a whisper. "I am lost under the desert sun."

Tanu for once was quiet as he looked back at the brightening sky. I turned to leave him alone with the gift Waikenu surely meant to give to everyone but me, but he reached for my hand and pulled me to him. His sudden closeness when there was no show to put on for his family made my heart skip a beat, and for a second too long, we could only look at one another. Staring into his dark eyes, it was as though we'd met before in another life and had only to meet in this one to rekindle whatever had once been between us. But when he shook his head slightly and spoke, the moment slipped away.

"Do you see that barn in the distance?" His outstretched arm pointed to a place far away where crops surrounded a thatched-roof structure. "I knew the man who lived there when I was still small. He would tell me stories about how he'd traveled to the ends of the world, where the ground simply stops and over the edge is only darkness. Of water that stretches farther than you could ever see, moving in waves as big as mountains. I used to love his stories. He left home for a long time before returning to take over the family farm."

"Why did he ever leave?"

Tanu turned to me with a small smile. "He didn't believe in the sun god's religion. He wrote to the high priests of our time to tell them how wrong they were. But I'll never forget the day he returned. He was worn from his life on the road and looked older than time itself, but when he saw the temple again, he wept like a child. He was so glad to be home."

My throat tightened with tears itching to be free if it weren't for my pride. "Why are you telling me this, Tanu?"

"Because the sun god never stopped letting the light shine when he was away." He shrugged, then added, "Because you can always return home, but you won't be the same as when you left it—hopefully, for the better. And maybe, because sometimes we think we're more lost than we really are."

It was a blanket statement for the two of us, but the man from his story did not risk death for returning, and that would forever be the difference.

In the courtyard below, a maid walked to a large bell in the center of the gardens and rang it three times. The mutter of life in other rooms followed.

"There's the morning bell." Tanu rubbed his face and let out a slight groan. "There are definitely some things I don't miss about this place. Everything is on a schedule. We'll be expected at breakfast within fifteen minutes."

Breakfast was served once everyone had washed up and marched down from the rooms. Once again we ate at the large outdoor table in the courtyard between the family apartments. While I managed to avoid sitting next to Salah, he ended up across the table from me. After we glanced at each other once and then twice, I made every effort to avoid looking in his direction.

At first, I thought his eyes reminded me of my gentle goats, but truly they were more like that of the wolf that had stalked the herds of Bahmisi. It took the men three days to catch him, and when they did, they skinned him for a coat for the high priest. But a day before his death, I had been alone in the field with the goats when the wild creature appeared. We had stared at one another, the two of us—girl and wolf—and his eyes were icy pools of water captured beneath glassy orbs. I thought I'd had a connection with him, until he leapt for a goat kid and made off with its ragged body. I spent many nights afterward crying with guilt, thinking of the ways I could have saved the kid.

Tanu's hatred of Salah might have stemmed from jealousy, but it was possible the man with eyes like a wild animal was every bit as stealthy and unpredictable.

After we'd eaten and the family dispersed, Ama Isla called Tanu to her end of the table where she drank her coffee in slow sips. She shot a glance at me as I trailed behind him.

"Oh, Akedia, dear. Your husband will be along shortly," she said, and while her tone was kind, I couldn't help but feel like I'd been sent to my room.

No matter, I thought. *I'd rather a minute or two alone.*

I returned to a room with fluffed pillows, a new tray of water, and sweet candies on the vanity table. The servants around here were like quiet elves lingering in the shadows. I popped one of the amber-colored candies into my mouth and voyaged to the balcony with the flavor of honey and ginger lingering on my tongue. Something about the cool breeze and lofty view of the city gave me a sense of peace in all the chaos.

The world below was more frenzied than it had been earlier this morning. Merchants passed with handcarts through the streets, while shoppers bustled through the maze of vendors with their spoils. It was a fascinating cacophony that I didn't necessarily mind at this hour, but it couldn't compare to sunrise.

In Bahmisi, the common people and even those who had become nobility through connection to an offering wore basic browns and tans. Only the high priest, priestesses, and templekeepers wore purple robes. But here in Tigrea, it seemed cloth dye was easy to find—everyone wore some kind of colored garment. Scanning the crowd, I could see reds, yellows, blues... Purple.

My heart hammered at the sight of that hue, and I ducked down behind the balcony banister. Anxiety had seeped so far into my being, it was braided into the structure of my bones. If the high priest's men ever caught and tortured me before leaving my body for the wolves, the beasts would probably taste it in my marrow.

Slowly, I dared to peek over the top to examine the man in a deep purple toga. I allowed myself a sigh of relief and stood at full height when I didn't recognize him as someone from Bahmisi. Maybe that ransom wasn't the best idea after all—we had essentially given them a map to find me...

The sound of bare feet padding across the marble floor gave me the signal that Tanu had returned from speaking with his aunt. I gave the city one last glance before slithering through the curtains and into the room.

"What did Ama Isla have to say?" I called, pausing at the looking glass to tuck stray hairs into place. A few wispy ones near my face always escaped from pins or braids. And the City of Tigrea seemed to hold more moisture in the air, unlike the ashy dryness of the sands beyond. I turned toward the door. "Tanu?"

No one answered, but the door was ajar. Perhaps he'd forgotten something and left it open in his haste. I opened a jar of oil and dipped my fingertips inside before lathering my forearms with the sweet-smelling liquid. Lavender and vanilla. I scooped a bit more to moisten the ends of my long hair.

"That fragrance is made here in the Batla estate." The male voice inside the room wasn't Tanu's, and when I jumped from fright, I knocked over the oil, sending it splattering onto the rug.

Salah.

Strands of his wavy hair hung loose around sparkling blue eyes.

Glancing at the spilled oil, I grabbed a nearby towel and crouched to clean the mess. "Oh dear..."

He bent to help me dab oil from the otherwise beautiful rug. "I'm so sorry to have startled you."

"Don't worry." I stood and looked down at my handiwork. The dark spot of oil was too noticeable, I realized, as I glared at the stain with my arms folded. "We should roll this up and take it outside for washing. What do you think?"

Without waiting for his opinion, I bent the rug, but he clutched my arm. I straightened at the touch.

"How long have you been Tanu's wife?"

It felt like a trap. Had he already spoken with Ama Isla? Regardless, I had to stick with the lies Tanu and I crafted. "Six months."

His eyes lingered over me, examining. "And you're not with child yet?"

Fortunately, my previous encounter had robbed him of the chance to catch me off guard.

"We will have a child when it suits the gods." Blaming my circumstances on the will of the gods would give me the chance to point the topic back to him with a threatening undertone: *Do you claim to know more than the holy ones?*

"In addition, Ama Isla is going to have her medicine woman examine me today," I added, remembering my lie and cringing when I realized that gnawing feeling from the night before was from forgetting to tell Tanu.

Salah stepped closer. "That doesn't seem quite right."

What if Tanu said something to spark suspicion and Ama Isla sent Salah to press the issue? If he said I was with child, because I messed up and didn't tell him, then my lie wouldn't make sense anymore. This had to be a test.

"If the gods will us to wait for children, who am I to question them?" I'd leave out the fact that I had run away to avoid serving them with the sacrifice of my mortal flesh, though.

"The gods sometimes do not intervene when you insist on making mistakes, like choosing the wrong husband." When he stepped closer yet again, I stepped back and bumped into the vanity. He reached for my face and stroked my cheek with his thumb. "When the men of Tigrea cannot sire a child, it is customary to send in a... *replacement*. Is that common where you are from?"

I'd once heard a story of an older nobleman who couldn't impregnate his young wife, so he called for the services of an *aide*, so to speak. But that had been a story, and if it was customary, it wasn't something people spoke of often. Either way, I didn't like how close Salah was and how his gaze wandered over my body.

"No," I said firmly, stepping aside. I marched toward the door, but he grabbed my arm again, fingers coiling tightly around me as he yanked me close.

"I can give you children," he whispered in my ear, his free hand wandering up my thigh. When I swatted him away, he grabbed my wrists. "They will look just like Tanu, since we're cousins."

"Let go of me!" I cried, writhing in his grasp.

I broke one wrist free and tried to slap his cheek, but he moved like a striking viper, blocking the swing and seizing me again. "Tanu is an incapable husband. He should have given you a child by now, but clearly he can't. And since he can't, you are to be paired with someone who can."

My cheeks burned with fury as I glared at him. "Who would decide such a thing? Get your hands off me!"

He pressed me hard against the vanity, his hand wandering under my garments. I took a breath to scream, but he snapped his other hand over my mouth.

"If I bring this matter to the council, a sire will be assigned. It is the way. But we could take care of this without a lengthy process..." He worked to untie the loincloth I wore under the chemise, pinning me every time I struggled. "It's what your husband would want—to bring this matter publicly would surely be an embarrassment. This way, no one would know but us."

He kept a hand over my mouth, and I could barely breathe through my flaring nostrils. Every time I thrashed, it seemed as though it took no energy for him to hold me. I shook my head, pleading for him to stop, but he just shushed me in a horribly calm voice.

The second his hand left my mouth, a volatile scream tore through my throat at a range I didn't even know was possible. Footsteps pounded into the room, and Salah jumped away from me as Tanu flew at him. I had never been so glad to see that scruffy face, scrunched with rage as he punched his cousin's jaw.

Salah doubled over only briefly before recovering to take a swing. He landed a hit in Tanu's stomach, but the blow didn't stop Tanu from striking Salah's face again.

I darted out of the way and searched for something that could double as a weapon. But before I could hit Salah on the back of the head with one of the long candlesticks, a flurry of people entered the room and broke apart the fighting cousins. Their chests heaved as the red-faced pair glared at one another while their family members dragged them apart.

Ama Isla was the last to enter the disheveled room. "Tanu... your presence has already reignited old feuds."

"He was trying to bed my wife!" Tanu yelled, yanking free of the one who held him, though he didn't charge for Salah again.

Salah glanced at me, then smiled like a devil wearing the robes of a mortal man. "I did no such thing. The woman invited me into her quarters, whining about her husband's infertility. I refused her three times over, but Tanu entered and jumped to conclusions as usual."

Everyone glared at me, confused, suspicious—accusatory in their silence. Panic shot through me as my eyes darted from face to face.

"He's lying!" I cried, my voice squeaking. Even *I* wouldn't have believed me. Why would anyone else?

Ama Isla waved a hand to dismiss everyone. "I will speak to the newlyweds alone."

The minute everyone had left, a sob broke free. "Ama Isla, I promise, I didn't..."

Tanu reached to comfort me, and while it was probably part of the husband act, it felt nice to feel the warmth of his embrace. Ama Isla stared at me for a long moment as Tanu kissed the top of my head.

"I know," she said simply.

Tanu froze next to me. "You do?"

The woman nodded, looking like a queen surrounded by the abundance of colorful robes. "Salah is my grandson. Don't you think I know when he's lying? The question is *why*?"

Tanu's arms shot in the air with exasperation. "The same reason he's always tried to step between me and every girl I've ever known. He likes the sport of it. He enjoys winning."

Ama Isla made a noise that confirmed she'd heard—not whether she agreed. "Tanu. You know I have loved you like my own. But maybe it's time for you and your wife to leave. It has caused strife amongst the estate, and I can't have that."

Tanu wrapped me in another hug and kissed the side of my head. "It's going to be alright."

I nodded and allowed myself to melt into him. Ama Isla would only see a loving couple, but I was soaking up the moment of a warm body between me and that bastard Salah. It didn't hurt that Tanu's calloused hands were papery smooth on my neck as he played the part of a tender husband.

Ama Isla gathered her gowns as she rose from her seat, taking her time to shuffle to the door. She paused before leaving and turned to us.

"At first glance, I wouldn't have believed you two were married," she said, making my heart skip a beat. "But seeing you together now, it is clear you truly care for one another. Tanu, before you leave, you must collect your inheritance funds for beginning your new life. Find a home, and stop dragging your wife from place to place. Perhaps that is why she has not become with child." Then she looked at me. "My medicine woman has arrived. If you still wish, I can have her examine you before you leave."

I saw Tanu's lips part as he inhaled to say something, so I wrapped my arm behind his back and squeezed his shoulder in warning.

"Oh, Ama Isla, I'm afraid I'm too upset right now," I said. "Your suggestion to settle down is fine advice."

Her eyes shifted to Tanu—probably searching for some kind of objection, as though I couldn't be trusted to make medical decisions for myself—then nodded before turning to leave.

Once she was gone, Tanu slowly released me, our closeness more apparent without a performance to put on, but he left one hand lingering on my shoulder and studied my face.

"Are you alright?" he asked. I just nodded and slipped away from him. "I'm sorry. I should've told you what he was like. I just never thought…"

I turned and looked at him expectantly, but he didn't continue the thought. "Never thought?"

"Well, I never thought he would attack you. He's always gone for the girls I've courted, but you're the first one to turn him down." He rubbed a hand over his dark beard and shrugged. "It figures the most loyal girl is the one who's pretending."

I squared my shoulders, a pang of indignation coursing through my chest. "I am a native of Bahmisi. We are a fiercely loyal people, pretending or no. The idea of betraying a marriage vow made me sick."

His face lightened with a small smile. "Of course."

"It's also why we don't take marriage lightly. It is arranged for many rains as the sun god ordains, with the couple getting to know one another in that time, and if the couple is not a fit, they are not united. Wedding celebrations are considered far better to nullify than marriages."

In my case, a wedding was never offered. Only death.

We packed quickly, which was easy given our few belongings fit neatly into saddlebags, and we made our way outside the estate gates with Pharaoh clopping along behind us. We still had two days in Tigrea to await Tanu's ransom funds, which meant we would need to find other lodgings. One of Tanu's older cousins suggested we stay at an inn in the heart of the city, so we headed in that direction after a tearful goodbye with Pagria. Seeing the young girl sob as she was forced to say goodbye to her favorite cousin made the bridge of my nose burn.

The only positive aspect of leaving the Batla estate early was that I wouldn't have to subject myself to further questioning about my fertility. We were simply leaving with funds in hand.

Once beyond the gates, I gasped when a sudden sensation filled my chest before a blue cloud hovered around me and dissipated in the air. Pressure pulled away from my ribcage like a spiderweb clinging to a duster and stretching from the ceiling where it had been built.

The second favor was complete.

Tanu's eyes darkened with a frown, and he remained silent as we walked. He should have been happy for that sack of gold in his pouch—he had used magic to force me into a contract simply to retrieve it—but from his sour demeanor, it seemed as though the prize no longer held valuable.

I didn't speak, thinking about the encounter with Salah, watching it over and over again in my mind's eye. His cousin was like a seed of poison in the family soil. I couldn't pretend to understand how that felt.

I followed along behind him, but a distant voice from behind caught my attention.

"Miss! Miss!" I could tell the speaker was short of breath as he ran up from behind me. When I whirled around, I saw a boy with light streaks of color in his hair. The mail carrier.

The boy bent over to place a hand on his knee and pant while handing me a single letter in a sealed envelope. His left eye was badly bruised and swollen shut. "I delivered your package. I'm sorry that I couldn't follow your instructions exactly. Strange men grabbed me and demanded to know everything about who sent it."

Darkness seeped into me like a poison snaking its way through my veins, searching for my heart. My fears had come to fruition. Before I could ask the boy another question, he darted away as though death followed me and would snatch him too if he got close enough.

I opened the parcel, panic swelling inside me as my fingers fumbled to tear the seal. Finally, I had it open and found my uncle's rock inside along with a letter. Tanu peered over my shoulder to read, his hair tickling my cheek.

Akedia Morestone,

There will be no ransom funds. As a runaway offering, you are hereby marked a fugitive. Your father has been interrogated and arrested for his aid in your departure. The bail on his head is your immediate return. However, should you not return by the rise of the fullest moon, your father shall be sacrificed in your place. Be it the will of the gods that Waikenu accepts the substitute.

High Priest Vikton

Familiar religious fear that had been washed into my brain since childhood rushed over me, but this time it was seasoned with the raw and unapologetic frenzy of a cornered animal. Everywhere I turned now, all I saw were flashes of purple gowns fluttering around building corners.

The fullest moon. That was only ten nightfalls away.

The high priest was onto the ruse, and my father was set to pay for it.

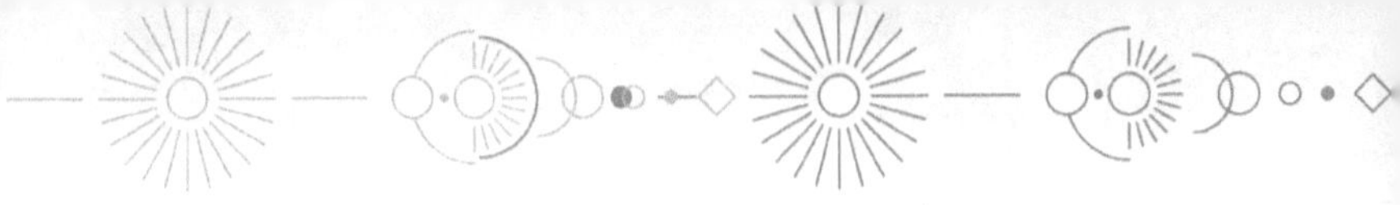

Chapter Fourteen

FAMILIAR FACES

I grabbed Tanu by the wrist and dragged him into the shadows of a narrow alleyway, leaving Pharaoh to guzzle water from a nearby trough. Every passing cart or shouting voice echoing through the crowded streets made me flinch.

"Akedia, the mail carrier only guessed we were still here." Tanu spoke too loudly. I hushed him, and he carried on in a whisper, gently placing one hand on the small of my back and the other on my stomach. The touch sent a shiver of comfort through me, though it couldn't dispel the anxiety. "But that doesn't mean the person who sent this letter knows where you are—only that this is where the ransom money was to be sent."

"The letter said I was being kept in a cave, but the high priest doesn't believe the letter." I released his wrist and paced, sending pebbles skittering across the ground. "If you were looking for someone you believed orchestrated their own kidnapping, wouldn't you look in the very city where they asked you to bring the money?"

That shut him up.

I searched the crowd, eyes jumping from face to face. One face in particular sent a roll of panic crashing down my spine as it dipped into the spaces between my knotty bones where some medicinal magic workers believed remnants of the soul lingered. In that moment, I believed it too, as darkness seeped into my being.

Nevario.

I slammed Tanu against the wall of the alley and whispered harshly. "The high priest's most loyal servant is already here." When Tanu turned his head toward the crowd, I tried to point him out. "Do you see the one in white linens with the deep purple trim of the high priest's color? The one who keeps a beard with a pattern shaved into his face and a point at the end?"

We watched Nevario speak with a vendor. All I could remember were the stories of people walking into the desert with him only to disappear. They were usually those the high priest deemed as sinners.

And the box of learning. I'd never forget he sent me there.

When Nevario finished speaking with the vendor, Tanu used his body to hide me. If he looked in our direction, Nevario would see only a man's back in an alleyway.

"We have to get away from here," I said. "The ransom letter has only led the worst of them straight to us."

Tanu tossed a glance over his shoulder before leaning closer. His mint and sage scent filled my nose, but it no longer smelled of unwashed man, thanks to the stay at Ama Isla's.

I dared to peek over his shoulder. "He's walking away. But he'll have men all over this city. I have to get away from here. If you don't want to come, I understand, but you'll need to release me from that third favor."

"Nice try. There is no getting out of favors." He looked over his shoulder again, then nodded down the darkened alley. "Come on. I know this maze like a trained rat."

We darted through narrow side streets, dodging dark pools of water that gathered in potholes and smelled of stank. Sewage. *These vile people must sweep it into the streets.*

We climbed over a fence separating two alleys when I remembered something. "What about Pharaoh?"

Tanu shook his head and didn't answer at first, but as we jumped to the other side of the fence he whistled three shrill notes. Two streets later, the black horse met up with us. Truly, I had underestimated the intelligence of the beast. My little camel, Coska, was smart but not enough to find me at the call of a whistle in a busy city.

We climbed on the horse's back and trotted. I wanted to kick Pharaoh's sides and urge him to gallop away from Tigrea forever, but pedestrians and carriages clogged the passages and stopped him at every turn. Three Tigrean templekeepers and one priestess walked in a slow procession with bells and incense, blessing the street and its inhabitants through chanted prayer. Tufts of purple clouds surrounded them as they moved. It was a customary honor to the sun god to bring this magic beyond the temple and into the streets for the benefit of the people. I once delighted in the tradition, when I was young enough to be wooed by the spectacle of it all. Now, I wished for them to be done with it and move out of the way.

Once they passed, more people clogged the road. Tanu sat behind me, his deep voice rumbling like thunder against my back as he bellowed for the horse to move—for the people to pass. For anything that meant something other than sitting behind a congestion of travelers and merchants. The power in his demands made me glad that, at least in that moment, we were on the same side.

A sense deep in my gut made me want to crawl into a sand burrow and hide away from the world and everything in it. Without thinking, I realized I had pulled part of my linens over my head and across my face like the far riders of the desert sands. If Waikenu truly did exist, perhaps He had taken mercy on me, because just as I felt the urge to hide my face, we crossed paths with a man of Bahmisi—one I had recognized by the opal jewelry alone.

He had either escaped to live life beyond my secluded homeland or he was here on orders. I tensed in the saddle as we waited for him to pass, and Tanu pulled me closer to his chest.

"Once we hit that open sand, we'll ride hard to the next town," he muttered into my ear. "Can you hold on?"

I only nodded. I didn't want the quiver in my voice to give away my supreme fear.

Somehow, away from the clay buildings that cut out the sun's glare, the heat ravaged the earth at degrees that suffocated the living. Clouds in the distance promised to dilute some of that brilliance, but in that moment—as Tanu commanded Pharaoh to gallop away from Tigrea—all I could feel was the shudder of powerful muscles.

Sand flew into my eyes, so I squeezed them closed and trusted Tanu (or at least his horse) to know where to go.

"*Away*," I whispered, knowing no one but the wind would catch the word.

Keeping my eyes sealed shut, I could feel the rhythm of the horse's thunderous strides and kept time with him as he bolted across the open sand. It was like the animal's heart had synced with mine—we were on the course together, and he didn't want me to throw his weight off by falling any more than I did. We were a team.

"We have a slight problem," Tanu said, his voice huffing from the work it took to ride a horse through a gallop. I couldn't answer. It took too much from me, but he carried on. "We have riders on our tail."

My eyes shot open, and I whirled my head around. I had to squint, but the specks in the distance were clearly horseback riders, chasing after us as we fled into the sea of endless sand.

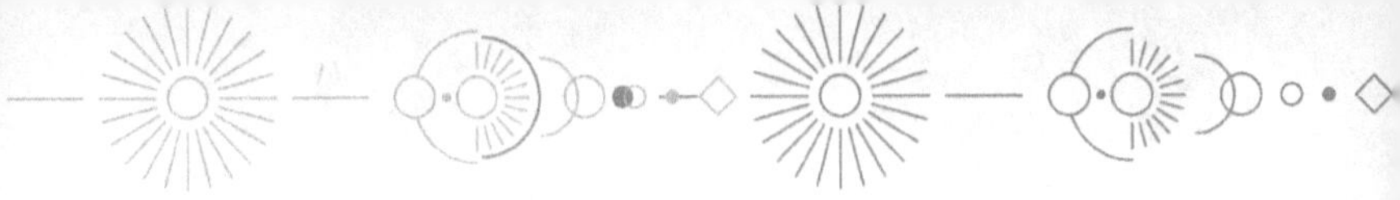

Chapter Fifteen
FINDING SANCTUARY

I bit my lip and faced forward again. "Are they... ?"

"They're riding far too fast to be ordinary travelers," he shouted over the wind. "It's probably because *we're* riding far too fast."

Tanu lashed Pharaoh's rump with the slack of his reins and shouted, making the animal jolt into another caliber. We couldn't let the distance close and discover the high priest's men were the ones who had decided to see why two people on a horse were fleeing the city. I could feel Tanu turn his torso around to look back.

He didn't say anything. But by the way he pushed his horse, he didn't have to. The group was hot on our heels, and the horses behind us carried only one rider each. Poor Pharaoh was quickly losing steam as we rode directly into the storm.

Clouds approached with their darkened ruddiness like a being intent on witnessing our defeat. Pharaoh didn't rear when a streak of lightning lit up the world and touched down to the earth in the distance. The tremor of thunder that followed, however, made him whinny.

"Keep on, Pharaoh!" Tanu shouted as fierce winds slapped our faces.

I chanced a look behind us and saw our pursuers veering away to the right. Maybe they hadn't been following us.

But when I looked to the left, I saw why.

"Tanu!" I screamed, pointing in the distance at a monstrous wall of sand as it came barreling toward us.

The race from the riders quickly became a race to escape the desert itself. As the wall neared, I saw tendrils of sand lurching and flicking from its top. It wasn't simply a sandstorm. The giabdens, demons of the sand, were out to play their wicked games. I gaped at the rumbling wall of creatures I'd only heard of in legends. The furious sand thrashing through the air made it difficult to see exactly what they looked like, but strikes of lightning lit up the sandstorm where shadows of the beings darted over and around one another like enormous beetles scrabbling for food.

Tanu didn't spend one second staring at the mass of reddish sand rising up from the ground and towering into the sky. He shouted at his horse again and clutched me fiercely with one arm.

"The demons will steal us right from this horse and consume us whole if we let them!" he shouted, his loud voice ringing in my ear. "Pray we make it."

I didn't have to ask where. In the distance, I spotted the lumpy curves of clay buildings crammed together. Another town. Walls. Safety.

The only problem was it looked impossibly far, and Pharaoh's fur darkened with sweat just under his bridle. I snapped a glance at the barreling sandstorm filled with writhing giabden monsters. The fears I'd had of them before were more than justified—the beings were far worse in real life. A flash of red eyes glowed at me through the sandstorm.

"We're not going to make it, Tanu!" I shouted.

"We have no other choice."

With that, I closed my eyes and felt the horse again. Maybe some of that old magic I'd learned through the village grandmothers and Matka would come in handy after all. I could bind with the creature and offer a bit of energy and encouragement, just enough to see us all through. Perhaps village grandmother magic was nothing more than prayer whispered into a void of nothingness, but I was going to try it either way.

I muttered to myself as the sand slapped my face and beat against my closed eyelids. The horse's energy was red hot and streaked with veins of wild green. Then Tanu shouted for me to get ready.

We neared the village with the storm demons snarling behind us. In that moment, my entire world became the heavy huff of labored horse breath and powerful muscles pounding hooves into the sand, our hearts racing in time.

The massive wave of sand reached for us as the giabdens within controlled its movement, and I felt its gritty lash when a tendril almost made it close enough to pull us from the horse. It must have brushed Pharaoh, because he whinnied and bucked before giving one last burst of speed at the threshold of the village.

We charged through abandoned alleyways between the clay homes with the sandstorm on our heels. Ahead a door opened, and I feared whoever had done it would succeed in aiding the giabdens while getting trampled at the same time. Instead, a woman flailed her arms at us and pointed inside.

"Pharaoh, in!" cried Tanu, yanking the reins to the right and kicking his left leg.

The horse's hind legs skidded as we made the sharp turn. Once through, Tanu tumbled from the saddle and helped the stranger shut the large wooden door. They pressed their bodies against it and worked together to secure the bolt.

The furious giabden demons of the sand howled with rage, but they moved on to find another victim. I slid from the saddle and walked Pharaoh in the small circles to cool him down until his nostrils stopped flaring.

When the howling subsided, the woman turned toward us. The oil lamp light made shadows dance above her high cheekbones, and for a moment, there was nothing but three strangers and a horse, trying to make the most of their limited space until the raging storm passed. Defeated and unable to venture within the crevices of the city to seek out victims, the giabden demons receded to the desert. They would leave heaps of sand in their wake, and maybe they'd been successful in dragging a victim beneath the earth's surface—maybe someone had been offered to appease their tempers—but it wasn't me. Not today at least.

"Kind woman, we thank you for taking us in," Tanu said. "How did you know to help us?"

"I was hanging laundry to dry on my rooftop when I saw the storm kick up in the desert and a horse running like a fury," the woman said.

She had grayish green eyes and olive skin, and her thin face had traces of fine lines. She had the elegant, somewhat bony beauty of a woman nearing her forties. Her thick dark hair was spotted with touches of gray.

"An eternity of gratitude for taking us in, dear sister," I said, still clutching Pharaoh's reins so he wouldn't crash his rear into anything in the house.

The woman frowned and gathered the reins from me. "Here, here, let's bring this creature outside."

She brought the stallion through the small home and opened a second door that led to an enclosure with chickens. Throwing down hay, she left him to feed and closed the back door.

"I am Akedia, and this is Tanu," I said when she walked back inside. "What is your name?"

"Morra," she answered, tying an apron around her waist and opening a cabinet to remove three dishes. "I can only assume you're hungry."

My mouth watered at the sight of the dishes alone. Had she planned to place a fried goat's tongue on my plate, I would have eaten it—the fierce rumbling in my stomach was like giabden demons whirling in the sands.

"Thank you, Morra," Tanu said.

We helped her prepare rice mixed with fried eggs and some grilled vegetables. At last, our plates had the steaming piles of sustenance I needed after that ride on Pharaoh. I remembered the kind people who had cooked outside and shared what they had on one of our first stops.

I folded my hands together and muttered the prayer they had taught me. "May we be fed in our hearts and souls, even when the platter's clean."

Morra lifted her brows approvingly. "So I see you are from Manitu."

"No. We visited briefly." I caught Tanu's dark eyes for a half second before we both looked down at our plates. Perhaps a girl who shamed the gods and a thief who shamed his family could only be anywhere *briefly*.

"I would love the chance to properly thank your husband as well, Morra," Tanu said. He scanned the room for other doorways from which a husband of a kind could enter the scene, but Morra snorted.

"I have no husband, boy," she said, rolling her eyes. "Is it not enough to thank me, a lowly female, for saving you from the sand devils?"

Tanu's lips parted to form an answer, but I seriously doubted his ability to not offend her at that moment, so I interjected.

"My husband means no disrespect, madam," I said but cringed the minute it came out of my mouth. Especially since Tanu winked at me when my eyes flashed to him and my cheeks flushed. By the gods, that man was easy to hate.

"Do you two wish to rest now?" Morra said, clearing plates and bringing them to the wash bin. She continued to speak over her shoulder as she worked. "I'm not much of a hostess, but there's a spare room to the right. You're welcome to it for one night. Take baths, be fed. But then you should leave."

"Thank you." I stood and walked to open the door with Tanu right behind me. Inside was a small bed covered with a worn quilt and a wooden trunk at the foot. When he shut the door, I spun around and practically snarled. "Now, you listen to me! We are not sharing that tiny bed, and I am not keeping up this wife act. From here on out, that's over."

Tanu's lopsided grin made me want to slap him. "You're the one who can't drop the act. If you want to be my wife, you may have other ladies fighting you for the title."

I looked behind him and then around the room. "Yes, I can see the *zero* women lining up to be your wife will be hard to sort through. How will you ever choose between all *none* of them?"

We glared at each other for a moment. Then he erupted with laughter and sat on the trunk. It was worse that he couldn't just be deeply wounded by the insult.

I walked to the room's window and examined the view—another wall ten feet away—before fiercely scrubbing my skin over the wash basin. I could hate Tanu, but certain facts remained: I needed his horse and, pride aside, his guidance. He knew the land far and wide. I knew only the streets of Bahmisi and tiny bits of the wild land surrounding it.

"Look," I started. "I think it's time we came up with a new plan—"

I swept my long hair onto the side of my neck and began to braid. "You will need to tell me what the last favor is, so we can change course."

When I looked at him, his eyes darted away.

"No, I cannot reveal that at this time, but it will be the one that ends the contract. It will be a large favor, and you must do it." He stood and ran a hand through his hair, eyes downcast under a frown.

I swung the finished braid over my shoulder and took a slow breath. "Tanu, this favor business is the least of our problems. We are hunted. I don't know what to do."

I wanted to sob into my hands. If only I could have a moment alone to fall apart, but he wouldn't leave me, like a leech clinging to its blood source. I sat on the edge of the bed and stared at the door, willing him to walk out. Instead, he rose from his place on the trunk and sat beside me.

"Listen, yes, I am a wanted thief. You're a runaway. And your people have picked up our trail." He rubbed his beard, thinking. "I'm not sure what we're going to do either, but we will figure it out together. We will go in the morning to refuel our supplies, and then we should leave for Carabna."

A tear formed in my left eye, thinking of my people—my parents, my father, locked away—but I turned my head and blinked until it decided to retreat. "Carabna? Why there?"

"It's one of the largest cities north of here. A person can get lost in the cracks, so to speak. Once there, we will find some friends of mine who can give us shelter and food until we determine the next step."

"I can't go with you, Tanu." Uncle Peko's stone sat on top of the letter on a small bedside table, and I reached to pick it up and hold it in my palm. Somehow the stone always had a hint of warmth like a piece of the sun had broken away and fallen to earth, and its smoothness reminded me of tender, calloused hands rubbing my cheek before bed at night. "I should return and take my father's place. We can't continue on this journey together. Ask me now for that third favor, so I can be free."

We stared for a half second too long at one another. Then Tanu grabbed the rock as I yelped in protest and jumped to swipe it from him. He blocked my attempts. "What is it about this thing? Why is it so important to you?"

"It was a gift from my uncle." Tears clouded my eyesight. "It was the last thing he gave me before he was sacrificed."

I could feel Tanu's gaze studying me as I looked away, my cheeks burning with shame. Then he gently grasped my wrist and placed the stone in my hand.

"I will not ask for the third favor yet—"

"But—"

He held up a hand to cut me off. "There might be a way for us to free your father without surrendering."

My heart skipped at the thought of somehow sneaking my family away from Bahmisi and starting over. No death. "But how?"

Tanu shook his head. "I'm not sure yet."

"Wait." I turned my head to the side and narrowed my eyes at him. "Why would you help me? What do you stand to gain?"

There had to be more...

He smirked and ran a finger under my chin. "You are still bound to me for that third favor. Make no mistake, it will be the best one of all."

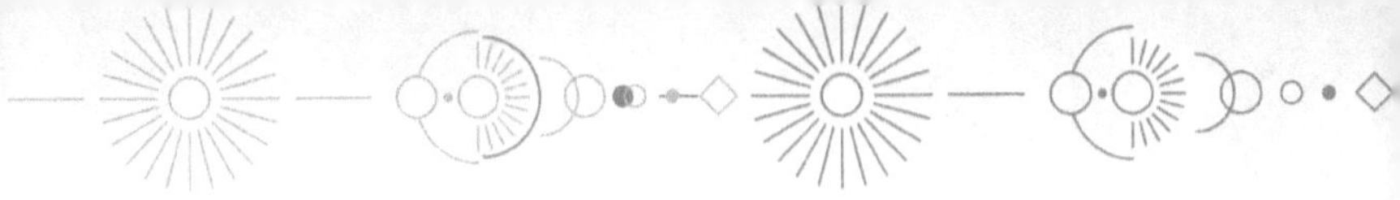

Chapter Sixteen

SKINWALKER LEGENDS

The one benefit of staying the night at Morra's was Tanu did not insist we share the bed, which was far smaller than the one we'd had at Ama Isla's estate. He slept on a pile of blankets and didn't stir until the sun poured light into the alleyway outside our tiny window.

"Good morning, wife," he muttered, mockingly. I threw my pillow at his face, which only made him laugh.

"I will not pretend here. We have nothing to lose."

He sat upright. "Except our cover."

I groaned. "I'm going to help with the meal. Make yourself useful and at least chop wood for the poor spinster."

When I opened the door and turned to enter the main living area, Morra stood in the doorway with an armful of logs, making me jump.

Her gray eyes glistened with mischief. "The *spinster* has already split the wood, thank you."

My cheeks burned, and I could feel Tanu hovering behind me. His hand on my waist felt warm, comforting, and unnerving all at once in a brief storm of feelings.

"Good morning," he said. "Please forgive Akedia's rudeness. She was kept in an underground hole away from humans most of her life."

I jabbed him in the gut with my elbow.

"You two should get better at this if you plan to make your lies believable," she said, glaring at each of us as she handed me a wash rag and Tanu the logs. "You must think my walls are made from pure stone with the way you talk. Now, you girl, help me clean while the boy starts a fire. Then you both can tell me the truth. *All* of it. Or I'll turn you in for coin faster than you can spit."

We told her everything. At least, I did. I couldn't speak for Tanu, whose past was as muddied as water that gathers between stepping stones, but Morra wasn't nearly as interested in Tanu.

"What made you decide to finally leave?" she asked, leaning forward at the table where we sat. "You still seem... conflicted."

I opened my mouth to answer, but the word *conflicted* echoed in my mind. "I *am* conflicted."

"Why?" Morra's response was abrasive, to the point. Challenging.

"Because I left my home, my family, and my faith all at once." Hot blood churned in my veins. What kind of fool's question was *why*? "Because what I left behind felt wrong, but what I'm heading toward does too. Nothing is right with me."

She nodded, and her face softened. So did my anger. She *was* challenging me but not in the way I'd thought. That blunt *why* had called me to bluntly respond with a real and raw truth.

I squeezed my eyelids closed and saw Lileena's bracelet on that skeleton's arm. "Because I can't get the image of those bodies out of my mind."

When I opened my eyes, I saw Tanu and Morra exchange a glance.

"Bodies?" Morra asked, frowning. "What bodies?"

I'd forgotten that part, so I told them about the cave and the high priest and how the orders for my sacrifice came shortly after the encounter. Morra's face lost all color.

"Child..." she began, glancing between the two of us. Tanu shifted with unease in his chair. "I've heard of your village and the stories of how the people there offer human lives to Waikenu." She slowly shook her head and looked at me with pity. "But... I've also heard the legend of the skinwalker."

A fierce wind slammed one of the shutters closed outside, and Pharaoh whinnied just beyond the back door. Tanu tried to pretend he hadn't jumped in fright by re-tying his knot of dark curls and clearing his throat, but I snickered with delight.

Morra looked toward the shutter, then back at Tanu. "It's just the wind, boy—not some ominous spirit I've trained to scare people on cue."

We both laughed, and for once the scruffy Tanu turned a shade of pink I hadn't seen on his bearded light brown cheeks. It was decided: I liked Morra.

"The skinwalker..." She paused with a finger suspended in the air for dramatic effect then shrugged when the wind behaved itself and shot me a wink. Tanu rolled his eyes.

"...was legendary in the village of Lakoma. The beast took the form of a man. He charmed the villagers into following his every whim, forcing them to give their lives for the sake of Rihi."

"Wasn't Rihi the god the uncivilized people of the desert used to believe in?" I interrupted.

Morra issued me a scathing glance. "There have been *hundreds* of gods known to our desert people since before the time of the long-toothed cats, and you think yours are the accurate ones? No. Now you just call them by different names and think yourself more civilized."

I wilted in my chair. I'd traveled from Bahmisi with guilt over my head for leaving my faith, and here she had made me feel foolish for believing in the first place. Waikenu still had pieces of my heart, even if believing in Him had also torn me apart. How could something feed and destroy your soul all at once? What lesson was I supposed to learn from this? I tried to imagine a day in my future when a simple question couldn't unravel me. Hopefully, the price to pay for that wisdom would not be a mind fenced in by new insufferable beliefs.

Morra ignored my pause and carried on. "The skinwalker twisted the people's love of their gods to fit his wicked design. Once they were killed, he would devour their flesh and drink their blood."

She stood from her chair and pulled an old book from a shelf on the kitchen wall that also held clay jars, a copper briki pot, and spices. The book's leather binding cracked and rippled at the spine when she carefully opened it and placed it on the table. It appeared to be a basic encyclopedia of spells and medicine, which were one and the same in most homes. She muttered to herself, thumbing through the pages, until at last she stopped.

"My family has been gathering this information and passing it along for over three hundred years," Morra explained. She placed her index finger just above a sketching with a scribbled attribution. "A native from Lakoma, my great-aunt, Izeliah, etched this one after witnessing the devil take its true form. Once exposed, it must be returned to the underbelly of the sands."

I stared at the image. The creature stood like a man, but its skin was gray and cracked like stone, and pointed ears protruded from its head. Its animalistic mouth curled into a wicked smile of pointed teeth. But the eyes—amber lined with black—seized my throat, making my breath short and staggered. A flash of the high priest's kohl-lined eyes made me shudder.

My heart raced as the pieces of hidden truths formed in my mind. Bahmisi only began sacrificing humans once Vikton came along and told us to twenty rains ago. The bodies in the cave had been either bone or decaying, but if this creature—this skinwalker—was responsible for the deaths, it could have been feasting on the bodies. It was keeping them in storage, snacking on their flesh between pretending to be human. My stomach turned as the taste of bile rose to the back of my throat.

"Did…" I began, scooting away from the image. "Did your aunt ever mention what made the creature reveal its true form?"

Morra nodded and turned one page, her finger pointing at the text.

"Right here," Morra said. "Roughly translated, I believe it to mean a counter-curse was uttered."

"That's it!" I bolted from my chair and made Tanu and Morra jump in theirs. "I need to find the counter-curse. No one back home knows what the high priest was doing with the bodies except for me. That's why he wanted me dead." I paced the floor feverishly. "A sacrifice? *Indeed*. He wanted me out of the way to keep preying on my people." I whirled toward her, and her gray eyes widened. "I think you're truly right about this skinwalker. Everything makes so much sense now. What's the counter-curse? That's all I need. Then I can return home and say the words. I have until the fullest moon. We can do this."

I felt inside my pocket and removed my uncle's rock, turning it over in my palms and seeing it in a different way. What if my uncle had begun the search for the counter-curse too? He had been sacrificed, but my father never wanted to talk about it in our home. All this time, I thought of the stone as a lovely gift, but what if he had been trying to tell me something?

Morra shook her head regretfully and closed the book. Her contorted brow formed creases in her dark olive skin. "Unfortunately, I've read this book cover to cover and have found nothing more than the mention that the skinwalker exists. The words my aunt wrote on this topic were in Lakonian, but I've worked them out to mean, 'The counter-curse was the creature's undoing. It was uttered by a knowledgeable one.'"

I frowned and continued pacing. A knowledgeable one? In Bahmisi, that meant someone who was permitted to read the scriptures.

"Oh no," I said, turning to them once more. "So the people of the temples? That means only the high priest and his men would know. Of course. Who better to guard the secret?"

I plopped back down in my chair and fought the urge to cry, even though the bridge of my nose burned with the effort.

Tanu put a hand on my shoulder, his warm touch radiating through my linens. "Even if Morra's theory is right, that doesn't mean *all* high priests and temple people are skinwalkers."

More nodded. "He's right. The counter-curse could be found in any of Waikenu's temples."

A bubble of hope wobbled to the surface as something inside me screamed for immediate action. "Let's go to your temple then."

I headed for the door, ready to walk to her city's temple, when Morra stopped me. "Where are you going?"

"To where the light first touches your city, of course. It's the proper position for a temple."

"There is no temple here, child," Morra said. "At least, there isn't anymore. And even if there was, you wouldn't be allowed behind the altar let alone permitted to read their holy books."

"How is it possible that no temple exists here?" I asked, pausing as I held the doorknob. I hadn't exactly planned on *asking* to sneak behind the altar to steal a holy book.

Morra walked to the kitchen and opened the window. Tendrils of fresh morning air curled inside, making me eager to begin the walk before the sun set to burning the ground.

"What do you notice?" she asked.

"That I shouldn't be wasting any more early morning hours on chatter." I huffed, but Morra shook her head.

Tanu's baffled face as he slowly stood from his chair made me wonder what I was missing. "It's silent... It's silent, but for the wind."

Morra nodded, and this time I listened too. It *was* silent. The telltale signs of a city were vacant outside her door. No children laughing in the alleyways. No men shouting in the streets. No women negotiating in the market for the best price. There was nothing but the hollow whisper of wind.

"I suppose you couldn't have noticed last night with the sandstorm demons chasing you, but I am alone in this abandoned place," Morra said.

Exiled? Was she a criminal?

We were in a ghost town with one woman who had our only horse locked away in her pen and who was somehow able to spot us coming into town from miles away. Now here she was, sharing a book with demonic pictures of creatures who eat humans.

My palms grew sweaty. "W-Why?"

I could tell Tanu was feeling the same unease, because I caught his eyes darting for the kitchen—possibly inventorying the selection of knives.

"You can stop staring at me like I'm some kind of monster." Morra closed the book and placed it on the shelf. "I was cast out by my husband two years ago for not bearing children."

I looked down at my feet then toward the door. It was a common and unfortunate story for many women. Even though monsters would certainly be inclined to lie, I had the feeling she was neither a monster nor lying. "I'm sorry, Morra. So you just live here by yourself? How do you eat?"

"I'm allowed to trade at the nearest market, though it's a long journey." She tucked a loose strand of wavy hair behind her ear and cleared her throat. "I sell eggs and vegetables. I get by."

My chest filled with heat, and I knew the skin around my neck had grown splotchy. "Why would your entire family send you away from your village just because your husband was horrible?"

"Because it was *his* village." Her gray eyes flickered with something fiery. "I was sent across deserts and jungles to become his wife when I was your age. The man was a swine." She turned her head to the side as though she was about to spit on the tile floor of her own home and then decided against it. "I welcome this life alone compared to that slavery."

Tanu rubbed his beard, frowning. "Madam, we should be on our way. Thank you for your hospitality..."

"I can bring you to a temple where the books are kept by my cousin," Morra said, her eyes glistening with excitement as she completely ignored Tanu's attempt to leave.

"You could take us there? Your cousin is a man of the temple? Would he allow us to read them?" I practically jumped to give the woman a hug when Tanu stood and clutched my elbow.

"Akedia… a word?" When we retreated to the bedroom, he shut the door. "We're not going to get the book."

"What?! Why not? You don't have much of a plan. Sneaking my father out of Bahmisi will not be a simple task. If this theory is true—and I feel it in my gut that it is, Tanu—then we will have the support of the village on our side when we reveal the monster." I paused and took a deep breath. "Then, I promise, I will go with you wherever you want and pretend to be whomever you want. It will work out for both of us. You'll see."

I turned to the door and cracked it open, but he pushed it closed and hovered over me when I whirled around to glare up at him with my back pressed against the wood. We stayed like that a long time, glaring with stubbornness until at last he dropped his arm.

Finally, I broke the tense silence. "*Please.*"

"It is not a risk I'm willing to take," he said. "We can't trust this woman. What if she's turning us in for coin, like she said she would? She's out here alone and desperate."

Morra's knock on the door sent vibrations through the wood and down my spine. "You two forget I can hear everything through these walls. If I may interject?"

Tanu's dark eyes held mine captive for a half second longer until I pushed my hand against his chest to scoot him away from me. His hand lightly brushed my wrist, but I swatted it away and nodded toward the door. He sighed.

"Yes, Morra," he said, sighing through his teeth. When she walked in, he grumbled. "This is a complicated matter..."

"Nothing a large pile of gold can't uncomplicate, I'm sure?" she asked, grinning at me as her eyes flashed to Tanu.

He frowned. "Go on..."

"Religion is big business, my dears. And who knows this better than the priests and templekeepers?" Morra's bracelets jingled against one another as they danced up and down her thin wrist. "The temple of Kuniki is especially wealthy. That is where my cousin resides. There is great fortune to be had within the temple walls. If you go to get that book with Akedia, you can fill your bags with more funds than you'd ever make pretending to be married."

Tanu considered the proposition, then narrowed his eyes. "What do you stand to gain?"

Morra sighed. "Being an exiled female doesn't exactly make one eager to bring attention to oneself with the authorities, now does it? What little coin your head would bring me wouldn't be worth the grief. Besides..." She hesitated, glancing at her feet. "Before I was sent away, I left a man I loved very dearly—my true love. My cousin mentions his name from time to time in our letters, and I've been meaning to return, but I've feared the journey alone. It's much farther than the market, and I've never had enough resources to make it." Then she looked at me. "Now that I've met you and heard your story of the cave of bodies, Akedia, I know for certain the legends are true. If they are, then it is only a matter of time before the skinwalker moves on to prey upon another village. We must end this now."

Something tightened in my gut. Morra was not only an outcast but separated from the one she loved all these years and now willing to take on a demon from the depths of Kakaura. Suddenly, a flicker of confusion reared its head. If I didn't believe in the gods and goddesses who breathed life and love into our world, where did I stand on demons? The constant questions running through my mind exhausted me. For now, I had to brush away the thoughts.

We had very little to go on in the way of another plan, and I had to believe it wasn't a terrible one.

I took a deep breath to ease my nerves. "We will go to Kuniki to find true love, gold, and hopefully, a book with a counter-curse to rid my village of evil."

Morra nodded. Tanu groaned. And I grinned.

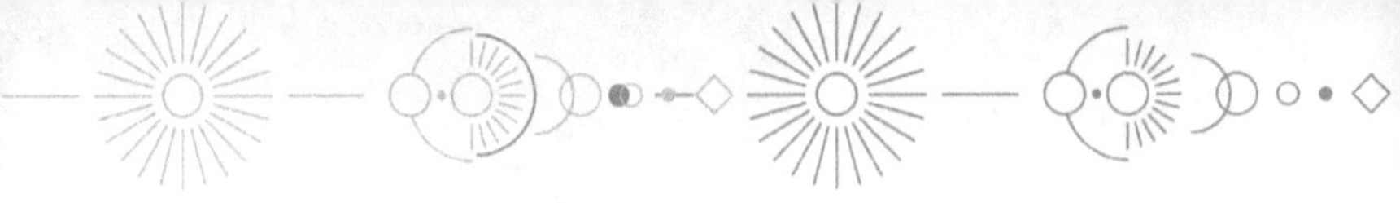

CHAPTER SEVENTEEN
ESCAPING THE CITY OF GHOSTS

We spent the remainder of the day wandering through Morra's ghost city, exploring the shell of a village that saw a mass exodus some fifty rains ago due to famine. Or so was the legend Morra shared of a place that was too far from food and water for life. Her husband had probably intended for this exile to become Morra's death sentence, but she proved too hardy to die. The nearest thing was a mountain range in the far-off distance. I couldn't imagine how long Morra's journey to market would take on a good day.

Wind sent sand dancing down the streets between sun-bleached clay structures that had once been homes. Some had remained intact far better than others, but mostly the place gave me the feeling that we were being watched by lost souls hiding behind darkened windows.

We found abandoned tools and wagons in one alleyway and a small garden of wild herbs and vegetables in another. One vine crept up the side of a stone wall, heavy with beans, and I realized this was where Morra grew her produce.

While we were exploring, Tanu caught a rabbit for dinner, and we brought it back to Morra who showed us a place in the center of town where a fire pit stood. As Tanu turned the small creature's carcass on the metal spit, Morra sat beside me and stared at the flames. Then she turned her head to look at me.

"What exactly made you question your people?" she asked me. "Were you suddenly afraid to die?"

I shook my head slowly. "I was sad when everyone else was celebrating my best friend's upcoming death. I think it might have started then, but probably sometime before. I was never the most obedient believer." I stared into the fire, remembering the way Lileena's skin shimmered with gold like a sun goddess on the day she lost her head. I met Morra's gaze. "When I heard the blade hit the altar, though, I knew. I was just in denial before."

Morra nodded. "It is very lonely to think you're alone in your feelings, in your thoughts." She picked up a nearby twig and picked at pieces of it to throw in the flames. "But you soon realize the feelings that make you feel lonely are the same that others have."

I thought of Lileena's brother, Athalo, whose words to me just after her death formed support for my reasoning to leave. Others were doubting but not speaking. It was impossible to know how many others in Bahmisi were questioning.

Once we'd cooked the rabbit and piled its meat on our plates laden with rice, I realized I had been hungry all day long with no respite from the gnawing pangs until then. Being able to quell hunger was a luxury not known by many, but the feeling of a full belly almost made me thank the gods. How easy it was to believe when basic survival needs were met.

Before we headed back to her home, Morra burned the remaining bones.

"We don't want to attract the meat-eaters," she said ominously, and I decided not to ask for the sake of my own sleep that night.

Back in the little bed at Morra's house, I could hear the wails of the giabden demons in the desert as they played in the night air, and a shiver rolled down my back. Their forms had been difficult to see through the veil of sand that moved like a walking mountain, but I had caught glimpses of horrible gnashing teeth and pointed horns and claws.

I tossed in the bed. The next morning would see us off on another leg of this journey, but I couldn't sleep. The weight of Morra's skinwalker revelation was heavy on my mind. Was I relieved? Horrified? What if she was wrong about everything, just like me?

Eventually, the cycle of endless thought wore me out, and I fell asleep without realizing it sometime after Waikenu was said to shift the world into the next day before He rose the sun again.

When I woke in the early morning, the sky was still black and Morra's face hovered only inches above mine as she hissed at me.

"Wake up!" she whispered.

I mumbled and sat upright. "Do we need to leave *now*?"

I rubbed my eyes and looked around. Tanu was already up and pressing his ear to the window that led to the alleyway. "People are here."

Morra nodded when I gasped. "Two riders passed my door and kept moving. We're lucky my backyard animal pen cannot be seen from the main streets or that your horse didn't squeal for attention when they passed. But we won't be safe here long if the people out there are the ones looking for you."

Tanu and I exchanged a glance and answered at the same time. "They are."

The bag Morra had slung over her shoulder made me think she had already suspected this much. A crash in the streets sounded like someone breaking through a door. They were searching.

"I don't know if you noticed, but some of the houses look lived-in still. I've kept up a number of homes throughout the town to throw off travelers," Morra explained through a rushed whisper. Then she rolled her eyes. "And also my former husband, should he change his mind."

The three of us moved about in the dark and crept to the front window to peer through the cracks in the shutters. I caught the flicker of purple-lined robes and slapped a hand over my mouth to keep from gasping aloud. Tanu whirled around and grabbed me by the shoulders.

"Keep calm," he whispered, giving me a slight shake.

Morra nodded to the back door. "Go get your horse. Follow the alleyway north. There's a road that will lead you out of town and toward the mountains. I'll try to give a whistle when it's a good time to bolt. When you hear it, go. Don't look back."

"What about you? Aren't you coming with us?" I asked, reaching for her slender hands before I remembered myself and pulled back. Perhaps she wasn't one for affection.

"If my plan works, I won't be far behind." She shooed us away, and Tanu grasped my elbow, edging me toward the back door. "Now go!"

I grabbed my bag, followed Tanu outside, and waited by the door as he placed the saddle on Pharaoh's back. While I waited, I peeked inside and watched Morra slip out the front. Her voice echoed in the emptiness of the village, asking the men if she could help them with something.

I shuddered to think what they would do to her should they discover she lived alone in this abandoned place. The childish trust I once had for those in high rank had been replaced by suspicion and fear. Without a witness in sight, I wasn't sure what crimes the high priest's men and Nevario would be willing to commit.

"Do you think she'll be alright, Tanu?" I asked as he pulled me onto the saddle and wrapped his arms around me.

"Probably not."

A sharp whistle cut the air, so before I could scold him for being a negative, rotten person, he kicked Pharaoh's sides and we bolted into the alleyway. I tried to look behind as we galloped through the maze of the abandoned city, but I couldn't see much.

"Are they following?" I asked, though the wind filled my mouth and swept my words away from my lips. If Tanu heard me, he said nothing.

Instead, we worked our way north as Morra had instructed. Just as we escaped the edge of town, I glanced back again and my heart leapt into my throat.

"There's a rider behind us!" I shrieked. A vision of those men dragging me back to Bahmisi before I could uncover the counter-curse racked my mind, making me wonder if I was doomed to become another rotting body in the high priest's cave.

Tanu didn't bother to turn around—he just shouted for the black stallion to run faster. I clutched the saddle horn and squeezed my eyes closed. I hated having to run at these speeds. Even though I was getting used to it, the flinging sand and dry air stung my eyes.

"Come on, Pharaoh," I whispered to the horse in what felt very much like a prayer to gods who probably wouldn't listen to me anymore.

I chanced a look around as we moved at breakneck speed toward the distant mountain range. After resting in Morra's stable, Pharaoh was a new horse. He flew like a phantom over the hard-packed soil outside the abandoned city. I looked back again and saw the rider behind us followed in the distance by two more riders. They were still a good measure away, but we couldn't stop if we ever hoped to lose them.

As we neared the base of the mountains, the terrain began to change from the sandy openness of the desert to the rocky incline of the land jutting toward the brilliant blue sky. Pharaoh proved to be a steadfast creature, tackling the narrow pathways of boulders and cacti with gleaming spines as the two of us leaned forward in the saddle for the incline.

Tanu's chest pushed into my back as we made the climb, his warm breath tickling the skin on my neck. "Around this bend, and they won't see us anymore. We can make it."

At the top of the hill that overlooked the land, we took a glance at our pursuers. I squinted and shielded my eyes from the sun.

"Is that... Morra?" I pointed at the rider on the gray horse who had been just behind us.

Tanu pulled a small telescope from his pocket. "Indeed."

"Well, should we wait for her?"

He tucked a stray curl into the low knot of hair at his neck. "No. We will find each other later."

I wasn't sure how that would happen, given the vastness of the land and the way its endless paths cut in every direction, but then Tanu pulled a piece of looking glass from his pocket and cast the sun's light on the ground near her.

"What are you doing? Won't you blind her?" I said, attempting to snatch the thing from his hands.

He put it away before I could. "I'm sending her a signal. When she sees that flickering light along the mountain range, she will know we are close. That's all I can offer at this point. We risk too much staying behind."

I steadied my breath. He was right. I knew he was right, but something still felt wrong about leaving her behind when clearly she had stolen a horse for our sake. Plus, we couldn't hope to get close to a holy book without her help.

We pushed on. The paths that snaked through the mountain cut around steep cliffs and over loose rocks. We crossed a narrow stretch poised hundreds of feet above a gully. Pharaoh lost his footing, making me yelp with surprise and cling to one of Tanu's arms.

He gave me a gentle squeeze. "We're fine."

But the concerted silence that followed gave me the impression he wasn't all too convinced by his own words. That, and he didn't loosen his hold on me until the path widened and we were able to pick up speed again.

We didn't stop to rest until Pharaoh conquered the last steep range and we could see for miles in the distance. Blue sky blanketed a vast land of yellow-orange sand. Morra's village. Somewhere far away was Bahmisi and my poor parents.

I'm going to help you, B'Ba. I'm coming back with the answer.

"We've come a long way," I whispered.

Tanu's voice drummed in his chest against my back. "Yes, and we have much more land to cover. *Look.*"

I'd been so busy looking at the path behind me, I hadn't noticed the terrain ahead—for as much as the sand had stretched on one side of the mountain, trees stretched on the other. It would take us some time to climb down the rocky slope before entering the region where greenness covered the earth, but this was the closest I had ever been to a place I'd only heard about in stories.

"It's a..." I had never seen such a sight. Tree after tree without an inch of land between.

"Jungle. The climate is drastically different on this side of the mountain," Tanu explained.

"The trees were placed here with seeds from the gods. They grew right out of the desert," I said, remembering the story of the god, Primi, who made giant plants shoot forth from the sand.

"Ah, but if you are from the jungle, the children there will tell you the desert was formed when trees exploded into millions of pieces to form the dunes," Tanu said, chuckling. "I suppose we only believe what we believe based on where we're born."

"I suppose," I muttered, glancing behind me to catch a glimpse of the desert before it fell from view behind the mountain.

Perhaps Tanu's casual mention of birthplace dictating faith should have angered me or made me feel like a foolish lamb who had been born and bred for slaughter, but I found the concept lifted some of the weight I'd carried since Lileena's death. Maybe Waikenu did exist, and He wanted me to question, to find more answers, because if I was cursed to suffer in Kakaura for doubt or even faithlessness, then it was not faith and free will to believe. It was fear. If Waikenu didn't care about free will as much as he cared about attaining loyal followers, why then wouldn't He create a world of believers? Was it the act of a merciful god—a god worth following—to create a people only to damn them to death and suffering for their innate curiosity He supposedly designed?

The questions drowned me in the black chasm they had opened, and my mind spun on the precipice of the endless void. I didn't know how to be whole anymore, but I was beginning to take solace in allowing the light to pour through my broken pieces.

Tanu's beard scratched the side of my face and neck as we rode, and I tried to ignore it for as long as possible. I figured he would make an offhand comment about my tendency to complain. When we stopped for the first time in two hours beside a river, he frowned and reached for my chin.

"Just one of your cheeks is red," he said, holding my face as he examined my skin.

I shrugged away the touch and continued drenching my arms with water to cool my skin. "It's from your beard."

His papery smooth hand reached for my face again and gently turned it to the side. I stopped breathing for a second as his thumb worked its way over my jawline.

"Here," he said, releasing the hold and reaching into his bag to produce a jar. "I have a cream made from camel's milk for chafing."

Given the nature of a rider's *chafing*, I eyed the jar suspiciously. "Well, I don't want anything to do with it if you've already dipped your hands in it more than once."

"I've been riding far too long to chafe there anymore." He unstopped the large cork that covered the opening. It was nearly the same surface area as my palm. "Just place a small amount on your skin. You'll thank me later."

The cream felt like a smooth river of coolness over the area I hadn't even realized was burning before. It smelled faintly of lavender and echinacea.

"You need to put some on your neck," he said, taking the jar from my hands and dipping his fingers inside. He removed a small portion and rubbed it on my neck. I tried to look anywhere but into his black eyes until he pulled away and replaced the jar's lid. My face flushed, making my other cheek feel warm like the chafed one. "We should be on the m—"

Before he could say *move*, the clop of horse hooves echoing through the mountain air made us freeze and stare at each other with wide eyes. Then I jumped to my feet, ready to hop on Pharaoh, but Tanu grabbed my arm and pressed a finger to his lips.

"Shh..." He tilted his head toward the sound. "They will hear us storming away. Let us see who it is and not make a sound as they pass through."

I nodded and crept toward the edge of the cliff on my belly. Tanu followed suit and lay beside me to peer down. The rider was blanketed in shadows at first, but once they moved into the light, I noted the gray horse and Morra's long brown hair. I wanted to call out for her, but I knew the echo could give our location away. In the far distance, I caught sight of the high priest's men who followed.

Tanu removed the bit of looking glass and made a spot of light flicker in her face. She squinted and looked in our direction, silently nodding when her gaze fell on us waving from the cliff. We pointed in the direction we would go, and she nodded again. I felt bad for pulling Pharaoh from the bits of grass he had found sprouting from the dirt, but we didn't have time to let him graze until his belly was full.

We zig-zagged down a path that eventually ran into the path Morra was on.

"Morra!" I said, still cautious with the volume of my voice. "How did you..."

"Steal one of the men's horses while he was investigating the home I told him you were hiding in?" She smirked, picking her teeth with her pinky nail.

Tanu chuckled. "Well, that answers that."

"We don't have much time," she said. "The mountain delayed them, but they're not far behind. We should head into the jungle." She led her gray horse in front of Pharaoh then turned to look at Tanu ominously. "Thief, have you ever crossed Binlu Jungle?"

"I prefer the name Tanu, and no. I've been near it, not through it."

When she leaned back in the saddle and placed her bony hand on her horse's rump, woven metal bracelets jangled down her wrist. "In that case, stay as close to me as possible. One wrong move could mean the difference between life or... being eaten." I looked past her to the looming jungle in the near distance and a shudder swept through my body like giabden demons rising from the sands. She looked at me. "You should ride with me and give that beast a break. My horse is still fresh."

"And to think I thought you meant Tanu," I said, chuckling at my own joke as I tried to slip down from Pharaoh's back.

Tanu held me in place and whispered in my ear while Morra spoke sweetly to her horse. "Don't get any ideas about running off with her. We still have a deal."

Hot anger flared and sent heat to my cheeks at Tanu's suggestion that I would run off with Morra. "In case you've forgotten, I *can't*."

"But will you be safe riding with her?" His voice softened, and his hold became more of a *touch*. I was suddenly aware of his chest rising and falling against my back as he breathed. "She won't be able to hold you like I can. Will you fall?"

A small smile lifted one corner of my mouth, but I quickly wiped it away. "I will be fine." I turned toward him, my own tone more gentle as I looked up into his eyes. "Really, Tanu. I will be safe."

His gaze shot away, before he released me so I could climb onto the gray's back. We carried on. I found myself smiling as I realized that Tanu had seemed to care more about me getting hurt than breaking the deal. That was paired with flashes of irritation. I was being a silly girl. Runaway offerings with the high priest's men on their trail should not concern themselves with the intentions of tall, dark, and bearded thieves with shimmering black eyes and long hair.

Morra's horse was large and strong, and there was room for me to sit behind her as we rode toward the jungle, but something felt... off. I hated to think I missed the way Tanu made sure I didn't slip from the saddle—his strong arms around me—because he had also made me his prisoner.

I looked back. His dark eyes held mine hostage as his grimace softened, his broad shoulders swaying side to side with the gait of the horse. A yap from somewhere around us snagged our attention, making us look away from each other. Morra held up her fist and halted her horse.

The yap came again, followed by another. Then it sounded as though something was chattering its teeth together.

"What could that be?" Morra said, looking up and around, as more sounds filled the mountainous space around us.

Movement flickered in the corner of my eye, and I snapped my head around to find the source of the noise. "I-I don't... know. But whatever it is, it's watching us. I don't like this."

Gleaming eyes appeared from behind a rock, scrutinizing us as we passed. I couldn't quite see what the eyes belonged to, but when I caught flashes of its long coat as it darted between the dry, dusty boulders, I could tell it wasn't human. The longer the creature watched us, the more bold it became—appearing for brief moments to glare before darting away. It was like a huge hairy human that walked on all fours, with two horns that curled like a ram's on its head. Blue streaked its pale scrunched face where long fangs emerged from a cruel mouth.

Then it stopped hiding and stared as more beings like it emerged. They reminded me of a beast Bahmisi hunters had found while voyaging far to bring us meat during the famine of my seventh rain. But that one had been a carcass, and I remembered feeling sorry for it. The way these very much alive beasts stared made my heart beat like lightning striking the desert, erratic and wild.

Another appeared from a different location overhead. Then another. Their chattering and squawks fell silent as they watched. The silence made goosebumps prickle over my skin as my arm hair stood on end—like raised hackles on a frightened dog.

I looked back at Tanu, who spoke in a quiet yet firm tone. "Don't look at them. Keep going. Look straight, Akedia."

"What are they?" I whispered to Morra, trying my best to keep from looking up.

"I don't know, but it would seem Tanu does." She was rigid in the saddle. "I suggest we follow his lead. Don't look at them."

When one of the creatures shrieked, its cry thundering through the canyon walls, Tanu shouted. "GO!"

Morra didn't hesitate for a second, kicking her gray horse hard and shouting as I clung to her waist. When I looked back, a fleet of the wicked-looking creatures poured down the mountainside, barking and howling as they descended on us, fangs gleaming in the sunlight. I couldn't scream or breathe or think as I stared behind me in horror at the beings so unlike anything that prowled the wild outskirts of Bahmisi.

"Don't look back!" Tanu cried. "Just get away from their land!"

My heart jumped into my throat as we barreled down the mountainside, its rough terrain making the gray horse lose its footing. It was a mistake to ride with Morra, I realized. I couldn't use the stirrups where I sat behind her, and I wasn't sure that I had the leg strength to keep my seat.

I hoped Waikenu still cared if I plummeted to my death, but I wasn't going to hold my breath for His mighty hand to part the heavens and stop the devils from chasing us. I could only count on the surefootedness and speed of our horses.

With every pounding gallop, I prayed alongside the gray's effort. *There is love, there is life, there is everything in between...*

One of the monsters bounded over the rocks and leaped in front of our horses, making them rear and squeal in protest as the thing barked and snarled at us. Tanu's shouts were muted, as though someone held my head underwater where I could barely hear his voice. The creature stalked toward us, walking on its front knuckles. The beast and I stared at one another, its hideous face and gleaming eyes capturing me. Was it a kind of magic or my own paralytic fear that kept me spellbound?

Morra reached into her cloak and produced a vial as our frantic horse danced in place. The bottle contained swirling purple mist, which expanded in the air when she unstopped the cork. A wispy cloud hovered before us as her faint mutter made it spin in place.

"Theloso!" she shouted, flinging her arms toward the beast.

The purple cloud burst into the shape of a wolf and charged. The animal's threatening snarl quickly morphed into fearful shock before it turned tail, barking at its comrades.

Morra looked back at Tanu. "It won't buy us much time. We're almost to the edge of the jungle. No stops."

Tanu nodded, and I braced myself for another long haul of galloping. The jungle loomed in the distance, a shadowy place that cut out the sun, and I couldn't help but feel like we were running from one monster and into the jaws of another.

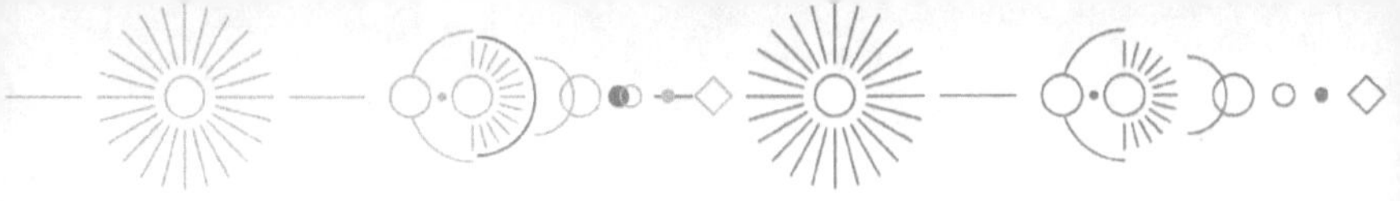

CHAPTER EIGHTEEN
WHAT HIDES IN THE JUNGLE

We had nearly reached the leafy terrain of the Binlu Jungle when Tanu pulled alongside us and waved for us to slow down. Looking backward, I realized we were a good distance from the mountain and the animals hadn't followed.

Tanu untied a waterskin from the back of his saddle and took a swig. "They probably won't follow us, but we shouldn't delay. They could change their minds."

"What were those things?" I held my hand out for a turn with the water, and my eyes involuntarily rolled with relief when the cool liquid hit my parched tongue and trickled from the corners of my mouth.

"Mountain devils." He shrugged. "At least, that's what I call them. I've passed them before without incident, but

I guess they felt threatened today. I've seen the deformed corpses of those who aren't so lucky to get away."

I shuddered at the thought of how close we had been to a similar fate. Then I remembered Morra's purple cloud that saved us.

"You're a priestess?" I asked as regret pooled over me. I had certainly not behaved in the manner one should before a priestess, never mind that I had clung to her for dear life only moments before. That ingrained sense of propriety from my upbringing was hard to shake.

"No. I am classically trained as a mage, however," she replied. "There are few of us left."

I wanted to sigh with relief but caught myself just in time. While still impressive, a mage could be any commoner who had completed their apprenticeship. Priestesses were more like royalty. In Bahmisi anyway.

We walked our horses into the jungle and dismounted. Leaves the size of goats protruded from the moist soil and trees overhead made for a kind of darkness I had never felt during daylight hours, but the break from the sun was somewhat welcome.

Tanu pointed out a pool of water and led Pharaoh to its edge when Morra shouted. She ran to the glistening pond.

"Just wait…" She threw a branch into the water and stared as it sank before bobbing to the surface.

I glanced between the floating branch and Morra. "Is something the matter?"

"Remember yourselves in this place," she snapped, eyeing the pool. "It's a good habit to make sure nothing is waiting in the water to kill us before we drink from it."

When nothing snapped its teeth around the branch, we let the horses drink. Morra sat on the bank by herself and rolled up her sleeve. She apparently didn't mean for me to see the welts that formed spiderwebs of dark bruising along her arm, because she covered her skin when she noticed me looking. That marking… I couldn't remember where I'd seen it before, but I did recall the ugly feeling that came with its memory.

Whatever it was, it wasn't good.

For Morra to have those marks just beneath the skin, I figured she had some kind of blood condition. Even if it wasn't in her blood, it was in her flesh. During the winter of my eleventh rain, an illness broke out and spread through the village. The sick ones were set up in a large home turned infirmary, and M'Ma had helped care for the sick ones. I wasn't allowed to enter, but it felt like a monster was creeping in the streets, waiting to dig its talons into me. Was Morra's arm infected from an injury, or was she diseased?

I tried to act casual and feigned a sudden interest in Tanu's work of removing Pharaoh's saddle so I could walk away from Morra. But he was too busy to notice the face I was making at him, so I hissed as quietly as possible.

"Hey," I whispered. He stopped and looked at me, frowning as he wiped a bead of sweat from his brow. "Did you notice Morra's arm? I think she has a disease."

"Disease?" He looked at her then back at me. "Why do you say that?"

"Her arm is full of dark marks. She covered it up the minute she saw me looking."

Thoughts of contagious diseases filling my lungs made me panic. We'd been in small spaces with this woman. If she were contagious, she should have had the decency to tell us so.

Tanu shrugged. "We're not dead yet. I'm sure it's fine."

"Tanu... A disease doesn't just kill you like that. Clearly it's slowly working its way through her body."

He pinched one of my cheeks patronizingly, his crooked smile an infuriating sight. "Well, you're the one who insisted on traveling with her to Kuniki. I plan to spend my dying days bathing in fine wine, surrounded by beautiful women. How about you?"

I slapped his hand away. "I hope whatever she has infects you first!"

Pushing him as he laughed, I marched away. I couldn't pick a better moron than Tanu to inherit a deadly disease, but even as I thought this, I wanted to take it back, afraid something would happen to him. The two conflicting thoughts left me confused and sent a flutter through my stomach before another thought hit me:

I was the one to touch her as we rode across the desert...

On some level, I needed Tanu's general disregard for, well, everything. I couldn't worry about the possibility of disease at this point. If I had been exposed, it was too late. Maybe she had some kind of condition that you didn't *catch*. She was, after all, our ticket to the holy book.

I needed her. I needed Tanu, too. He didn't know the jungle, but he was an able guide in every other land we'd touched. A sigh heaved through my lungs as I looked at the sorry pair, my last hopes.

Jungles are disgusting, sweltering, hot, sticky messes that no human should ever be forced to enter. At least, this was my opinion going on two hours of walking the horses through mucky trails that hadn't seen a rider in many moons. The leaves hadn't been hacked back, and everything pulled at my clothes and clawed my skin. Something constantly darted past in the corner of my vision.

A shimmering black snake as thick as my thigh coiled in a tree overhead and snatched a colorful bird right out of the sky. Something in the distance growled, followed by a horrible squeal. And general cries of wild things filled the air, promising violence, blood, and savagery.

But it was the large, fuzzy spider dropping onto my shoulder that made me scream loudly enough to spook the horses, which earned me a lecture from Morra and Tanu. As though either of *them* would want to cuddle the thing with long fangs and beady eyes.

I was still grumbling when the path opened and the jungle gave way to an open canyon. A bridge made entirely of rope spanned the distance from one side to the other. Morra turned to her horse, stroked its long gray face and whispered something before giving it a kiss and sending it away.

"From here on out, we won't need the horses," she said.

"Not possible." Tanu stepped closer to Pharaoh, as though Morra would make the beast disappear into thin air if he didn't protect the animal. "I've had Pharaoh since he was a colt. You can go on alone from here, if that's what suits you."

Morra lifted a brow and stepped toward the bridge. "Can you find a way to bring the animals across?"

A strong wind made the bridge sway and ripple. Had they been pigmy goats, it wouldn't have been a question, but the horses were large and heavy. One stumble or bout of panic and they were bound to topple over the side—not to mention they probably wouldn't set a hoof on the thing in the first place.

I walked toward the bridge, and Tanu grabbed my arm. "*We* stay behind."

In his eyes, there was a hint of asking, but mostly he was telling.

I yanked my arm free. "Where exactly should we go, Tanu? The high priest's men are not long off. I suppose we can wait around here until they catch up. Then we can swing from the gallows together—me for running from sacrifice and you for being a thief."

He clutched Pharaoh's face and stroked his nose, and something in my heart softened. A tiny, grain-of-rice-sized part of my heart.

"Morra, is the bridge the only way across?" I asked, watching Tanu's dark eyes as I waited for an answer. I thought I saw a creature in the corner of my eye again, but when I looked, nothing was there. I desperately did not want to spend an extra day in this jungle. It was as though everything inside of me itched to be free of this damp prison and bolt into the sun's light.

Morra was already crossing the bridge and her voice echoed along the walls of the canyon as she shouted back to me. "Yes, but the point where you can safely cross is miles from here!" She paused, the bridge swaying with her movement. "If you want to chance it, go around. It will take you a full day longer."

Tanu patted Pharaoh's neck, then whispered in his ear. With a slap on the rump, he sent the animal away.

"But Tanu..." Without realizing it, I'd placed a hand on his shoulder but pulled it away when his firm muscles flinched beneath my palm.

"I told him to meet us on the other side." He ushered me closer to the bridge with one hand on the small of my back.

"We have distance to cover. But that horse could find my scent across the desert. If there's another path across, he'll find it. I just needed to know it was there." He smiled at me and squeezed my hand. "Thank you."

Tanu was so confusing. Half the time, he made me insane with his arrogant comments, and then sometimes he showed hints of being a decent person. Whichever one he was, I hated the fact that my face burned from his touch.

I walked on the bridge behind Tanu, scratching my neck where a cursed bug had bitten me. The rope fibers creaked with our weight, sending pangs of fire through my belly as I tried not to think about the last time the structure had been serviced. Five thick ropes tied together with smaller ropes made up the narrow space where we placed our feet one in front of the other, and two thick ropes on either side with netting in between offered a handrail. Up close, I could see there would have been absolutely no way for the horses to cross, even if they'd wanted to. Morra was almost all the way across when she turned and shouted back at us, pointing.

When I looked behind me, I saw the ruffle of jungle foliage as something emerged from the dense growth. I couldn't move on the bridge as I watched, waiting for whatever it was to appear.

At last, the quivering leaves produced a small boy. He had maybe seen eight or nine rains as the sun god ordains, and he wore red and black paint over his light brown skin and nothing more than a loincloth. His hair was very curly, but it was the lightest shade I'd ever seen on a human—it was no darker than his complexion and nearly yellow at the ends where the sun touched it. Like the golden lion the hunters once caught for meat, fur, and bone.

I didn't have much time to consider his striking appearance before a group of his people appeared behind him, holding spears and knives. Many of them had the same light hair as the boy, but most had black hair like mine.

Their paint was foreign, terrifying. Most people of Bahmisi painted their skin for celebration. These people looked fierce and wild, even the young boy.

"Everything comes with a price," Tanu grumbled half to me and half to himself as he moved in front of me and reached into his pocket to produce a gleaming piece of gold. Then he shouted to the people. "Many thanks for letting us pass your bridge. May you accept our payment and be blessed."

He flung the coin with clever accuracy, and it landed at the feet of the boy. An adult bent down, picked it up, examined it, then threw it over the cliff.

"Hey!" Tanu cried.

The men started with a low rumble, banging their chests in rhythm with one another. Then the women wailed a melancholy cry.

"What are they doing?" I clutched Tanu's shoulder, hoping he'd seen these people somewhere before and would know what to do.

"I-I don't know, but the spears make me worried..." he said just as those holding weapons poised them for attack.

"We should run then?" I asked.

"Yes."

We swirled around to run down the rope path only to find another group of these people, one man holding Morra's limp body in his arms.

The wind rocked the bridge as Tanu and I looked back and forth, realizing we were completely surrounded. I felt three sharp needles pierce my skin in the brief moments before everything went dark.

Chapter Nineteen

Mark of the Mialinis

I was first aware of the sun shining on my face, its brightness through my closed eyelids pinkish and warm as the darkness slipped away. I had dreamt of beheaded bodies crawling after me in the night. They had pawed at my nightclothes; one managed to steal a shoe as I screamed. But now, slowly stirring and blinking away the blurriness of the sleeper's realm, I realized I was in a real nightmare.

Bamboo bars surrounded me. I was in some kind of crate inside a hut where the sun poured through cracks in the structure that was also made of bamboo. A small fire smoldered in the center of the hut, its smoke swirling toward the hole in the ceiling.

Where were Tanu and Morra?

Light flooded inside when someone parted the large leaves that dangled in the entrance to form a door. An elderly woman appeared, chuckling. She removed a ring of keys carved from bone and unlocked the cage door. "I hope you don't mind being locked up, dear. There's no telling how people will react to the medicine."

"You mean the sedative?" I grumbled, feeling the sharpness of its presence in my body when I tried to sit upright. Everything stung as I crawled from the cage.

"No, I meant medicine." She grabbed a stone mortar off the shelf and a bottle of leaves then plucked two from the jar and began to grind them with a pestle. Her skin had trails of wrinkles forming lines throughout her face, and her gray hair looked like it had once been black. She had a tattoo of a skull on the inside of her wrist. "You and your friends are lucky we caught you when we did."

"What do you mean?" Pain radiated through my head as though my brain were inflamed and pushing against my skull. I cradled my neck and grimaced.

She took the powdery leaf remnants and poured them into a bowl of water before handing it to me. "Drink."

I took the bowl and lifted it to my lips. It smelled like a musty mint plant. Had she wanted me dead, I would've been dead already. So I drank.

Every drop was bliss. The pain leaked away as though the tonic had washed it from my insides.

"Now," the woman continued. "We've been watching you lumber through our jungle for miles. We intended to let you pass, but... You were *marked*."

I stopped drinking. "Marked?" The word made me freeze. A million thoughts raced through my mind like white river water crashing over stones. What if the high priest had found a means for marking me as property of Bahmisi? Or perhaps I'd been wrong to doubt Waikenu and He had marked me unfit to live. Was it something other people saw? Since Morra and Tanu hadn't noticed, maybe only pure believers could see it.

She nodded. "We couldn't be sure at first, but those blue dots on your neck are from the shooting quill snake."

Concerns of High Priest Vikton and Waikenu were immediately forgotten only to be replaced by another. "A shooting quill snake?"

"It shoots its victims with quills so thin you can't feel them pierce your skin, or it feels like an itchy bug bite.

Then the snake catches up with you once the venom kicks in. You had little time left. And sometimes the venom makes people violent, so we had to keep our distance in order to bring you here to administer the antidote, which can also have adverse effects. My apologies if it was a rather brusque capture."

"But... I'm fine now?" My fingers grazed my neck, searching for the wounded area.

"Oh, yes, you're recovering well, but your friend, I'm afraid, is not."

"Tanu?" My heart quickened. I realized he couldn't have been far from me if I wasn't feeling any pressure in my chest from the spell. "Is he alright?"

"He is rather volatile," the woman continued. "He will be fine, but we haven't let him out of his cage yet—not until he takes the medicine I just gave you."

Of course, Tanu was being stubborn. "That's probably for the best. But I'll talk to him. What about the woman I was with?"

"The last time I checked, she was still sleeping. I suspect she will wake up at any moment, if she isn't already out and about." When the old woman grinned, I could see she was missing several teeth. "My name is Huma."

"I'm Akedia," I said, immediately regretting my lapse in secrecy.

Huma led me from the hut and into a village. Adults sat around cooking fires, while children ran through alleyways between bamboo huts in a small clearing surrounded by dense jungle trees. It was a tiny village—easy to miss, easy to hide. The air smelled like spices and smoke from smoldering wood.

My stomach rumbled with hunger.

I found Morra drinking from a cup of something steaming while sitting on a log beside a fire. A man about her age spoke to her, smiling flirtatiously as he listened to her talk. When she noticed me approaching, she reached for my hand and gave it a squeeze.

"Akedia," she said. "Are you feeling better?"

"Yes." I glanced at the man beside her. His eyes were gray and flecked with black, watching me. "But it seems Tanu didn't react well to the poison or antidote, rather. I'm going to go check on him."

Morra shrugged and turned back to speak with the man.

Huma pointed to a hut at the edge of the jungle. When I approached the entryway, she nodded, and inside, I found

Tanu clutching the bars of his bamboo prison, sweating profusely.

"Tanu," I whispered.

He lifted his head—eyes bloodshot and drooping. Locks of dark hair were plastered to his forehead with sweat, and he took staggered breaths. "Ak..."

I searched the hut for water and found some in a bowl made from a coconut shell, which was perched atop a small wooden table. "Here, you need to drink something. You look terrible." I grabbed one of the rags next to the coconut shell and dabbed his forehead through the bars before handing him the drink. "They said you weren't reacting well. I didn't think you would be in this bad of shape."

"Akedia..." He could barely mutter my name, but he clutched my hands and squeezed. "We have to..."

Suddenly, Huma flew into the hut. "It's not time to release him. He's been violent. Best to give him time to recover."

I spotted another coconut shell drinking bowl on the floor next to toppled items as though someone had thrown it in a fit. Probably Tanu. But he didn't seem dangerous to me.

"He needs care. Look at him," I said, removing one of my hands from his grasp and placing it on his hot cheek. "He's incredibly warm."

"I will send in my healers to tend to him." The woman smiled and placed a gentle hand on my shoulder. "In the meantime, you should eat something, child."

Tanu looked at me pleadingly, a desperation in his dark eyes at the suggestion of my departure. His fingers tightened.

"I'm not hungry," I lied. "I will stay on to assist your healer. I think he needs a familiar face."

Tanu sighed and loosened his grip, though he grabbed for my other hand and held them both again. He watched Huma leave.

"Akedia, listen—"

The leaf door flung sideways and a man entered with a mortar and pestle. He nodded at me while grinding something into a white powder.

"My name is Luca," the man announced. His eyes were a stunning shade of green next to his dark olive skin and light brown hair, which he kept shaved on either side of his head. "Your friend has not been very accommodating, but maybe you can try? He needs to take this medicine for the fever." Luca held the bowl out to me, his chiseled jaw pulsing with sinewy muscles as he gritted his teeth. "We've tried and tried to explain it to him, but he won't take anything. Have him eat the powder—we shouldn't dilute it with water at this point. It's been too long."

I nodded and looked at Tanu, head leaning against the bars of his bamboo cage as he clung to my hands and heaved with labored breaths. I pulled one hand free to accept the bowl Luca offered.

"Tanu?" I said. "Tanu, you have to take the medicine. You need to get better. *Please.*"

He slowly looked up at me, then down at the bowl and over to Luca. When he looked back at me and nodded, a rush of relief washed over me. If he wasn't the most stubborn man under the sun...

I dipped my fingers into the fine powder and lifted the substance to his mouth. "It's going to be okay."

His lips parted, allowing me to wipe the white residue from my fingers onto his tongue. He stared into my eyes, before I looked away and dipped my hand into the medicine again. When I fed him another handful, I kept my gaze focused on the floor, but I could feel the burn of his stare as his warm tongue absorbed the remainder of the medicine.

"He can have water in just a little bit. Allow his body to absorb it first," Luca said, his voice like clapping thunder in the hut where I'd forgotten I wasn't alone with Tanu.

I eyed the coconut shell from which Tanu had sipped earlier and realized there wasn't much water left.

Luca must have watched my glance. "I'll go get more. But since he took the medicine and seems to have calmed down with you here, I'll unlock the cage."

The medicine man produced his own set of bone keys and fiddled with the lock on the crate until the bolt turned and the door drifted open. This time he spoke directly to Tanu as though he had finally become his own person. "Rest on the bed until you've fully recovered if you'd like."

When Luca left, Tanu pulled me closer and took a breath to speak again. "We have to... leave."

"You're not going anywhere but onto that bed." I pulled free and opened the cage door, pointing at the bed. It was nothing more than a mattress of large leaves, but when I walked over and pushed down on the surface, I realized it was surprisingly plush. There was also a pillow and a light cotton blanket. I fluffed the pillow and placed it at the head of the leaf bed. "Come on. Lie down."

For once, Tanu listened and lay down, his eyes fluttering once his head touched the soft pillow. I sat beside the bed with the rag and continued to wipe sweat from his forehead.

"Just sleep for now. We'll continue on our way as soon as we can," I whispered as I stroked his face and watched his eyes fight the urge to close.

His hand grabbed mine. "Akedia—"

"Shhh... sleep."

He couldn't resist any longer. As his breath went from staggered to long and peaceful and his temperature dropped, I sighed with relief and draped the cotton blanket over his legs.

I sat beside him until the afternoon light faded and the promise of nightfall tinted the sky. Hunger coaxed me from the hut. Luckily for me, the people there loved to eat, and they had food cooking over nearly every fire throughout the village. Luca spotted me wandering and waved me over to him.

"How is the stubborn one?" he asked, ladling some soup into a bowl and handing it to me as I approached.

I chuckled, taking the offer. It looked like a mix of vegetables and some exotic roots. "Stubborn, indeed. He's asleep at last."

"Good. I didn't get your name earlier." He lifted a spoon of soup to his lips and blew at the surface.

"Ak-Akmali," I stuttered, keeping in mind the delicateness of my situation. A girl's name from my village popped into my head before I uttered my own. But the pride in my quick thinking fizzled when I remembered I'd already told Huma my real name.

"Nice to meet you, Akmali. Will you stay here long?"

"No." I took a sip of the soup to give myself enough of a break to think of an excuse. "We're visiting family far away, and we really should be on our way."

Luca frowned and stopped mid-bite. "Morra said you were delivering goods to a market in Swenyi for your master."

"Oh, y-yes. We are. But we are also visiting family, hence the tight schedule." I smiled—perhaps a little too sweetly—and then returned to my soup.

If he was bothered by the conflicted story, he didn't show it. "Well, I'm afraid your friend will need more time to rest before you leave."

"I see." For now, it was easier to play along than to snub their hospitality.

Music from a string instrument resonated in the air, interrupting the awkward conversation at hand, as someone began to sing. Other voices joined in and dancers stepped into the circle that had formed. The women wore jingling jewelry and flowing garments, not unlike the women from Bahmisi, but there was a different strut of their bodies, an archaic abruptness in their movements.

I laughed when I saw Morra step into the circle and flick her wrists right along with them. The flirtatious man she'd sat with before wasn't far off, hovering around her like an insect to a creosote bush flower. Luca grabbed my hand and brought me into the flurry of movement.

"We will honor Waikenu tonight with dance," he said, smiling.

My heart skipped at the mention of Waikenu, but I didn't let my smile falter as Luca pulled me toward the circle of dancing villagers. They formed an opening to let me in as one man pointed toward the center, inviting me to center stage.

At first, all I could do was sway from side to side. How foreign it felt to rigidly recall the movements I had once made with such love and pride for my gods. I squeezed my eyes closed and took a deep breath before performing the choreography of the faithful. Each move felt like ice breaking all around me until I was fully thawed and twirling, laughing, and trilling my tongue in the true spirit of a Bahmisi woman who honored the sun god with her very life.

My feet flew over the ground to the rhythm of the wild drumbeat. I was lighter than sparkling dustmotes. I was faster than the desert hare. I was the center of attention as the people clapped to the rhythm of my worship dance. Waikenu may have cast me out of His kingdom forever. And maybe that was fine with me now, but for the first time since Lileena's death, I remembered the love of my culture—all the pieces stitched together to make up who I was—and allowed myself to rejoice in it despite the messes made by men.

"Tanu?" I stumbled into the darkness of his hut and reached blindly for the foot of the bed where he slept. "Tanu, are you feeling better?"

There was sure to be a light source nearby. I groped the wooden table and felt a drawer on its front. Inside was something cool and curved—a metal lamp. There were pieces of flint inside the drawer as well. I placed the lamp on the table and scraped the flint together to create a spark. The oil in the spout came to life with a tiny flame.

Tanu stirred, and his eyes scrunched close as he grumbled. "Akedia?"

"Are you feeling better?" I scanned his face, which didn't look as sweaty as before. The bags under his eyes had lightened. "Why did you refuse to take your medicine? "

"Akedia, listen to me." He coughed to clear the scratchiness of his voice and sat upright in stiff, staggered movements. "We have to get out of here."

"You didn't answer me. Why didn't you take the medicine from the healers, but you took it from me? Were you delirious?"

He shook his head and waved his hand. "The pain had finally gotten bad enough. But trust me, we don't want to stay around for long."

I narrowed my eyes at him and turned my head to the side. "Why? The people here have been so kind. They went out of their way to take us in and heal us."

Tanu straightened, his chest bare as he searched for a tunic. He stood from the bed and began searching for his clothes. "We've already seen how different regions make different sacrifices to Waikenu, yes? But these people do so by consuming flesh. *Human* flesh."

A dark demon of panic pooled into my blood like an inky poisonous cloud. Dispersing, merging. Conquering.

"B-But"—He pressed a finger to my lips, so I lowered my voice—"but why would they bother to give us medicine to help fight off the snake's venom if they intended to kill us either way?"

"First of all, there was no snake. They needed to sedate us in order to bring us back to the village. Second of all, the 'antidote' was merely a canceling agent, meant to rid us of the sedative before cooking our flesh." When laughter from people outside passed the tent, he paused. Once they were gone, he turned to me again. "Would you eat a chicken with toxins in its blood?"

"How do you know all this if you've never been to this jungle?"

"You forget I've traveled far and wide. I've seen and heard many things. And legends are often rooted in truth. The legends of Bahmisi were true after all. Did you see the old chieftess's tattoo?" he asked, pointing to his wrist—the place where I had seen a skull painted on Huma. "It's the mark of the Mialinis, the flesh eaters. Akedia, for the last time, we *have* to get out of this place."

Chapter Twenty

SNEAKING AWAY

I peeked outside the hut and watched Morra—flirting with the man. Pulling her away without raising the alarm was going to be difficult. If Tanu was right about these people, clearly the man's purpose had been to distract her. In fact, all of them had tried keeping us distracted. And separate.

Tanu and I decided it was best if they believed he was still recovering. If they suspected he was still afflicted with their tranquilizing poisons, it would buy us time before the *feast*. Part of me doubted that Tanu was right. He did like to pretend to be all-knowing. Part of the legends he'd heard of Bahmisi involved drinking the blood of babies, which I knew to be tall tales. But I didn't want to find out the hard way.

I left Tanu and headed toward the crowd. People still danced and drank spirits while others sat around fires speaking. Did they have parties like this every night? Or just on the night they planned to eat three human beings? Was it an offering celebration like we held in Bahmisi?

I took a seat next to Morra on the log where she sat. "Hey Morra. I had a great idea I wanted to share with you about the horses."

Morra's brow furrowed. "What are you talking about?"

"The horses. You know, the ones we had to leave behind? I was thinking of a plan to find them again." It was a weak topic, but I aimed to bore the man out of listening to us.

When her suitor turned to speak with an elder who had joined them at the fire, I seized the opportunity to lean closer. "Morra, I need to talk to you *now*."

Morra's gray eyes glistened in the firelight, searching me. Even if she'd been annoyed by my interruption, I saw the concern and understanding there as she nodded and stood to follow me.

"Where are you going?" the man asked.

She smiled at him, practically fluttering her eyelids. "My little sister wants an escort to do her business in the jungle. I wouldn't dare send her into the dark alone."

"Don't leave me waiting too long," he said, grinning.

Waikenu, I'll sacrifice myself *if I ever become this nauseating...*

We walked away, holding hands, and neared the edge of the jungle where I was supposedly planning to do my business. We were almost to the jungle when Huma stepped in our way. I glanced at her skull tattoo and hoped she hadn't noticed.

"Do you need help finding something?" she asked, eyes darting between us.

"Oh, no, mother," Morra began, showing her an old-fashioned courtesy. "We are on our way to *pass the seed and plant a tree*, as they say."

I scrunched my nose. I had been raised in a cult, yes, but at least the isolation of my upbringing had shielded me from that exact phrase.

"Of course." Her voice seemed so kind. I couldn't imagine her roasting human beings. "Just mind the snakes."

Once she was gone, we darted for the trees. I felt relief in their darkness and cover though more wary than ever of the places where I couldn't see my feet.

Once in a position where we could see the village, but they could no longer see us, I grabbed my fake sister's arm. "Morra, these people are—"

"Cannibals? Yes, I know."

"What?! You knew? Why have you been sitting around flirting with that man if you knew he meant to eat us?" I hissed through a whisper. For all I knew, they had placed spies in the trees.

Morra stared through the foliage at the man by the fire, who was now laughing merrily with the group. "I've crossed paths here long ago and heard tales from travelers who had encountered them. They are evaluating us right now. There will be no decision for at least three days, and we will leave before then. I figured there was no use running off without a proper meal, especially since Tanu wasn't feeling well."

"Well, he refused medication." I rolled my eyes and sighed. "So what now? Tanu and I planned to pretend he was still ill to buy us time before we escaped."

"That's a fine plan," she said, her voice monotone while watching the man beside the fire.

"What of him?"

At last, she looked at me. "He was a distraction. In case you didn't notice, the young man named Luca was yours. Had Tanu left his hut, there would have been a pretty little maiden ready to make him extend his stay. I had to pretend he had me." She stared coldly at the man before turning her attention to me. "I am good at pretending."

The next morning, we feasted on the plants of the jungle and a type of grain and bean. There hadn't been a single meal with meat in it, which seemed strange for a group of human-eaters. Perhaps this was the fast before the meal.

Envy pulsed through me at the thought of Tanu pretending to be sick in bed while Morra and I had to play the part of gracious guests—never guessing for a moment that we were their next victims. Luca hovered around me, casting playful glances my way, but I didn't have much heart to throw myself into the act the way Morra did.

The old woman chieftess held up her bowl of grains and smiled at the crowd. "Together we shine..."

"Let us chase away the foe," came the response from the crowd. "In community, we triumph and glean all that we know."

I leaned toward Morra and whispered. "Are we the foe?"

"No. Wickedness is the foe. You see, they too sacrifice human life, but by consuming it, because they must believe they are casting away evil by feeding their young." Morra seemed far too calm, considering we were the ones they planned to feed to their children.

"Morra, I need to get you out of here before you decide to volunteer to become the next entree." My eyes flickered to Tanu's hut and around the village, wondering only briefly which maiden would have been tasked with keeping him *distracted*.

"Nonsense. I still have my wits about me, but I'm not going to pretend the whole thing doesn't fascinate me to some extent." Her gaze settled on a pregnant woman. "I suppose if you're raised to believe that is the way to honor Waikenu and feed your children all at once, you do it."

After an hour, the crowd slowly dispersed after cleaning up the mess from the meal. When a girl passed us en route to Tanu's hut with a plate of food, I jumped to intervene. Something burned in my gut at the thought of her spoon-feeding him while batting her lashes. It was *certainly* not jealousy, though.

Morra followed, and when we caught up with the maiden, I realized she'd only seen ten to twelve rains.

"I will take the food to our friend," I said to her.

"He needs a familiar face to ease his pain," Morra added in a motherly tone.

The girl was either too young to argue with strangers or saw the request as a relief of her chore, because she shoved the plates into Morra's arms and ran off. We found Tanu inside, sleeping.

"Do you think he's actually asleep?" I whispered, sitting beside him on the bed.

Without opening his eyes, he answered. "No. But I'm bored out of my mind." His eyelids fluttered open as he groaned and sat upright. "So I tell you ladies we have to escape because we're in the company of cannibals and you decide to extend the stay."

"Oh, stop your complaining," Morra snapped. "It just feels longer because you're stuck in this hut."

"Indeed." He sat up and stretched. "We leave now. No more waiting."

Morra crept to the doorway and peeked through the leaves. "Everyone must be napping. No movement. Tanu's right. It's a good time now."

"We should refrain from telling Tanu he's right too often." I nudged him with my elbow.

Tanu smiled and flicked me on the arm, before walking to the door. "Let's not waste another minute then."

He slithered between the palm-leaf door, and we followed. Dappled rays of light poured through the dense jungle vegetation. It seemed close to midday, but no one was out.

"Is everyone in their huts?" I whispered.

Morra frowned, reaching for her belt as though it held a concealed weapon. "I don't know. Something doesn't feel right. Things slow down after the fast-breaking hour, but when was the last time you didn't see a single person about?"

"What if they're waiting for us to escape?" I searched the jungle for signs of movement, but *everything* moved—it was a place filled with animals and foliage fluttering in the breeze. Then I realized it didn't matter if they were waiting for us. We were dead either way if we waited for them to return. "Let's just go now."

"I like that plan," Tanu said, running toward the dense wilderness.

The three of us ran hard into the jungle. I didn't know where we were headed other than away. This plan was probably no more sound than the one I'd had the day I fled Bahmisi, but at least I could carry this one out with confidence and not a single tear in my eye.

Morra sprayed flecks of mud on my face as she ran, her feet suctioning to patches of the moist ground we crossed. The wind whistled through the trees amid shrieks of animals in the distance, but the most deafening of all was the thud of my own heart, raging like an angry storm in my ears.

A flicker of movement caught my eye. Someone or something ran alongside us while hidden by the overgrowth. I prayed it wasn't the cannibals. Leaving the way we did would signal we knew the truth, and if we knew the truth, there was nothing left to do but eat us...

Without saying a word, Tanu and Morra ran faster.

They saw it too.

When the two of them rounded a bend in the path and disappeared into the overbearing leafiness of the jungle, I heard a cry. Only seconds behind, I came upon a scene that made me shriek—Nevario and his men holding Tanu and Morra by their throats.

CHAPTER TWENTY-ONE
SECRET BARGAIN

For a long time, I could only stare at those sinister brown eyes and pant away the exertion I'd just put my lungs through. His smile curled at the ends not unlike his black mustache.

"You," I gasped. "Why have you followed me all this way?"

"I trust you received the letter, Akedia?" he purred. "I'm here to make sure you get back in time."

Nevario stalked closer to me and traced a finger along my jawline. When I swatted his hand away, he gave my cheek a stinging slap. Tanu thrashed as a large man contained him and Morra shouted.

"That's enough!" she bellowed. "Leave the girl alone."

Nevario ignored her and continued staring down at me. "This girl is wanted for crimes against the sun god. It is within my duty to return her for punishment." He leaned close to me and whispered. "Besides, your father can't die for your crimes, now can he?"

Rage and despair made my nose burn with the threat of tears, but I couldn't let him see that. I couldn't let him win.

"And it would seem you're traveling with an unsavory crowd these days, Akedia," Nevario continued, removing two folded papers from his cloak.

When he opened one, I saw a drawing of Tanu's likeness on a wanted poster. For thieving, as expected, but when he opened the other to produce Morra's slender face, I gasped. *Wanted: Morra Khili for the illegal transport, purchase, and sale of stringer.*

I flashed a glance at Morra and remembered the track marks along her arms. "What exactly is stringer?"

She nodded to her arm, unable to move it while the man held her. "An illegal potion. I need it for my... condition. And I know others who need it too."

Nevario snorted. "Your sickness is self-inflicted. I have no pity for your kind. Now, come along. I have rewards to claim."

When he grabbed my arm and tugged me away—back to Bahmisi, to my death—I held together the emotions swirling inside me and walked with my head held high. Even if every living thing in existence hissed as I returned and cheered as my head rolled into the dirt, I wouldn't die with shame.

Even if every doubt I'd had was wrong and Waikenu was mightier than He was imaginary...

The feel of that snake's grasp around my arm brought back memories of lying in the dirt in the box of learning, watching slivers of sunlight fade and reappear between slats of the wooden door before my parents were allowed to free me. I had been so hungry and cold as the desert chill crept in. All I thought of that night was hating Nevario and, gods forbid, the high priest.

The tall, lean man who held Morra suddenly gasped. Nevario and I turned around just in time to see him wilt to the ground.

"Daikata! Stand up!" Nevario barked, but the man didn't move. A dart with blue and yellow feathers stuck out of his back.

Something whizzed through the air, and before I could see what it was or where it had come from, the man who held Tanu crumpled as well.

Left alone with his captives and invisible assailants, Nevario's glance flicked from me to Tanu and Morra before he bolted away.

I stepped in front of Tanu and placed a hand on his chest when he sprang forward.

"A man like Nevario is never far from more accomplices. Let him go," I said.

"He slapped you." When I looked up at him, he averted his gaze. "And he's bound to make trouble for us again. He knows everything about us."

Morra stared at the ground, rubbing her wrist.

"What we need to worry about now is who or what attacked these men," I said, clutching both of them by the arm to drag them from the area.

But we were too late. The leaves shook, and Luca and some of the villagers appeared.

"We're not going back to your tribe," I snarled as prickly fear pumped through me at the sight of him. No more playing along.

"You don't have to…" Luca replied, crouching beside one of the darted men. "But that seems like a strange thank-you for saving you from these men."

Tanu stepped between Luca and me. "Save us? Why? So you could eat us before they dragged us off to prison?"

"*Eat* you? Oh, yes, the rumors." Luca and the people behind him laughed.

My face burned. Why did I ever believe Tanu? And now we'd gone and offended the people who saved us. Twice.

Huma emerged, and all grew silent. "You may have noticed you weren't offered meat once during your stay? That is because we never eat it, regardless of the creature." She gave us a once over and smirked. "However, being a small tribe, we've kept ourselves safe from intruders by moving quickly and quietly through the trees, concocting some of the best tranquilizers plants can offer, and spreading fun rumors."

"But what about the shooting-venom snakes? Are they real?" I said, wondering whether that information fell under fact or fiction.

"Oh, they're real. Too real." The lines on Huma's face deepened in different places when her smile morphed into a frown.

My fingers reached for my neck again. "Thank you for saving us. I'm sorry we, um, thought you were going to eat us."

The woman smiled, chuckling softly as though she kept a secret too rich to share. The way her skin crinkled around her eyes warmed my heart. "You should be on your way. We sensed the intruders and silenced the camp as our warriors surveyed the jungle. You should be safe for now, but the men who are after you will no doubt return."

"What about *these* men?" I asked, glancing at the ground. Their eyes were rolled back in their heads, showing slivers of white. "Are they..."

"Dead? No. But they will wake with pain in their heads like none other."

"I can attest to *that*," Tanu grumbled.

"How can we repay you, mother?" Morra asked, shouldering her pack and glancing toward the road ahead. The man who'd flirted with her stared at the ground. Maybe he had genuinely liked her after all.

"Keep the nasty little lies about us alive and well," she said. "As far as anyone need know, you barely escaped with your lives."

We smiled and nodded before forging into the jungle. Nevario would head back for more men and supplies and possibly send word of my whereabouts to the high priest. The more I thought of him as a skinwalker from Morra's family spellbook, the less I could think of him as a priest of Waikenu's temple. He was an imposter—a serpent lurking in the shadows beneath layers of rotting skin.

After half a day's journey, we approached the rope bridge again, and I realized the Mialinis had taken us back over land we'd already crossed. Half a day's journey in the wrong direction. But at least they hadn't really intended to eat us. They'd also set Nevario and his henchmen back a few days.

As we stood before the bridge, a flash of panic made a sheen of cold sweat coat my skin. I couldn't help but imagine what kind of danger awaited us on the other side of the bridge. Morra went ahead as I stood frozen on the solid ground as the dangling mass of rope swayed in the breeze.

"Come on," Tanu whispered, the warmth of his breath barely brushing my ear. "I'll go first."

He held my hand and tugged me along, crossing the bridge one step at a time. I had to look down at my feet.

The height didn't bother me. It was the jungle filled with shadows on the other side—the vulnerability of crossing the bridge in plain sight on a network of ropes—that made my hands shake as they slid across the rough handles. Plummeting into the cavern below, oddly enough, seemed the better death than crawling into a predator's jaws or surrendering to Nevario's men.

"Almost there, Akedia," Tanu whispered.

Just look at your feet, Akedia. One in front of the other.

But then I looked past my feet and down at the drop below. When I froze, Tanu placed a gentle hand on my lower back. "You're ok. Keep moving. We're almost there."

At last, I felt solid earth and gasped for air. Stepping on the other side felt like a million knots inside me untying all at once. I wrapped my arms around Tanu's waist and pressed my head to his chest in a tight hug.

I loosened my grip and let him go, suddenly feeling aware of our closeness in a way that hadn't mattered only seconds before when I was just grateful to be alive.

He cleared his throat. "See? We made it."

"Come along you two," Morra called from ahead, breaking the moment of tension with distraction.

From the bridge, we walked until the black veil of night covered the sky, casting out Waikenu until He could return to reign supreme, as some would believe. Or perhaps, the light had simply disappeared.

I stopped walking and craned my neck to gaze at the sky. Tears misted my eyes. I longed for B'Ba and M'Ma and home and the bleating of goats as the herds converged in the morning to drink from the river. I missed watching the sunrise over Bahmisi from the highest cliff during the days when my faith was stronger than my suspicion. I had yet to long for my complacent ignorance, however. I could only hope that one day I would know more things than I did in that moment. Or at the very least, make my peace for not knowing them.

"Akedia." My name on Tanu's lips jarred my thoughts, scattering them into nothingness. "Akedia, we must move on."

I nodded, tearing my gaze from the stars, and followed the two through thick curtains of foliage as noises from the night creatures rumbled to life.

"We should build a fire as soon as we find a clearing," Morra announced, then she pointed to a tree with round fruit dangling from its branches. "Let's gather some of those for supper."

I still didn't know what to say to her. She sold and used an illegal potion. Illegal potions were said to be thick with dark magic. For a long while after the fire roared and crackled with life, no one spoke. I had a feeling Tanu didn't care about Morra's stringer addiction as much as he cared about avoiding conversation in general. But Morra refused to look at me.

Finally, I couldn't take the silence anymore. "So is that why you want to get the holy book?"

Morra slowly lifted her eyes. "Excuse me?"

"The holy book. You told us you'd take us to Kuniki because you needed passage to find your true love—"

"That should've been your first hint she was lying." Tanu chuckled and took a bite of fruit. "Anyone going on about *true love* to strangers has ulterior motives."

I ignored him and stared at Morra. "Am I right? Are you trying to get the book to craft more stringer with dark magic?"

Morra rolled her eyes. "Your isolation from the world thus far is obvious. Holy books only give direction on how to repel dark magic, not conjure it and use it for recipes.

And not everything you've been told is 'evil' is wholly evil. You must remember as you grow beyond the confines of your upbringing that you were made to *fear* far more than you were made to *believe*."

It stung a little, her words. I was wiser than all of my village for spotting the proverbial wolf in the goat herd, but she was right—I was still learning where the brainwashing stopped and my own beliefs began.

"Very well," I said, lifting my chin. "Tell us. Why did you offer to help us then?"

Morra rolled up her sleeves to expose the bluish mass of bruising on her arms—like ink seeping into her blood just beneath her skin's surface. "My husband didn't just cast me out. He poisoned me with magic that will eventually kill me. I use stringer because it slows the process; kills the pain at times. But I need to undo what he did to me. I need to reclaim my life. There are answers in those forbidden texts."

I nodded, lacking anything wise or comforting to contribute. Tanu lay on his back and covered his face to signal his attempt to fall asleep.

Morra rolled her sleeves down and lay on her side next to the fire. "We should probably get some sleep."

To say I *slept* in a jungle of hisses and howls and rattling leaves that danced angrily on command would have been an exaggeration. I closed my eyes and hoped for daylight between bouts of something resembling a nap. It was strange to feel so warm during the dark hours in that place of constant moisture where minuscule beads of water clung to everything. In the desert, we knew extreme heat and extreme cold.

I turned in the bed I'd made of leaves. They couldn't hide the fact that I was on the ground, which was still hard even if slightly mushy. Fortunately, the moon's light was brilliant that night, and it poured through the leafy canopy overhead and gave the otherwise dank jungle a soft bluish glow. I turned to see how my fellow travelers were getting along and saw Morra's shadowed form, rising and falling gently as she slept on the ground beside me.

Tanu, however, was nowhere to be seen.

"Tanu?" The whisper felt like thunder rumbling through my hoarse throat, breaking barriers of silence.

Only the flutter of wings from some night creature swooshing overhead responded to my call. Immediately, I feared the worst—something large and hungry had dragged Tanu from his bed. I crawled to the place where I'd last seen him to search for marks in the soil that would indicate a struggle or invasion. All I found were his sandal tracks, leading away from our campsite.

I crouched over Morra, ready to shake her shoulder, but then I heard the deep timbre of Tanu's voice. I stood and walked slowly toward the distant sound, careful to keep my feet from dipping into a large hole or stepping on a snake. As I got closer, I heard another voice. Had he been awake in the middle of the night talking to himself, I would have been alarmed, but it was equally alarming that he was awake in the middle of the night talking to someone else.

I inched forward until I was in a position to see the moonlight on his face as it cast blue shadows under his eyes and cheekbones. Another man stood with him, but I could only see the back of his head.

"Are you sure it's her?" the man asked, his voice making the hairs on my neck rise.

Tanu didn't utter a response. Instead, he nodded.

Immediately, I knew the *her* was me. Was Tanu turning me in after all this time? Had we crossed deserts together only for him to surrender me for coin?

The memories of the world I'd left behind swirled around me: voices of High Priest Vikton and Nevario chastising me; Lileena dancing around a fire beside me during harvest days when we were still young; my parents showing me in measures large and small how they loved me, even though I couldn't understand it at the time. In all of its darkness—all of its sinister twistedness, all of its breathtaking beauty—that place was calling me back.

Air staggered through my nostrils as I attempted to keep quiet and take in the possibility that Tanu was ready to betray me, but I wouldn't go without a fight.

Spell or no, I refused to stay bound by invisible shackles.

I watched Tanu exchange something with the man and wish him a safe journey through the night. Then leaves rustled as he made his way back to our camp.

I intentionally stood where he would bump into me on the rugged path, and he shrieked when he did. "Akedia, you scared me halfway to the spirits' world."

I crossed my arms, mainly to keep from swinging my fist at his face. If I hadn't been furious with him, I would have laughed at his terrified scream.

"Who were you talking to, Tanu?"

He faltered and shifted his weight from one foot to another. "What do you mean?"

"I heard you talking to someone." My frown deepened. "Who was it?"

"I was talking to myself." He lifted his chin as though he knew I knew he was lying and was challenging me to call him on it.

His eyes sparkled in the moonlight, but I wouldn't be swayed by their otherworldly depth. Fury burned within me.

"You won't even bother to come up with a decent lie?" I said through clenched teeth.

"Well, I suppose if you insist I'm lying—"

"You *are* lying, Tanu! I saw you speaking to a man just now. Why did he ask you if you're sure it's *her*?" My chest squeezed with anxiety and rage as we inched closer and the anger grew.

His thick brows were dramatic in the blue shadows, illuminating his expression in the dull light. "Fine. I lied. But it's not your concern what I was doing."

I scoffed with indignation. "Truly? I'm traveling with you and you dare say a secret meeting with a stranger in the jungle doesn't concern me?" He turned to walk away, back toward our camp, but I followed close on his heels. "You were going to turn me in, weren't you? Weren't you?!"

He stopped suddenly, making me bump into his back, before he whirled around and grabbed my shoulders. A twinge of that pressure I'd felt from his spell returned to my chest, making me gasp. Was he using it against me again, or was I just upset?

"Stop asking me about it," he growled through his teeth.

Our eyes locked in a glare. I swatted his hands away from my shoulders.

"You *were* going to turn me in—"

"Akedia..."

"You were. Why else won't you answer me? But I'll not stand by while you sell my head for coin. I'm done being used as your treasure trove." Tears blurred my vision as I whirled around and charged away through the jungle.

Tanu ran after me and grabbed my arm. "But the spell. You haven't completed the favors. You can't leave."

"I don't believe anything you say anymore. Your magic is a lie. You're nothing but an unwashed thief!" I spewed venomously, trying to pull free.

"Akedia, stop. You must believe me. It *will* kill you," he said, his voice a near growl as he struggled to contain me.

I writhed, but he continued to clutch me until we both slipped in the mud and fell to the ground. Covered in mud, I stopped struggling and pawed the ground for a rock as he lay on top of me. There were only clumps of dirt caked together between plants. Finally, my hand found the smooth surface of a stone. It wasn't large, but it would have to do.

"Let it crush me then," I uttered between breaths. "You sentence me to death one way or another."

I took a chance. It was a small window and he was very strong, but I swung the rock at his head and darted free when he shouted and recoiled in pain. Then I ran with every ounce of strength I could muster through the blackest night.

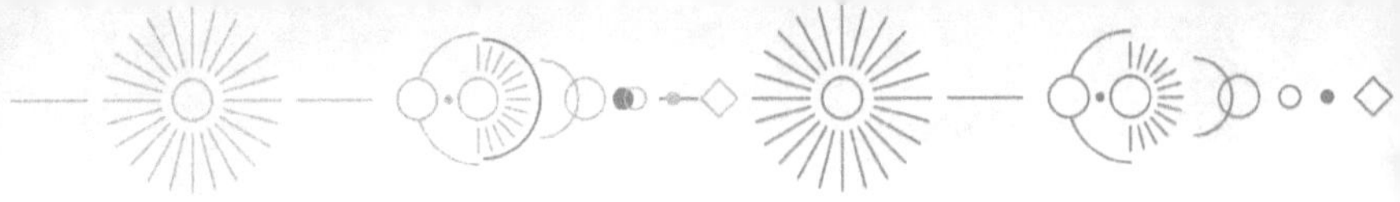

CHAPTER TWENTY-TWO
A NEW OFFER

All I could hear was the heaving of my own breath and the whip of leaves and branches as I tore through the jungle like a blind and wounded animal. Tanu followed closely behind, shouting my name, so I ran harder, desperate to get away. I made sharp turns to run in different directions to throw him off, but I could still hear him behind me, rushing through the foliage like a beast of prey. I wanted to scream for him to leave me alone, but I knew it would only lead him right to me. My advantage was the dark. I made another sharp turn and darted into bushes for cover. *Hold still, Akedia... maybe he will pass right by you.*

I heard feet approach and felt every muscle in my body tense. If I was going back to my village, it would not be from his doing. It would be because I had made a plan to rescue B'Ba.

"Akedia." His voice boomed, making me flinch as he walked slowly around the dense vegetation. "Akedia, I know you're out here. Listen to me—"

Something not too far off scurried through the bushes, and Tanu bolted away, probably thinking it was me. I planned to stay still and wait. *By morning, he will have forgotten about me.*

A tear rolled down my cheek and dripped from the edge of my jaw onto my chest. A stupid, infuriating, pointless tear. My heart had been softening toward that thief, and there he was ready to turn me in for coin. I scolded myself for letting my guard down. He was nothing more than a criminal, and I had been nothing more to him than a naive girl who could be used.

Exhaustion from a restless night and running, combined with the time I spent trying to hold completely still in the cover of the bushes, finally created a force strong enough to make me sleep. I awoke to daylight, a thin layer of drool coating my face, and the sound of someone calling my name in the distance. I wiped my palm over my cheek and listened a few more times.

It was Morra. But she only called my name, not Tanu's. If Tanu never returned to her last night, she would be missing—and calling for—both of us. Tricky. Tanu was definitely with her, but he wasn't about to give away his position. I wished I could run into Morra's arms, but she didn't fully understand the situation. He probably told her we had a fight and I wouldn't answer his call because I was too stubborn.

I couldn't return to her. To him. I slithered from hiding and stretched, ready to put some distance between us. I would get to the next village on my own and search the temple with or without her inside connection.

Hunger was the first thing to strike me after a few minutes of jogging. The water fetchers in Bahmisi who filled large jugs to return to Moruka Temple ran everywhere they went, as though walking consumed too much time. I'd seen them pass and thought nothing of them. Now, so far away from home, that once-common component of my life—that passing background image of men with dark arms somehow jogging from the river to the temple with heavy clay containers on their shoulders—seemed like a significant memory as stitches of pain filled my sides and my chest heaved with the pressure of lost air. How had they done that day in and day out? How many other jobs in Bahmisi had I overlooked and not appreciated?

Morra's calls moved farther away as I carried on, and I allowed myself to ease into a walk. I needed to find food. As I walked, the piercing pain in my sides diminished, but the pressure in my chest remained. I hadn't run for that long or far since I was a child with skinny legs and mud-crusted hair. I was not used to running anymore. That was the reason.

It had nothing to do with Tanu's magic—curse, more like. Maybe if I kept calm and in control and told myself that he was not the reason the pressure grew, I could conquer its power, if it existed at all.

After an hour of trudging down a path and watching the sun pour rays of light through the dense canopy of leaves, I found a tree with fruit dangling in its boughs and picked one to tear open with the side of my nail. Its skin was thick, but its bright innards that smelled of syrupy sweetness made my mouth water. If it were poisonous, I figured it to be a far better death than the torture I was sure to face at the high priest's hands or slow starvation.

Opening the fruit from the ragged tear like a ravenous animal, I touched my tongue to its fleshy innards to gauge its taste. Poison would taste bitter, I assumed, and since it was nothing but the blissful flavor of perfect ripeness, I sunk my teeth into it and hoped I wouldn't feel horrible pangs in my gut that evening.

A twig snapped, making me freeze. My skin rippled with bumps as I listened. Something was out there. Well, *everything* was out there, but something in particular was watching me where I stood. It had become too quiet. Nothing scrambled away like an animal would with time. It sat there in the brush, silent and watching me. I could feel its eyes piercing my soul.

"Tanu?" I whispered, glancing from one shadow to the next. I waited, then cleared my throat and found more courage to challenge the invisible intruder that I could only feel and not see. "I'm not going back with you, Tanu. I just want to be left alone."

Nothing.

Dropping the fruit, I bolted away, and the rustle of bushes followed close on my heels. I wasn't wrong to feel watched, because I was most certainly being followed. Fear jolted through my blood. Tanu would have spoken, his words dripping with arrogance, but he would have spoken. Whatever followed me felt foreign and hostile.

Even though my thighs burned with the work, something fiery inside me made me move at a speed I'd never felt before, and my feet flew over the ground. I had almost fooled myself into believing I was going to make it away from whatever predator stalked me when something snagged the back of my chiton and sent me rolling to the earth. When I turned to see my captor, I gasped at the sight of piercing blue wolf eyes.

"Salah?"

He didn't say anything at first. His breath was heavy as he pulled himself upright. He reached down and offered a hand, a bizarre gesture given the reason I was on the ground in the first place was because he'd tackled me.

"Akedia," he said, still panting. "You must know something…"

I ignored his hand and stood, wiping slabs of mud from my clothes. The only good thing about being away from home was there was no one to lecture me for my state of uncleanliness.

"Salah, for all that's holy under Waikenu, what are you doing here?"

He reached for me, his hand softly grazing my arm as he spoke. "I followed you from Tigrea. I just had to find you and warn you."

"Warn me about what?" I waited, almost certain that he would try to tell me I traveled with a thief, which of course I already knew.

But then he snatched my wrist, and his eyes narrowed.

"You have a lovely bounty on your head," he hissed, holding my wrist with increasing pressure as he pulled a piece of papyrus from his coat to reveal a notice with my face painted onto its surface. "For sins against the sun god," he read from the notice then bared his teeth at me. "Tanu has married a criminal, but I will reap the reward."

I shook my head and squirmed. "You don't understand! My people are being controlled. I must return to help them. I'm no criminal, Salah, but they will murder me like one if you bring me back. *Please*. Reconsider."

"That doesn't sound like my problem," he said, pulling rope from a bag he held and winding it around my wrists. He paused. "Unless..."

The muscles in my neck tensed at the word. *Unless* held too much meaning. *Unless* was hope dangling in front of my nose but filled with something vile.

"Unless *what*?" I pressed.

"You bring the case of your marriage to the temple and have it erased," he said. "The lack of a child is enough to sway the council, and as you have an immediate replacement, it is most likely to pass."

"Immediate replacement?" He nodded, and I caught the meaning. My wrists stung with the pressure from the rope, but anger pooled into my lungs and chest, filling every organ with an inky blackness of rage. "You wish for me to end my marriage to Tanu and become your wife instead? Why? Why must you have whatever Tanu has?"

Darkness clouded those icy blue eyes. His fingers wrapped around my wrist again, making me cry out as a pinched nerve sent a flare of pain to my elbow.

"It isn't a matter of wanting what Tanu has!" he roared. "Why would I want what he has simply just to have it? I am someone who knows what I want—I always have been. Can I help it if my fool of a cousin loses everything and then blames me for the mess?"

Still, he frowned and looked away.

"You *are* jealous," I said, snorting with disdain and a pinch of amusement.

He pulled me close and spoke within an inch of my face. "Tanu will tell you all day that he is the favored son of our family tribe, and he may be right, but I will never be jealous of someone like him."

The pain I felt in my wrists and the threat in his tone made me keep the retort I had in my mind from escaping. I had to think of a way to escape, not enrage.

"Tanu never said such a thing. He spoke only of how close you were as children," I whispered. I breathed a small sigh of relief when he loosened his hold. "Perhaps you have misjudged your relationship."

"Perhaps." He seemed to weigh the thought before it disappeared and the expression full of darkness and revenge returned. "But the offer is still the same. I can either turn you in for the bounty or turn you into my wife."

"What will I earn from the latter?" I asked, trying to extend the conversation until I could think of an escape plan. At that moment, I just needed to keep Salah talking until Morra and Tanu caught up with us. "You will bring me to my death if I say no, but a lifetime of service to a *beast*? I'd rather die."

He scowled with distaste. "A beast? What makes you think you know what kind of husband I would be to you?"

"The kind who forces me to choose between marriage or death." I turned my face to the side and spat on his shoes then glared up at him, welcoming retribution. Bahmisi had made me who I was—somehow equal parts whole and broken and disgraced and proud—and I would not cower to him.

To my surprise, he only smirked, but he didn't have time to truly respond, because the leaves rustled around us.

Tanu.

I flashed Salah my own devilish smile, which faded the minute I saw it wasn't Tanu hiding in the bushes.

The man Nevario had called Daikata stepped forward, tall and lean as he towered over us, and I searched the trees for any sign of his master, the one from my village who would drag me back to the skinwalker. More rustling, and I looked up in horror when I realized Daikata was not alone. He came with a party of men.

Not being from Bahmisi, Salah couldn't have known the evil awaiting us at the hands of these men, so even though I couldn't forgive him for the choice he left me, I looked desperately into his wolf eyes.

"Run!" I twisted in Salah's grasp to dart away, thinking at least he would follow my lead if not release me entirely at the sight of the intruders.

When he clutched me and dragged me back, laughing, a sick feeling pierced my gut.

"Daikata, welcome," Salah said, his tone still amused by my confusion. "Our captive is rather feisty. I will need your help."

My throat tightened as though an invisible hand closed around it. "So you're working together?"

"I stumbled upon a rather fortunate opportunity while drinking at the taverna after you and Tanu left the Batla estate. These men were willing to pay a hefty fee for your *safe* return," Salah said. He reached for my face and dragged his thumb along my cheekbone as he spoke. "Only thing is, I've made a side deal with Daikata and his comrades here."

Daikata was either going to help Salah drag me to the temple for marriage or to Nevario for coin. I glanced at the man, but his face held no expression.

Salah's thumb stopped caressing my skin just before he struck my cheek with the force of a thousand angry gods. I shrieked and bent forward, surprised by the attack. He grabbed my hair and pulled me upright as tears welled in my eyes.

"Don't ever spit at me again." His hand returned to my face, once again soft and stroking. This man was unpredictable. Ravenous. Wild like a wolf. "Now, what is your choice?"

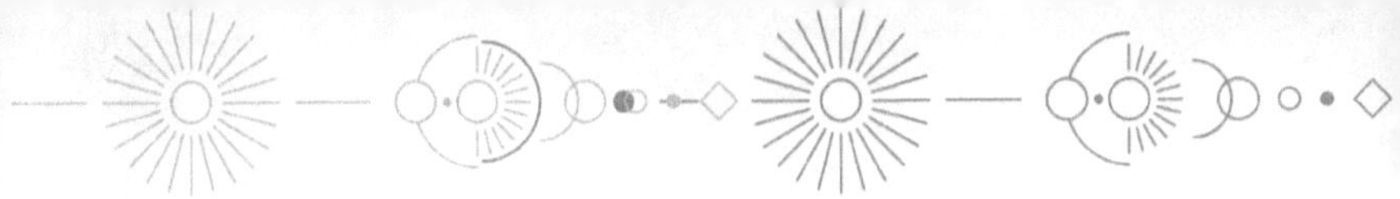

CHAPTER TWENTY-THREE
CLOSING THE DISTANCE

I chose death.

Salah was determined to make me pay for this choice. Perhaps he had considered the bounty the lesser prize compared to harming his cousin, who was more loved in the Batla family and far more handsome. And he no doubt expected me to choose marriage over public torture and execution. But I had refused him. For that, he kept me tied to a tree as the day wore on, and Daikata and his scoundrels teased me as they ate wild boar. I clenched my stomach muscles to keep my belly from rumbling with hunger and turned my head as they chewed loudly.

A dull tightening pain burned in my chest and worked its way up my throat as though it were growing, feeding on my fear. The laughter of the men faded into a dull background noise. The sense that I could fall away into the darkened corners of my mind and ignore the pain—ignore the humiliation—flooded my senses, even though the pain festered and radiated like an infected wound.

Tanu? Am I too far from you?

I shook my head. Of course not. This wasn't his magic and believing that it was only made me prey to it. I was strong. Stable.

Drowning in the thunder of agony in my own ears, I breathed deep, slow breaths, willing away the pain. Distraction was my friend, I realized, as I looked toward the evening's newest stars to see how many had poked through the fading sheen of the sun god's light.

Distraction was also my enemy, as a man from the group staggered toward me, unsteady with ale, and stroked my hair.

Salah grabbed him by the throat and threw him aside. The others in the group laughed.

The drunken man had deep shadows under his dark eyes, which were red with tiny veins, and his hairy chest heaved with rage. I thought he would fight Salah, but instead he returned to sit by the fire like a dog with its tail between its legs.

Eventually, Waikenu's light fell from existence and darkness saturated the jungle. The wild things came to life. The men lit a fire and became more drunk.

Tanu, where are you?

If I wasn't too stubborn to cry, I would have right then.

I kept revisiting the moments before I fled from Tanu, wondering if I had overreacted. He had been trying to tell me something, but I hadn't listened. What would he have said if I hadn't left in a fury?

Salah sauntered over to me and collapsed in the soil beside the tree. "Are you rethinking your choice now?" Daikata and his accomplices seemed more filthy and grotesque as they sat around the flames laughing like fools and shimmering with sweat. Salah leaned close. The stench of alcohol was thick around him. "I will keep you warm and safe tonight."

He pulled a knife from his belt and cut the rope from my wrists at long last. I couldn't help but gasp with relief.

He grinned. "Better?"

I could only nod, rubbing my skin where the ropes had left a mark. How many hours had it been? The muscles in my shoulders burned from keeping my arms behind my back.

Salah pulled me into his arms and onto the ground. He was so drunk that within a few moments, he was snoring in my ear. When I tried to pull free, his arms tightened around me.

"Sleep," he grumbled.

Daikata and his group also became more quiet as the liquor set in and the fire died. Soon, I was the only one awake, wrapped in the dead weight of Salah's arms. Every time I tried to move, he roused and tightened his hold.

I had to think. I needed some kind of plan. Magic wasn't my best option—I wasn't that talented. I was scarcely capable.

"Pssst!"

My head snapped in the direction of the noise. No one was awake, thank the gods, but someone had hissed.

"*Pssssst!*"

It had called again, sharper, louder.

"*Akedia...*"

The night was mocking me, playing games with my mind as I grew weak with hunger. The wind itself sounded like Tanu. Did I want to hear his voice so badly that I was imagining it within the spirits of nature?

"Akedia."

I lifted my head, daring to hope. Salah grumbled and his arms squeezed.

"Tanu?" I whispered.

"Akedia!"

This time, I turned completely toward the noise and blinked hard, forcing myself to wake from my dazed state. It *was* Tanu, and as he crawled toward me, tears streamed down my face.

"You found me," I whispered.

Tanu held his hands out and clutched mine as he pressed a finger to his full lips and revealed a fistful of colorful darts. Before I could make sense of it, he'd stabbed Salah in the arm. When Salah gasped, Tanu slapped his palm over his cousin's mouth and shushed him like a baby. "Why must you always have what's mine?" he whispered.

"Tanu, you..." Salah's voice trailed off as the drug took effect, making his face droopy on one side.

His anger and racing heart must have kept him awake a little longer, because he didn't drop off quite like we had when the cannibals had captured us unaware at the rope bridge. Tanu rubbed Salah's face and continued to speak to him in that mocking tone.

"Salah, Salah, Salah... Let me make something clear to you," Tanu said. "Don't ever touch Akedia again, because even if she wasn't my wife, she's too smart to want an idiot like you."

Tanu dropped his cousin's head. I slithered out from beneath Salah's heavy arm and stood, throwing my arms around Tanu's neck and reveling in the scratchy feeling of his beard on my face. The fear melted from the tip of my head to my feet as he held me, and I allowed myself to believe he was real and not a mirage of the night. It truly was Tanu, every bit of him.

"Tanu, I—" I started, but again he pressed a finger to his lips to quiet me, nodding to the other men around the fire. He held up a handful of feathered darts. "Swiped these from the cannibals. Thought they'd come in handy," he whispered. "I have more work to do."

One by one, he walked from man to man and stabbed them in the neck, shoulder, or back with a dart. Some grumbled when the needle hit their flesh, but it was so sharp and thin—not to mention potent—that they fell back asleep.

Tanu turned to me and grinned once he'd sedated each of the men, then sauntered over—proud of himself and just a bit boastful as he smiled flirtatiously at me. When I put my hand in his, our eyes locked for a moment. His dark eyes seemed to search every inch of my soul.

He cleared his throat. "Come on, my little runaway offering, we've got to find that book of yours."

Then we walked through the jungle, clutching hands as Tanu led the way. Insects stung our skin to drink our blood, and the web of roots underfoot tripped us over and over again, but I didn't care. I was never more happy to see that unwashed thief.

"How long will they be asleep for?" I asked when I thought we were a safe distance away.

His dark eyes gleamed in the moonlight, never looking away from mine. "I don't know. Akedia, listen... I wasn't trying to turn you in. I was buying stringer for Morra." When I frowned he nodded as though he understood how bizarre it sounded. "She didn't want you to know—I didn't understand why, I didn't ask questions. She just said a man from the cannibal tribe was going to bring it to her after his shipment came in, if he was able to track her. I heard someone coming while you both were asleep and realized it was him. So I went to take care of the deal."

"But why did he ask if you were *sure it was her*?" I asked, my arms crossed.

"He had asked to see her face, but I didn't want him to wake you after I'd told Morra I would keep her business private," he replied. "The man hadn't really seen me when we'd stayed with their people, so he was worried he'd reached the wrong group. He described Morra, and I said yeah that's her—that's when he said *are you sure it's her*. Akedia, please believe me. I promise I wasn't turning you in."

I wrapped my arms around his neck and squeezed, grateful for everything in that moment—his scent, his rough beard against my cheek... "You didn't leave me to die." Tears rolled down my face as gratefulness swelled inside me.

He chuckled and his warm palms cupped my cheeks as his thumbs wiped away the beads of salty water. "Leave you? Akedia, I've been following your trail since you left. I can't let you go."

"Why? I'm the one who will die from your magic, not you." I couldn't explain it, but my tears flowed endlessly and silently as we stared at one another, the bright moon making his eyes sparkle.

"Akedia, are you really that stubborn?" he demanded, shaking his head in disbelief and holding my face between two tender hands. "Or are you really too blind to see it?"

I leaned my cheek into his warm palms, allowing myself to feel comforted by him. I *had* been stubborn and guarded. Because if I allowed myself to open up, I would have seen that his eyes were like sparkling pools of his soul, peering into mine as though we had known each other for eternity before our worlds aligned to bring us to that exact moment. Everything was as it was for a reason. The pain, the leaving—it all had purpose. I couldn't pretend to know what it was,, but I saw a snippet of clarity staring back at him.

Our lips crushed together and moved in harmonious rhythm as his fingers wove into my hair. His tongue was smooth inside my mouth, and I bit his bottom lip gently, while the world blurred around me as though we were melting into one.

A twig snapped, and we jumped apart.

He grabbed my elbow and pulled. "We have to keep moving. I don't know how many more men were working for my cousin."

CHAPTER TWENTY-FOUR
WRITING ON THE WALL

We held hands and walked on. He paused twice to kiss me.

"They're not going to find you again," he whispered.

I smiled even though I knew he couldn't promise me that. So there we were, pretending to be brave and pretending to be comforted for the other's sake.

The sun was rising when we decided to pick up the pace with a jog. Something about that jungle was suffocating—I just wanted to find the end of it to be free. Finally, Tanu stopped.

"We're getting close," he said.

"Close to what?"

He pursed his lips together and issued three sharp whistles. We were quiet for a long moment before the tree branches shook with the approach of something large.

"Tanu..." I began, unsure if the thing coming at us was set to attack.

He just held his hand up, calm as ever as it approached. At last, his beautiful stallion appeared.

"Pharaoh!" I cried. "How did you ever find him?"

"Find him?" Tanu winked at me. "More like he found *me* while we were tracking you. Morra should be close."

I ran my hands down the horse's thick neck and gave him a hug even though I knew he liked to nibble my hair. Behind him appeared the gray horse and a face I had longed to see. Morra.

I ran to give her a hug too.

"Morra, you can't know how happy I am to see you," I said through her hair.

She chuckled and tightened her arms around me. "I know it, girl. Me too." She pulled away and looked me over. "They didn't hurt you, did they?"

I smiled. "Nothing I won't recover from."

Morra nodded. "Well, we should keep on. This jungle will eat us alive if we let it."

She led the gray in front, and we followed. We walked until the denseness of the jungle receded and didn't ride again until we could mount our horses without scratching our faces on the low-hanging branches. Soon the muckiness of the moist lands turned firm and gritty as it transformed into something more like the earth in Bahmisi.

As the sun rose higher in the sky like a lion with a fiery mane, we found ourselves on the precipice of yet another world.

We'd reached the edge of a hill, and below lay a city made of clay domes built between trees with trunks thicker than the homes themselves and gnarled branches that twisted into the sky. The land here was hilly and flat, bright and shadowed, green and dry—as though its creator had thrown odds and ends of ingredients together and stirred it into existence.

Morra gave us a knowing look. "We have arrived."

I swallowed hard. It was one thing to run for my life for a lack of faith. It was another entirely to steal a holy book from the holy men. If I was wrong, eternal penance in Kakaura would not be pleasant. But if I could spare my family and the whole of Bahmisi, I was willing to pay that price.

We descended the hillside as the sun baked the earth. Heat waves danced in the distance, which never seemed to close between us and the city, but when Morra covered her face with some of her linens, I knew we would arrive soon.

Her voice was muffled as she turned on her horse. "You know nothing of my name here. I am your sister, Koula, and I am mute if anyone asks. Understand?"

We nodded and allowed her to pull ahead.

Sitting behind Tanu on Pharaoh with my arms wrapped around his waist, I whispered in his ear. "What are the odds she's still lying to us?"

He only shrugged and was quiet for a long moment before issuing a real response. "Whatever her secrets are, they are her own. Everyone is entitled to their secrets."

"What are *your* secrets, Tanu?"

His voice tumbled against my chest as he laughed, its deep timbre making my heart flutter. "They are my own."

"Fine. But what of that final favor? Surely, that's not a secret between us anymore?"

He snorted. "That secret is most certainly still mine."

My heart stopped fluttering and dropped into the pit of my stomach. Not knowing what he would eventually ask of me was like standing at the end of a rug and watching him clutch the edges to pull it out from under me. Or not. I just didn't know. And that was worse than the fall.

I slapped his chest hard enough to make him yell in protest and make Pharaoh spook, but I wouldn't apologize for something I was likely to do again.

Morra turned her horse around, eyebrows furrowed. "Stop acting like fools, the both of you! We're approaching the outskirts of Kuniki."

We entered the city as it came to life. Women and men crowded the marketplace with children underfoot. Vendors set up their wares, and a few began the first calls of the morning, hollering the deals of the day. People brought laundry outdoors and tended to vegetable gardens in neat little boxes beside their homes. In the chaos, no one noticed three travelers with waterskins in need of refilling.

Morra brought us to a taverna with a water trough around the side. "Water the horses. I have business with the man indoors."

Tanu took a moment to dismount and stretch his legs as Pharaoh and the gray lapped up water. But I couldn't keep my eyes from the door.

"Aren't you curious about what she's doing in there?" I said, taking a step toward the entrance.

Tanu lifted a brow and glanced at the taverna's door. "You're the one who wanted to follow her out here, Akedia. Do you have another plan if you want to part ways with her?"

A million thoughts pulled me in different directions. I *had* been the one to insist we embark on this mission with her, and I'd genuinely missed her when I was captured by Salah. Did the fact that she used and sold stringer make her any less trustworthy? Or was it the fact that she failed to mention her criminal status when she already knew ours? That she'd asked Tanu to buy some for her and keep it from me was bothersome.

Before I had the chance to explore the different possibilities, Morra rushed from the taverna with a pouch in her hand. "My cousin will meet us at the temple when our shadows disappear."

We walked our horses by their reins through narrow roads of flagstone. In some less affluent neighborhoods, the roads were sandy and unkempt, but the tiny homes had an indescribable charm. Perhaps the circular windows with lacy curtains fluttering in the breeze made the dome-like structures look like overgrown beehives. The gates built with scraps of metal and twisted into unique patterns offered a homey touch.

I found myself wandering closer to Morra as we made our way through the streets. I could feel her glance at me from the corner of my eye.

"What is it then, girl?" she said at last. "If you have something to say, be out with it."

My lips parted to protest the accusation at first, but my defense fizzled before it could form. "Why didn't you tell us about the stringer? Why make up a lie about *true love*?"

Morra sighed deeply. "You are still in the age of black and white. I didn't know how you would respond. At my age, I've seen enough to at least understand things are not always so simple as purely good or purely bad. Stringer heals. But in bringing it to the afflicted, I have become a criminal."

"If the potion helps people then why is it illegal?" The dark potion had never reached Bahmisi in the outer reaches of the desert, as far as I knew. My limited understanding and new exposure to the concept left me conflicted.

"Don't you think it's interesting that the law of the land permits a husband to plague his wife with wicked magic, though it prohibits the very thing that cures it?" The fine creases around Morra's thin face deepened when the word *husband* passed over her lips. "It allows the lawmen to abuse the farmer and doesn't allow him to produce a crop that can feed his family? There is far more money in fining the offenders. In an unjust world, I have no qualms with being a criminal."

I nodded. A few children ran past, squealing with the lightheartedness of an era that felt like only a second in the past as much as it felt like a lifetime. Lileena and I were like them not too long ago, before that sweetness was ripped away and replaced with the ceremony of something vile. Look what being a law-abiding citizen under corrupt leadership got her. Dead and decaying in a monster's cave.

I stopped walking and touched her arm so she would do the same. "I think I understand."

A weary smile worked its way to her lips as she nodded. Then we both carried on.

We waited outside a beautiful temple of sandstone columns and arches just as our shadows disappeared beneath our feet and the heat became unbearable. Morra kept her face covered as though she expected a sandstorm. There were some who burned in Waikenu's rays if they weren't careful, and with Morra's olive complexion, she could pass off her face covering as protection from the sun. I desperately wanted to join her in hiding my face—and Tanu's too—but I was afraid it would be too obvious that we were trying to hide. As we weren't riding through the open sands and the day was pleasant enough, save for the heat, a group of people shielding their faces would be suspicious.

Tanu removed a blade from his boot and ran his hand along Pharaoh's back, gliding toward his rump to let the large animal know he was moving alongside him. Then Tanu picked up one of the back hooves to dislodge rocks from the animal's feet.

"Oh, poor Pharaoh," I said, stepping forward to pat his neck.

"He's fine," Tanu said, moving to another foot. "In a minute, we'll need to check the gray's."

We worked on Pharaoh's hooves in the shade of the temple before cleaning the gray's hooves. It made me cringe to watch Tanu dig the knife into their feet, but I knew the hooves were like giant nails with no feeling.

"My cousin approaches," Morra said, and when I looked up at her, I saw her staring down the road at a single rider who had diverted from the main flow of traffic to venture toward us.

"Are you sure?" I squinted. Could she even see his face?

"I would know him from a mile away." She waved at the rider, and I felt a small wash of relief when the person waved back.

It still made me uneasy to think of waiting for him to approach—it felt like a trap, and the rider took his time. I kept thinking I saw movement flash in the corner of my eye, as though people gathered in the shadows around us, but every time I looked, it had been only a leaf blowing in the wind or a stray animal darting away.

"Cousin!" Morra called once the man was close enough to see his features.

The rider had light brown skin and black hair that was so straight the strands bounced individually with every move he made. I found myself watching it; it was so shiny and much unlike the various curls and wavy textures I had seen growing up—the hair didn't cluster together. The man's light blue temple robes fluttered in the breeze. His eyes were either light brown or hazel, and the beard he kept was somewhat sparse in patches on his face.

The man slid from the saddle, laughing as he ran to lift Morra and spin her in a circle. When he put her down, he took a step back and looked at her.

"My little cousin," he said. "I haven't seen you since they sent you away. I've missed you, dear one."

Tears shimmered in Morra's eyes as she nodded and pulled him into another quick hug. When she released him, they both looked at us.

"Allow me to introduce you to my cousin, Lazo, the bookkeeper for the holy men of Kuniki," Morra said, pointing at the man who wasn't much taller than she. "Our mothers are sisters." Then she nodded at Tanu and me. "Lazo, I am indebted to this young man and woman. They have freed me from isolation and helped me journey here to you."

Lazo's eyes widened before he placed his hands together and gave a slight bow toward us. "If you have helped my cousin, you have helped me. Let me know if you are in need of anything at all."

"Cousin, I must admit, we *have* come to you with need this day." Morra looked over her shoulder and drew closer to him. "And we have matters to share with you that cannot be said in the open."

Lazo led us through the temple doors to reveal a set of wide stone stairs that led below the earth's surface. The structure we'd seen above the ground was simply the entrance to the temple, not the temple itself. As we followed him into its depths, I was amazed by how much light was able to pour through a glass window at the top. The staircase wound down the side of an enormous cave wall filled with religious carvings. Everything centered around an underground waterfall, which filled the area with the sound of rushing water. Several tunnels led away from the waterfall—evident by the dots of darkness that filled the wall around the beautiful centerpiece.

"I will bring you to my quarters to speak," Lazo said over his shoulder as we neared one cave tunnel lit with torches flickering in sconces along the walls. We approached a wooden door and walked inside when he unlocked it with a large metal key.

The peculiar cave room was like a tiny study chamber. It had a desk with writing tools and scrolls, and books lined the shelves. There was also one small bed.

Lazo shrugged meekly. "It is not much. But I am happy with the work I do. And I want for nothing."

Morra placed a hand on his shoulder. "It's lovely. Now that we're safe, I must tell you our predicament."

She explained the details of our meeting and the journey since. She told him of my crime for running away from sacrifice, that I was now being chased by the high priest's men, and that we needed protection. But she intentionally left out a significant part of the story: our need for the holy book that Lazo could access.

I didn't say anything until Lazo left to get us food. Once the door latched, my eyes shot to Morra.

"What game are you playing?" I asked. "Ask for the scriptures and let us be on our way."

Her hand flew up as she hissed for me to be quiet. "Lazo is a man of the temple. He would not betray his oath, nor could I ask him to. But don't you understand you are closer to the holy books than most people will ever be allowed in their entire lives? We will use the access he's granted us to do the rest of the work on our own."

I huffed with frustration. Once again, this was not what she had led us to believe. I knew we planned to steal the book, but I thought her cousin would at least aid us in the heist.

Footsteps echoed in the hallway, and the door's metal latch rattled as it opened before Lazo entered with the promised food. My mouth watered at the sight of bread, olives, and cheeses in the basket he carried. Even in the years when rain was scarce and the harvest was small, I had never experienced hunger as much as I did on this journey. No matter where we stopped, I ached with its constant pangs.

Before I could grab anything, Lazo held the basket over his head. His voice took on the cadence of one praying publicly, so I bowed my head.

"Waikenu, thank You for this feast and this time with family and new friends," Lazo said. "We are but humble servants and grateful for this splendor."

I opened my eyes, ready to snag a bread roll, but he took a breath to carry on, so I closed them again and pulled my hand away. This happened about seven more times as the man rambled on to Waikenu in the highest, and I imagined the templekeeper turning around at last to share his food with a trio of skeletons, which then made me snort through my nose. Tanu bumped me with his elbow, and Morra glared at me, so I mouthed *I'm sorry* at her. Fortunately, Lazo was none the wiser.

His final sentence, however, sounded less like an off-the-cuff monologue and more like a customary prayer: "*We are many. But we are one. We are whole.*"

At last, the basket circled the three of us, and we dug in for morsels of sustenance.

The templekeeper watched with a pleased smile as we devoured his gift. We spent the next few hours basking in the comfort of full bellies and conversation. Only when the lamp oil ran low did Lazo clear his throat and stretch.

"It's getting into the evening now, my friends," Lazo said. "I understand your unfortunate situation, but I will not share it with my brothers of the temple. I fear the information would only put them at risk. I will see if I can procure another sleeping mat."

A few more men wearing long blue robes like Lazo entered to bring us fresh linens and a wash basin and towels. Tanu and I placed our sleeping mats on the floor, so we could give Morra the real bed. Our eyes met as we arranged the bedding to make the corner of the room somewhat comfortable, and I thought of the bed we'd shared in Tigrea—tinged with the hint of his scent and the warmth of his closeness. His hand reached for mine and gave it a squeeze, before Lazo's voice pulled our attention away.

"I will take another chamber until I can think of something more permanent," the templekeeper said. None of us had the heart to admit we wouldn't be there in the morning. A pang of guilt eroded my confidence in our plan. He had been so kind, and we were about to sneak off in the night with one of his holy books. It would have been better if we'd never met him and entered more like the thieves we were.

As Morra worked to straighten her sheets and wash her face with a frown embedded in her brows, I got the impression she was feeling the same. Dabbing her cheeks with a dry towel, she walked to the shelf and selected a scroll from the wall before settling in her bed to read. My lips kept parting to speak, but I wasn't sure exactly what I needed to say.

Tanu was already resting on his side when I went to lie down on my bedding beside him. He stroked his hand across my cheek and smiled before giving in to the fatigue that made his eyes flutter and his breath deepen. I wasn't so ready to fall asleep, even though I was probably exhausted and depleted from anxiety and racing thoughts. Morra kept the scrolls in her lap as though she were reading, but there was something in the air that hinted she was only pretending. Finally, her voice cut the rigid silence.

"Akedia." Morra's smooth voice rumbled in the darkness. "If I am to betray my cousin, I must know something…"

"Anything," I replied, staring at the ceiling.

"The book might not contain a cure for me—I have some other plans up my sleeve if it doesn't. But I'm certain it holds the information you need. That said, I must trust that you have found the bravery to claim your truth." We were both silent for a long moment as I digested the comment. When she finally spoke again, her words made my heart skip. "If you will not go to your people with the truth, I will not risk my neck and my cousin's trust to seek it, especially if I remain plagued even after we get the book."

I understood her meaning, but I wasn't sure how to convey the fire that burned inside me. "I will not leave my father to die in my place. And I cannot return home without the truth if I hope to live. My only option is to speak the counter-curse."

"I know you wish to return to Bahmisi." She sighed and fell silent for a long moment. "But your new truth could mean you will never return *home* again. Your life there may never be the same as it was before you left. That may be for the better... but it may be what sets you apart and makes you alone in your own home. "

A single tear rolled down my cheek, and I thanked the gods for the darkness that hid it. She was right. I struggled with words dancing at the end of my tongue until someone knocked and Lazo and another templekeeper appeared in the doorway.

"I'm sorry to disturb you just before bed," Lazo said. "But we have some urgent news." The two looked at one another before Lazo continued. "We've just received news of a break-in."

I nudged Tanu, who woke with a start. We all sat upright.

"What does that mean?" I asked.

Lazo and Morra frowned at one another. He took a deep breath. "It means someone or something has broken into the temple without permission from a templekeeper." Then he looked right at me. "We fear it's looking for you."

"Me? *It?*" My throat tightened, and air caught in my chest and squeezed my heart with pain. "Why would you assume it's an *it?* And why would it be looking for me?"

The templekeepers exchanged another sinister glance before the other spoke at last. "Something tore through an old escape route and entered through the back of a long series of tunnels before it came across the waterfall of holy water and shrank away."

"So what does that have to do with me?"

"You *are* Akedia Morestone, correct?" Lazo asked.

"Yes..."

"Your name was written in blood on a tunnel wall."

CHAPTER TWENTY-FIVE
TREASURE IN THE LIBRARY

The templekeepers ushered us to the waterfall and pointed up the steep stairs leading to the surface.

"Whatever seeks you has been wounded by the holy water," said Lazo, nodding to the noisy waterfall and the tracks around it that showed evidence of a dragging foot. "It has recoiled. But if you stay here, it will try to return. And it now knows where the river runs. It will not make the same mistake twice."

Morra nodded and held his hand. "Cousin, I wasn't going to ask, but I'm afraid we have no other choice... We need to enter your library of holy books. We have reason to believe this thing that seeks Akedia is a skinwalker." The templekeeper beside Lazo sucked in a quick breath of air, and Morra nodded gravely. "You know I wouldn't ask this of you if I didn't believe it was necessary."

Lazo heaved a shaky sigh. "I-I don't know... No outsiders are permitted to enter, cousin. You know the ancient law." He looked at his associate, who was at least two inches shorter and kept a clean-shaven face. "What do you say, Marco?"

"It is forbidden," Marco replied, wringing his hands as his beady eyes darted between us. "Lazo, I'm afraid if you permit this, you will face the wrath of the templekeepers. In fact, I'm afraid you all should leave. Your presence here has already disturbed our righteous safety."

"I understand, brother." Lazo shook his head while staring at his feet.

"We should meet the others to see what should be done about the damage." Marco bowed to us. "I regret not being of more help to you. You must try to understand."

Marco disappeared into the cave tunnel, the torchlight casting eerie shadows on his retreating form. Morra and her cousin shared an intent stare.

"I wouldn't ask if it wasn't absolutely necessary," she whispered.

Another moment of silence followed as Lazo looked down the tunnel. Then his eyes snapped back to us.

"Three tunnels over from the right-hand side of my room, you'll find a wider tunnel," he whispered with urgency. "Follow that until you hit the first fork. Keep right twice." He removed a large metal key from his pocket. "You stole this from me when I wasn't looking."

Morra rose on her toes to kiss his cheek. "Until we meet again, cousin."

Then we ran down the tunnels, staying right both times the path forked. At the end of the path was a wooden door, but unlike the one at Lazo's chambers, this one was carved with intricate designs and images of the gods. Waikenu was at the center of the carving, surrounded by other gods and goddesses. The image of the sun-bearing god was different than the ones I'd seen in Bahmisi. His features were more rounded at the edges—less jarring—but it was Him all the same. Everywhere I went, there He was. I had crossed desert, mountain, and jungle, and Waikenu was at the heart of everything, even when He was perceived differently across the lands. As I stared at that more jovial depiction of Him, I wondered if perhaps He existed in ways no human could truly understand. What if He had given us pieces of an elaborate puzzle and sprinkled them throughout the nations of humankind, not asking that we determine a winner of truth but that we work together to put the clues in place?

Morra slid the key in a hole in the door and turned it until something clanked. We all glanced at each other before voices echoing in the halls made us rush inside.

I'd expected another room with chilly stone walls and lamps that could scarcely chase away the dark, but once inside, I gasped in awe at what we found. The moon's brilliant light poured through an opening somewhere at the top of the cave walls, which had shelves carved into their faces and sconces full of flickering light. Each bookshelf was crammed full of leather-bound books with colorful thread woven into their spines. Another much smaller waterfall allowed a trickle of water to flow through the library.

"Beautiful," I whispered, looking upward to see where the shelves ended. They twisted and turned with the natural rock, but they went all the way to the top. A small bat flew inside the cave opening and retreated when it saw us.

Morra snorted. "More like *terrible*. How do you ever expect to find the one book with a counter-curse for a skinwalker in all this?"

She was right. The picturesque plethora of books could very well mean we would never find the one we needed before someone found us.

Tanu pointed at one of the shelves. "Medicines."

"What?" I frowned at him, but he pointed again until I followed the direction of his extended finger. Along one wall, carved above a section of books, read the word *Medicines*.

"Of course!" I cried. "B'Ba always said that books should be kept in some kind of order. We never had enough in the village to warrant a need for full sections, but this makes sense."

Morra nodded, head tilted upward. "We'd better hurry. Look for a section on demons. Or counter-curses."

"Or high priests. Or monsters that eat people. Or perhaps that pile of gold you promised me would be here," Tanu said just as Morra and I had begun to search the shelves. "Whatever happened to that treasure you said would be here, Morra?"

Lines around her mouth deepened as she smirked. She grabbed a book from a shelf marked Lore and threw it at him.

"This time, I spoke the truth. I just didn't say what kind of gold would be piled up around here," she said, grinning. "Take a closer look."

Tanu frowned, but he examined the book as she instructed, holding it up in the light. Then he opened the pages and stared at the center where the thread held them together. His eyes widened.

"This is... This is extraordinary," he said at last.

"I know." Morra went back to searching.

But I couldn't see anything extraordinary. "What? What is it?"

Tanu walked over to me with the book and turned it around as he spoke. "This book is a work of art. *Expensive* art. The pages were sewn together with golden thread. Their edges were dipped in gold as well. And take a look at this leather cover."

The book had designs embossed in the leather, which was stretched with mastery. Its beauty made the high priest's book look like a dingy doorstop in comparison.

Morra climbed a ladder that went straight to the top of the opening fifty feet above. "Those will go for more than their weight in gold. Fill your bag with two or three."

Tanu slipped one into his bag and then grabbed another off the shelves. Blood boiled to my ears as quickly as it faded into a hollow feeling at the base of my gut. He was here for payment, and he'd never lied about that fact, but things were different between us now. Weren't they? Or had I let my feelings for him cloud my better judgment? I was in a hurry to find the right book, and I wanted him to help search, not worry about stuffing his bag with loot. Was he even worried about leaving room for the book we actually needed?

On the other hand...

This was his only chance to get payment. As much as I hated to think it, we would all need the funds if we kept traveling together.

After closing his bag, he joined us in searching the library and snapped his fingers. "I think I found something."

I hurried to his side and read the inscription above the shelf where he stood. The word *Creatures* made me nod and search the spines for some noteworthy title burned onto the spine. I pulled out one with etchings of trolls inside and flipped through more pages until Morra called to us from her perch on the ladder.

"Whatever you think you found—it isn't it. Come up here."

Tanu and I looked at each other and then closed our books. We headed for the base of the ladder.

"After you," he said, grinning.

I rolled my eyes.

"What kind of gentleman would I be if I didn't offer to catch you if you fell?"

"The kind who doesn't look up ladies' skirts. Now up you go." I gave his arm a swat and then waited until his feet reached the fifth rung before I followed behind. My eyes wandered upward only once. Maybe twice.

Once we reached Morra, I realized she stood on a narrow ledge near the ladder. She waved us toward her.

"Come look at this," she said, inching her way along the impossibly narrow ledge.

I didn't want to follow given the fact that we were almost at the top and had a long way to drop, but then she disappeared into the recess of a cave. I took a breath and placed a foot on the ledge. It was wider than I'd expected, and someone had carved a railing into the wall for support. Once I finally made it to the point where Morra disappeared, I found the cave and stepped inside. It held more books, lit by another row of mounted torches. Tanu followed shortly after.

"Look." Morra pointed at the section title signs. "Demons, Evil... Curses and Cures."

"Which one should we take?" I asked, pulling a book from its place to flip through the pages.

"I say at least one from each." Morra read a spine and then slid a book from its place, leaving a rectangular hole of darkness on the shelf in its absence.

A loud slam made all of us jump. Footsteps echoed through the cave. Slow. Methodical. Then voices followed.

"Your Eminence," a man said. "It is such an honor that you have come to visit us here in Kuniki. It is always a joy when other priests visit our humble temple. Please feel free to browse through our library. Is there anything I can get for you?"

A cold voice that pierced my skin like a million shards of glass replied. "I am looking for a particular book, and I've heard that your temple is the only one to house it."

I pressed myself against the wall of the cave and held my breath, sweat beading on my brow. Tanu frowned when he saw me and stepped closer. His hand held mine as he mouthed, *are you alright?*

I could only shake my head. No. No, I wasn't alright. I leaned over the edge of the cave, down to the depths of the library below, and caught a flash of purple robes.

High Priest Vikton himself stood just below my feet.

Chapter Twenty-Six

SIN AND WICKEDNESS

"Tell me, Your Eminence, of the holy book you seek." The other man wore blue temple robes like Lazo's and was significantly shorter than the high priest.

High Priest Vikton strolled arrogantly, surveying the books as though they were unimpressive trinkets. "I seek a book with a passage on eradicating demons. Skinwalkers, even."

"Skinwalkers? I pray you are not in need of this book for practical reasons." The man fluttered behind, his short legs stumbling to keep pace.

"I do worry for one reason or another," the high priest purred. "I would like to see this book."

The templekeeper cleared his throat and chirped a happy reply. "Of course, of course. I am not the librarian. We are shorthanded right now due to... unexpected circumstances. But I will retrieve the master ledger to see if we can determine the section. I will return shortly."

The man scurried away and left the High Priest in the library. I couldn't keep from watching him as he stalked through the aisles, staring at the section markers with kohl-lined eyes.

Morra nudged my arm and dragged me back into the cave. She whispered no louder than a sniffling mouse, but I somehow heard it. "We have to get out now."

I nodded and followed her lead of stuffing a couple midsize books into my bag before heading for the ledge. Morra pointed upward. We were going to escape through the opening in the roof, but the ladders didn't reach that high. We'd have to rock climb like goats.

The stone that made up the walls was porous—its pockmarked surface made finding holds easier—but it was still a looming distance over the ground. We lurked in the shadows where the torchlight didn't reach. My foot groped the rough surface for a safe place that could bear my weight, but I kept looking down to where the High Priest stood. Black gems on his black head cloth glistened in the torchlight that chased away the darkness of the cavernous library.

Tanu's hand on my waist made me turn to him. Our eyes locked, then he nodded upward. *Climb*, he seemed to say.

I nodded and looked up before pushing my weight upward with my legs and searching the wall for another hold with my hands along the way. Every time the high priest moved, we paused, frozen where we clung like a trio of cave bats. His shoes clicked across the stone floor with the heaviness of expensive material as each step echoed to my ears.

Morra's feet disappeared when she pulled her body through the opening and out of sight, which gave my heart a leap of hope. We were almost out.

Then the door slammed and footsteps entered. The voice of the templekeeper who had left squashed that hope.

"Your Eminence," the templekeeper said, panting as though he'd been running. "Thank you for your patience. We have a special section on demons, evil spirits, curses, and cures," he said, pointing in our direction.

Tanu and I climbed faster, both obviously thinking the same thing and throwing any caution we'd had about falling to our deaths to the wind. We were dead if they saw us.

"Excellent, show me," High Priest Vikton said.

The opening was so close. I just needed to find another hold that could help me.

One of my feet slipped and a pebble tumbled free from the wall, clattering as it bounced to the bottom. I found another secure place to put my foot, but my hammering heart made moving impossible.

Then I felt the pull of hands on my wrists and realized Tanu had climbed ahead and was now pulling me upward with help from Morra. They dragged me through the opening and into the night air, where gusts of wind made it impossible to hear what the men were saying below.

Had they noticed us? We couldn't know, so we had to assume the worst and flee.

From the temple top, it felt like soaring above the world with twinkling lights from the city below and stars above.

"I've never..." I gasped.

Tanu stood beside me. "It's pretty amazing."

"Sight-seeing is for tourists and dead fugitives," Morra snapped, and we followed her down a path on the mountainside.

I hadn't realized how large the underground temple was when I was inside, but we were nearly a mile from the entrance. The library's cavern was part of a hilly terrain that abutted a rocky mountainside and more wilderness beyond the city.

"Wait," I said just before we took off. "What about the horses?"

"Pharaoh will find me eventually," Tanu replied. "The gray will either follow or find a new home. Come on."

We ran with our bags full of six to eight books between us all, and I prayed to anything that would hear me that at least one of us had stolen the right one.

Morra was right about not building a fire, but the desert was as brutally cold at night as it was hot during the day. I tried to conjure memories of burning in the sun, but it didn't take away the sting of discomfort.

Somehow Morra fell asleep, but Tanu inched closer to me and wrapped an arm around my back, making my cheeks burn.

"You shiver like a frightened rabbit." He rubbed his hand on my back quickly, and the friction helped to warm me. Then he held still but left his arm in place as we faced one another.

"Thank you," I whispered. A thought crawled into my mind and fed on my happiness like a parasite until I was no longer a sufficient source. It had to escape. "Why are you holding onto that last favor, Tanu? I don't understand what you're gaining. If it was just about the gold, you could have forced me to steal for you and left by now. Why go through all of this?"

Tanu's grip loosened a little. "I... I cast the spell because I was desperate for funds and needed to get as far away from my homeland as possible."

"Because you're a thief?"

He didn't speak for a long moment. "Because I pretended to be one for someone who never asked me to."

"I don't understand..."

"My little brother got in a bad way. Stole from the wrong people. I knew he'd been struggling since our parents died, but I didn't realize how badly." Tanu mindlessly played with my hair as he spoke, sending shivers down my spine. "I took the blame for his crime with the lawmen. I knew I had a better chance of surviving. And I knew I could run and take the search away from our home."

"To get them to stop looking for your brother?"

"Correct."

The silence that poisoned the conversation left a bad taste in my mouth. "But?"

He chuckled derisively. "*But*, indeed. I took the search away from Proctah, my home—away from the lawmen—but the other criminals weren't so easily fooled. I received word of his murder one year ago. I couldn't even return for his burial."

I grasped the hand that wasn't fiddling with my hair and squeezed. "Oh, Tanu. I'm so sorry."

His jaw rippled with sinewy muscles when he clenched his teeth together. He puffed a short snort through his nostrils.

"What can be done? Nothing anymore. So I figured out a way to live like the criminal I was painted to be until I truly became one."

I glanced at Morra and thought of her words about being a criminal in an unjust society. The three of us were nothing more than glorified outcasts with bounties on our heads.

While he hadn't technically answered my question about the final favor, I didn't press it at that moment.

Tanu squeezed my hands. "At first light, we'll search those books for the counter-curse."

I knew he was trying to change the subject and uplift my spirits in one move, but the mention of those books made the anxiety I'd been ignoring harden into a rock of pure fear. What if we hadn't grabbed anything useful? We would be back to our starting point. Or we'd have to figure out a way to get back into the temple when we had more time to search. That would prove difficult, as by now Lazo had probably told his brothers of the faith that we had stolen his key. We would not be welcome to walk through the halls.

Tanu's hand pulled away from mine and stroked my cheek. "Hey, we'll figure it out."

His eyes were like the purest ebony—the kind the woodworkers of Bahmisi would pay an extra coin for at market. As he looked into mine, electricity coursed through my veins. He glanced at my lips and leaned closer until Morra's abrupt snore made us jump. We both laughed.

"Here." Tanu sat upright to open his bag and remove a small blanket. "I'm sorry, I just remembered I had this." He draped it around my shoulders and flashed a crooked smile at me. "Goodnight, offering."

"Goodnight, thief."

The morning would bring the sun as it had since the creation or coincidence of life itself, and I rejoiced in its warmth as it chased away the bitter cold. Soon it would replace that chilliness with unbearable heat, but in that tender moment of the day, the temperature was perfect for travel.

I was the first to wake and begin studying the books. Tanu had carried four from the library—two to sell from the lower shelves and two hopefully helpful volumes from the above-ground cave. The ones from the *Demons* and *Evil* sections had reddish leather. I searched those first and found that most of the chapters had something to do with morals and teaching people about how terrible they were. As it would turn out, even my strict upbringing had taught me nothing about sin as it was written in these holy books. For example, selling wool at market two days after a holy day; returning borrowed dishes without washing them three times; staring at anything for longer than one minute. Anything and everything. So it would seem my sin of running away from offering duty was just one of hundreds of other transgressions, which oddly enough, made me feel better. In a world where everything is a sin, might as well choose a good one.

Tanu stirred and went to wash his face with water that ran through a small stream. When he returned, he helped me flip through the pages of the other books. Then Morra awoke and joined us. For the next hour, we searched the chapters, hoping to find something about skinwalkers and the evil residing inside them, but every time we thought we were close because we'd find pages with sketchings of monsters with horns and scales, the concept turned back to wickedness and living a life full of perfect behavior. Books from the *Curses* and *Cures* section seemed to cover household remedies for the common cold.

I sighed and leaned against a rock. "Some of this is pretty terrible."

Morra chuckled and snapped a book closed. "It's fascinating to me, but I can't say I miss any of it."

Tanu searched through his bag and removed a piece of cured jerky. He ripped it into three pieces and shared two of them with us. As I chewed the salty bit of dried meat, I stared at the collection of eight books we'd stolen from the holy library.

Sin. Definitely a sin.

One of the spines caught my attention. It had a circular emblem of a snake eating its own tail. Or was it regurgitating itself? I snatched the book from the ground. It was one of the two Tanu had planned to sell, and it was from a section marked Lore, but I hadn't checked either one yet.

The binding creaked when I opened the book, as it probably hadn't been read in over a hundred years. The images inside made me gasp.

"What is it, Akedia?" Tanu rushed to my side. "Did you find something?"

I nodded. It was a book of *folklore*. The story that matched the spine's symbol was about a creature that could shift its shape. It went from rabbit to snake to crocodile to wildebeest to lion... to human. It changed many times to serve its needs, tricking its brethren creatures in order to feast on them.

"Morra, come take a look at this!" Tanu called, and she rushed to read over our shoulders.

"This may only tell the tales of such things, but keep reading to see if there are directions for exposing them," she said.

As I turned the pages, we all quietly read together. Each one detailed more trickery by the skinwalker, but with every page, we seemed to inch our way toward a solution.

I jabbed my finger on a page with text I was sure would add up to something. "Here! Look at this! 'A man named Joleni, son of the people of the sea, once captured the skin-walker by its tail. He whispered the words that transcend all barriers.'" I looked up from the jumble of letters and smiled. "This could be it! The words!"

I was just about to turn the page when Tanu gasped in pain and fell forward.

"Tanu!" I cried, dropping the book as he plummeted onto his face and a single dart stuck out of his back.

Morra fell next. Only a sliver of the whites of her eyes showed as she lay on the ground with a similar dart. I whirled around and screamed when I saw the person responsible: Nevario, flanked by no less than a dozen men and that bastard Salah.

"Akedia, my dear, I'm afraid your trial awaits you." Nevario rushed forward and seized my wrists as his men scooped up my unconscious friends.

"My payment, Nevario?" Salah asked, his wolf eyes taunting me for my choice to refuse his marriage ultimatum.

Nevario glanced at him. "Your award is kept safely in Moruka Temple. You will return to Bahmisi with us if you want it."

His words said one thing, but his eyes said another. With a terse nod, Nevario's men crowded around Salah. One removed a knife and ran it through his stomach before he collapsed in a pool of his own blood.

In the last seconds of his life, he extended an arm toward Nevario and choked out incoherent words filled with rage and something indecipherable.

"It will come for you, the thing you fear," he said, spewing blood from his lips.

Nevario's left eye flinched, a brief lapse in his uncaring expression.

I turned away from the sight and tried to work through the metallic taste in my mouth that signaled potential vomit.

Then Nevario returned his attention to me. "The high priest will be pleased to see your beautiful face. We must avenge the crime you've committed against the sun god before He decides to punish us all."

"Nevario, you have to listen to me!" I cried. "Look in that book and read about the skinwalkers."

"Skinwalkers?" He frowned, and a flash of fear coated his otherwise stern eyes. "What of them?"

Hope filled me with lightheadedness. I knew I had to speak quickly and convincingly, which made the words feel like sludge in my mouth. It all hinged on making him listen for long enough to hopefully believe.

"One has infected our village, Nevario. High Priest Vikton is not who you think he is." I paused as Nevario and his men stared at me. "He's a skinwalker. He's been feasting on the remains of our sacrificed offerings. I found them in a cave down the river. We were all tricked by the master of trickery. Those poor people never ascended to live with Waikenu. They were murdered and... eaten."

The men glanced at one another. One with widened eyes seemed to believe me, and even Nevario's hold loosened.

"That's not possible," he said. "Th-The skinwalkers were banished long ago, before our grandmothers' grandmothers' time."

I shook my head slowly. "One has returned then. Just look in that book over there. The one with the gold thread. All of the signs are present. But we can bring that book back to Bahmisi and destroy him!"

Nevario sighed. "I will not look in your foolish book, because it proves nothing, Akedia. Writers have taken an old and buried truth and turned it into something for entertainment. Whatever you've read is most likely a far cry from the reality it once was."

I shook my head. "No! Please, just read page one hundred forty-seven. How can you call these stories foolish when you believe in the holy books and call them truth?"

The sharp sting of a slap cut across my cheek, and I gasped with pain.

"You will not speak such vile words," he spat, looking at me as though I were filth of the earth. "The holy books contain the purest messages from Waikenu."

"I meant no disrespect, but you must listen to me about the skinwalker. Please read," I urged, nodding toward the loot we'd stolen from the temple library.

He glanced at the books on the ground and everywhere but at me as he waved some of his men forward. They clutched my arms as Nevario walked directly to the book of lores. "We must bring this felon back to Bahmisi to avenge Waikenu."

"Nevario, please. You have to listen to me!" I shouted over my shoulder as the men dragged me away. He still wouldn't look at me, but the frown he wore made me think there was still room for some convincing. "Why do you think no other village in this wild desert land sacrifices human beings—amongst villages full of people who worship the same gods?"

Nevario looked at me for once. "Why?"

"Because it is not needed. The skinwalker has only made us believe this. But this faith doesn't need to exist around death and fear."

"Wait," Nevario barked. The men stopped walking and turned me around to face him. He stooped to pick up the book of lores and thought for a long moment. Then he looked at me with weary eyes. "The people of other villages do not sacrifice because they do not know how to properly honor Waikenu. They are wrong. And wicked."

"No, Nevario, for once, think outside what you have been spoonfed to believe. *We* are wrong." The men held me tightly on either side, and pain radiated in my arms.

I thought I was getting through to him. I thought maybe he was taking a moment to reflect on a life wasted with false righteousness. Instead, he waved his hand in a circular motion and called the magic of flame into his palm. He held the book over the flame, inches away from its fiery tongue.

"I'm sorry, Akedia. Fairy stories will not save you. You've been away from Bahmisi too long. The sin and wickedness of the world has clouded your mind. You keep company with criminals and steal from holy men. You have ventured down the wrong path, but I won't be fooled by your lies and deception," he said, his voice filled with the authority that helped keep order in Bahmisi under the skinwalker's rule.

"No!"

Then he burned the book, its pages curling as they blackened. My hope of finding the counter-curse and saving my people went up in flames as the men dragged us in the direction of Bahmisi, where my homecoming would become my certain death.

Chapter Twenty-Seven
THE THIRD FAVOR

Nevario had come equipped with a wagon and a cage for me, though it was clear he hadn't planned on acquiring two extra captives. We sat crammed in the prison for hours as we crossed different lands.

After the first five hours of travel, Tanu and Morra awoke from their drug-induced slumber. They took one look at my tear-stained face and the cage and wrapped their arms around me.

"We'll manage something," Morra said, stroking my hair. "You'll see."

Even when Morra pulled away, Tanu held me tightly and kissed the top of my head over and over again. "I won't let them hurt you."

I knew their words meant to calm me. I knew Tanu *believed* he could protect me. My fate was sealed. The men were dragging us back to a world where ignorance was king over reason, and the one hope for showing the villagers the truth was gone.

Time became nothing to me as the animals dragged the wagon onward. Sometimes we ate, but it tasted of nothing. Sometimes we drank, but it never quenched my thirst. Perhaps I would die before we ever returned. Would this nothingness death be better than the torture I was sure to face at the skinwalker's hands? At least the latter would allow me to see my parents before my demise.

We journeyed for days upon endless days. My stoic state of being somehow made the voyage back over lands I'd crossed before seem like an eternity and nothing all at once. We cut through the jungle, and I felt nothing. We climbed a mountain, and I didn't yelp with fear when the wagon teetered at the top of a ravine. The men growled insult after insult to me as Tanu held me in his arms, and all I heard was the beating of his heart. I had felt *everything*—every miniscule pain—for so long as I ran from my homeland, but now, returning, all I felt was empty.

One late afternoon, the men set up camp. They released me from the prison to relieve myself. I was allowed to walk through a curtain of trees and bushes to the edge of a cliff not far away. I was finally alone. I stood at the precipice and looked out at the land—mile after mile of diverse terrain that I knew held lies and truths and beauty and ugliness in every corner. The sun, Waikenu's beautiful light, began to set and cast brilliant orange, pink, and purple across the enormous sky above. Sunset was a time of peace, and here I was at the top of the world, knowing I was soon to die. As the numbness melted away, I knew I was not at peace with it.

I looked upward and whispered. "Help me."

The wind played with my tangled hair, and birds cried in the distance. As the sun faded, the horizon became more lovely, and I could think only of B'Ba, who once said this time of day was when Waikenu whispered to a busy world, *I am still here, if only you'll listen.*

Fresh tears streamed down my face. I missed my father, and somewhere beneath the muck of religion I'd come to loathe, I missed Waikenu—the one I knew in my own heart, not the one fabricated by men to control other men and mostly women. I finally understood the tears I'd seen in B'Ba's eyes when we had placed the candles by the icon in what seemed like another lifetime ago.

"I'm listening now, Waikenu," I said. "What should I do?"

The sun god's light continued to shift as it began to depart.

"Answer me!" I shouted into the sky as tears rolled down my neck. "I'm asking you for help! Why won't you answer me?"

At last the light fell beneath the horizon, and a dull glow was all that remained of the once-beautiful sunset. As I sobbed for the horrid hollowness that now remained in my soul, one of Nevario's men came to drag me back to my cage.

Tanu and Morra tried to speak with me in the following days, but I had nothing left to offer them. Nevario had plans to throw them in prison until their bounties could be collected, so in being connected to me, they were doomed as well.

The sight of the river I'd known since childhood made my heart feel a weak throb of life. I said goodbye to it and the herds of goats nibbling fresh grass as we rolled past and onto the road that would lead us into town. In the daylight, people were cleaning laundry and repairing homes, going about their daily lives. When they noticed me in the wagon, they began to hiss and jeer, following us along the road into the center of town.

These people—many who had contributed a hand in raising me in our desert village by the river—shouted things about looking forward to my death and how I would burn for all eternity.

Tanu wrapped me in his arms and whispered into my hair. "Ignore these fools, Akedia. Just count my heartbeats." Then he pressed my head to his chest and covered my other ear, so I wouldn't hear the other horrible things they would say.

It helped for a little bit, at least until we arrived in the center of town and the wagon halted before the podium where a grim figure looked down on us.

The high priest's wicked face curled with delight at our capture. Then he waved to Nevario, who stood at attention.

"Bring forth the girl's parents," he commanded, and Nevario disappeared.

M'Ma and B'Ba looked dirty and defeated as they trudged into the town square, and I realized that they *both* must have faced imprisonment for my crimes. Once they saw me in the cage, their eyes came alive, and they ran to my side, hands reaching through the bars.

"Akedia!" they cried in unison.

"M'Ma! B'Ba! I'm so sorry. I'm so sorry," I said through tears.

"No, no, Akedia, shhh," B'Ba said, his own eyes glistening. "There is nothing to be sorry for, my girl."

M'Ma held my hand with desperation. "*Nothing* to be sorry for. I thought I would never see you again. Akedia, please forgive *me*, if I was not the mother you needed me to be."

"Oh, M'Ma, don't say that—"

"The time for reunions has come to an end, I'm afraid," said High Priest Vikton, his voice like a thousand knives in my heart. "There will be a torture and a sacrifice in the name of Waikenu. And then He will be pleased."

As the crowd cheered and my parents angrily shouted at the villagers, Tanu turned to me and clutched my face with both hands, speaking urgently. "Akedia, I have to be honest with you. I never knew what that third favor was going to be. I just didn't want you to leave me. But I know it now, and I command you to listen."

"Tanu, what are you saying?" I cried as he stood hunched over in the short cage.

"High Priest! *High Priest!*" he shouted. When High Priest Vikton finally noticed him above the noise, Tanu spoke quickly. "I will sponsor this criminal's crimes and take her place on the altar—"

"No!" I pawed for his clothes, as though I could take back his words if I could shut him up.

The high priest evaluated Tanu with cold and calculating eyes. "Who *are* you?"

"If I take her place, allow her and her parents to live," he said, swatting my hands away as I continued to plead with him.

The skinwalker evaluated the offer, eyeing Tanu. "Why should I agree to this?"

"Because my blood is of a noble line. I am Tanu Behman of the Batla family of Tigrea." He paused and nodded when the high priest cocked his head to the side. "There would be no better offering to Waikenu in the highest."

High Priest Vikton stroked his pointed beard. "If I allow this, Akedia must be sent away forever. Banished."

"I agree to these terms," Tanu said before pulling me into his arms and squeezing me hard. His gruff voice was tender as it tumbled through my hair. "This is my third and final favor: I command that you allow me to take your place without arguing with me."

Words failed me. I felt them clog with pain in my throat. I *wanted* to argue, but—bound by our magical contract for this last command—I couldn't. All I had were my silent thoughts that begged to be heard. He didn't deserve to die for me.

"Tanu, how could you?" I managed at last. My face hurt from the puffiness of sobbing. I hurt everywhere in every way.

He leaned forward and pressed his lips against mine before pulling away to look at me. "I had to, Akedia. It's another desert code of the unwashed thieves—to die for the ones we love." The corners of his mouth lifted into a tragic smile that broke my soul. "Your life will go on, Akedia. It must."

"*No!*" I sobbed.

The men opened the door and removed Tanu, throwing me back inside when I tried to fight my way out. While most of the villagers shouted and jeered at us, I saw a few walk away from the scene. Maybe not all of them wanted to watch this display after all.

Morra cradled me in her arms as I sobbed and the last strand of pressure living in my chest dissipated. I was free of his favors. And it felt horrible. How could I ever leave Bahmisi behind, knowing the things I knew—knowing my people would continue to feed the skinwalker and that Tanu was dead while I lived?

Something hard hurt my hip as I leaned against the cage bars. I reached into my pocket and found the rock from my uncle. This stupid rock had once been my comfort in better days when remembering words from Uncle Peko was all it took. Things weren't nearly as complicated then.

Tears streamed down my cheeks and over my lips as I thought of my uncle's words, *There is love, there is life, there is everything in between.*

The men bound Tanu's hands as I held the stone in mine, remembering how it had once been part of the bartering chip to our original agreement. This stone had seen me off on a voyage into the world beyond my own, where people lived together just as we did, but differently. I looked at the stone's smooth surface again then up at the skinwalker as he glared at Tanu.

Thoughts of Uncle Peko made more tears burn the bridge of my nose. What if my uncle was sacrificed because he had searched for the counter-curse too? Was he sacrificed because he'd gotten too close to the truth? My father never wanted to talk about it in our home, but it made sense. Despite my fear and the roar of the crowd that was eager to watch him die, I tried to remember my last conversation with him. How he wanted me to have a physical reminder of his words. *There is love, there is life...*

"There is everything in between," I whispered to myself.

My thoughts came faster now as pieces began falling into place. His saying was one of love and tradition. As Tanu and I traveled through faraway lands, I'd seen so many different ways to show love and honor traditions. What if the means to banish evil had been hidden in plain sight all along—woven into the very fabric of our societies?

My heart hammered with excitement. I had voyaged all across the desert, and the one thing that was always the same was how humans sought out community. I flashed through the many encounters I'd had, from Manitu to the cannibals of the jungle to the temple where Waikenu was worshiped by holy men. Each custom, each prayer—they were all parts of a whole fractured into pieces by time and distance. It was just a matter of putting them together...

I stood in the cage and stared at the skinwalker as the electricity of everything I felt in that moment pulsed through me. There was always the possibility that I was horribly wrong and my punishment would be a life without Tanu, but I had to try.

"*There is love, there is life, there is everything in between!*" I shouted at the high priest. His eyes snapped to mine, a wicked glower on his face. Fear fluttered in my chest.

"What are you doing? Someone silence her!" he bellowed.

"*May we be fed in our hearts and souls, even when the platter's clean,*" I continued, then I turned to the crowd. "*Together we shine, let us chase away the foe. In community we triumph and glean all that we know...*"

"Stupid girl, we must avenge the insult you have issued Waikenu before He destroys us all!" the skinwalker hissed.

I turned back to him and smiled. "*We are many. But we are one. We are whole.*"

The stone in my hand glowed and then faded. The high priest stared at me, still scowling. I expected him to burst from the seams, exposing the skinwalker's true form beneath. So when nothing happened, a terrible feeling clamped around my throat as I slid the stone back inside my pocket. It wasn't the counter-curse.

The high priest nodded to the assassin to begin with the torture, and the man raised a stick filled with nails to issue the first blow, but just as the weapon reached its highest point—ready to swing down on Tanu's flesh—a horrifying screech split the air.

I whirled around looking for the source and found Nevario writhing on the ground. His skin began to bulge and stretch before it split and blood gushed from the openings. Everyone watched with terror as something emerged from the pile of skin and grew larger by the second.

Underneath, something with greenish-gray skin shimmered with moisture and blood, and a creature emerged. Its pointed ears stood upright like the singing coyotes of the desert, but its face was a mix between monster and man, standing on two hind legs. Pointed teeth hung from its open jaw as it looked at me with bloodshot eyes.

I had been right about the counter-curse. We didn't need the book. The answer to expose evil had transcended the generations.

But I had been wrong about the skinwalker—it was Nevario, not the high priest, who had been pulling the strings. As it continued to grow, glaring at me furiously, I also realized the counter-curse would only expose the demon for what he was.

That wasn't going to stop it.

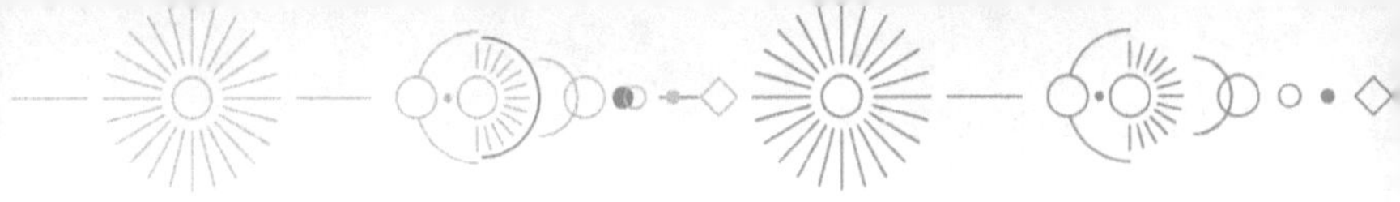

CHAPTER TWENTY-EIGHT
SCARS OF THE EARTH

The beast stepped from the human skin it shed and shook its head. For one terrible moment, the village could only stare in shock. Then a baby cried, and a woman with three small children screamed before ushering them away, which set off a chain reaction of panic. Men grabbed spears and some of the women joined them while the most vulnerable citizens fled.

The skinwalker hissed and growled as it stretched. My parents opened the cage to free Morra and me, and I ran to untie Tanu. His designated assassin had dropped a blade in his haste to flee, so I used it to cut the rope.

"Tanu, you stupid fool!" I gasped between breaths, wrapping my arms around him once he was free.

"You can call me names later, Akedia." He kissed the top of my head. "We need to take care of that."

The skinwalker roared once more, swinging a massive arm and knocking over a vendor cart as it ran toward me.

"Akedia Morestone." Its terrible voice boomed through the village, and it sounded as though a thousand demons spoke at once. *"I will especially enjoy feasting on your flesh."*

The high priest waved his arms and shouted at the creature. "Nevario!"

The skinwalker's head snapped toward the high priest, who looked far more worn and broken than he'd ever let on, before it rushed toward him. B'Ba launched a spear at its side. It sliced the beast but didn't land a fatal blow. The open wound dripped green ooze before resealing itself within seconds. Then it went for my father. I ran forward and screamed.

"You don't want any of them, skinwalker!" I shouted, standing with fiery rage in my chest. Any fear I might have had fizzled when I saw him try to attack B'Ba.

The demon turned, its glowing yellow eyes watching me with pleasure.

"Aw, the faithless one. Yes, it is you I want." The demon stalked toward me, grinning wickedly. *"But let us make an experiment. Ask Waikenu to spare you from my clutches. If you think He will do it and if He appears, I will leave."*

I had already asked Waikenu to speak to me in my hour of need, and He hadn't.

Or maybe...

He had?

Nothing manifested from the sky as I'd always imagined it would, but I had pieced together everything I needed for the counter-curse in time to spare Tanu from a horrible death. What if Waikenu was more of a presence lurking in everyday life than some kind of magical creature who could grant me wishes?

"I don't need to."

"What was that?" Its revolting body was now taller than the rooftops of our homes, and it stared down at only me as the villagers threw spears at its flesh.

"I said I don't need to!" I shouted. "I have nothing to prove to you, demon! Go back to where you came from!"

The skinwalker grew and grew, its hand now large enough to wrap around my entire body. It snatched me from the ground and lifted me to eye level. Its horrible voice was even deeper and louder now.

"Oh, you do, I'm afraid. Because without Waikenu, I will not leave. I will stay to drink more and more blood."

I could hear my mother's scream from below as the demon held me above the ground like a doll. I squirmed in its grasp and reached in my pocket to search for the stone. It was just a rock, but I felt compelled to hold it. The skinwalker tightened its hand. I could barely breathe. Spots sparkled at the edges of my vision. The demon brought me closer and whispered in my ear.

"I have feasted like a king in this ignorant village. Now you've gone and ruined it."

Lileena's happy face before she walked to the altar of her death made tears well in my eyes, but anger chased them away. She died at the mercy of this demon, but I couldn't stand the thought of him mocking the pride she felt in serving her people.

My hand finally found the rock. The minute my fingers wrapped around its cool surface, the skinwalker shrieked and dropped me.

The fall to the ground from such a height knocked the wind from me, and the stone bounced from my hand with the impact. When I looked up at the skinwalker, it was no longer as tall. Seeing that, I knew I needed to get that stone back. Something about it had altered the demon's state. We both leapt for it, dust clouding in the air around us as we tumbled in the dirt. The skinwalker tried to grab the stone and howled with pain upon contact.

I dove and grabbed it before pressing it to the beast's skin. The wail that resounded through the village pierced my ears, but I wouldn't let go. I had to hold that rock in place. The skinwalker shrank as it thrashed.

Finally, the thing collapsed, shaking the ground with its massive body. I panted, staring at the rock and down at the creature. It didn't move. I took a chance and nudged it with my foot and felt only the fleshy give of its lifeless body. Dead.

Spears lay scattered around its form. The villagers drew closer. My parents rushed to me, kissing my cheeks and holding me in the center of their tight embrace. I inhaled their scents—remnants of lavender from M'Ma's hair oils and the frankincense that always perfumed B'Ba's clothing even when it smelled mostly of body odor from a hard day's work.

"I missed you both more than you'll ever know," I cried, wiping tears from each of their faces. The creases in their skin as they smiled and sobbed with joy were like badges of hardship and love and hurt and laughter and sacrifice and a wisdom I could only hope to earn one day when the beauty of my soul would finally trace its presence on my face.

Behind them, Morra and Tanu waited, reminding me that they still didn't know the people who raised me. "Morra, Tanu, these are my parents."

M'Ma hugged a surprised Morra before looking at her. "You must have had a lot to do with keeping my girl alive."

"To be honest, she had a lot to do with saving my skin too." Morra winked at me when I smiled.

B'Ba bowed his head at Morra and then turned his attention on Tanu, who fidgeted under the sudden scrutiny. "I couldn't help but notice you kissed my daughter in front of the entire village."

"Well, sir, I was worried I'd never see her again and—"

B'Ba held up his hand to interrupt. "But I also couldn't help but notice you were willing to sacrifice your life to save hers." He grasped Tanu's wrist and pulled him close to wrap an arm around his back. "For that, I thank you... Just not for the first part."

M'Ma and Morra laughed while my ears burned. I didn't have much time to be embarrassed, though, as people rushed around us.

One man removed his hat and stared at his feet as he spoke to me. "Forgive me for the things I said when you entered this village."

A few others apologized for their words as well. In truth, I wasn't ready to forget just yet that the people who had watched me grow from an infant were so willing to turn on me, but I knew I could find forgiveness. Eventually. They had been nothing more than puppets dancing along a line their entire lives.

A few men had gathered around the beast, gathering closer to confirm its death. They nodded at me and walked away, talking about building a fire to dispose of the body.

"Akedia, you must be famished," M'Ma said, wrapping an arm around my shoulder and pulling me from the sight.

We were just about to retire to the mess hall for a meal when something thick and warm wrapped around my ankle and dragged me to the ground, pulling me across the dirt as I screamed. When I managed to twist myself around to see the source, I realized the skinwalker had awoken from what I thought had been death and sprouted a snake-like tail. It reeled me in as Tanu and my father tried to clutch my hands.

Its horrible echoing voice filled the air from every direction.

"You will not be rid of me so easily, little human girl. I have seen the sands of time and the depths of the least holy places. I will not be defeated by a child."

The villagers took up their spears from the ground and tried stabbing the thing, but it wasn't mortal. It couldn't be killed like a mortal. It drew me closer, opening its hideous jaws as I neared.

I tried to get the rock and press it to its skin again, but the thing was smarter this time. It ripped the stone from my hand and threw it so far, it disappeared into the sky. Some of the people darted after it, perhaps thinking they needed to help regardless of the futility, but I knew the monster would finish me before they ever returned. Tanu grabbed an abandoned sword and sliced through the end of the tail, freeing my ankle and pulling me upright.

"Run, Akedia!" he shouted at me.

I ran as hard as my feet could manage, but when I glanced over my shoulder, I saw the skinwalker shove Tanu aside and dart after me. My parents, Morra, and Tanu followed, shouting at the monster that ignored them as it pursued me for vengeance.

A swipe of the creature's claws sent me tumbling into the sand. It pounced on me, teeth bared as its jaw snapped. The others tried to jump on its back, but it flung them off.

"You have nothing left, girl."

Its hot breath was foul with rot and death. I turned my head to the side and saw more rocks scattered across the reddish dirt.

The one thing that had changed my uncle's stone into something extraordinary had been the counter-curse. It wasn't the rock itself. I rolled to the side from beneath the skinwalker and grabbed a pile of pebbles from the ground before bolting away. It shrieked, and at first I thought I'd angered it by slipping through its grasp by a hair, but when I turned, I saw Tanu had found a large stick and smacked the creature across the back of the head. B'Ba taunted it to get its attention.

Without wasting another breath, I whispered the counter-curse as quickly as possible and watched the stones in my palm. Only two lit up from the entire pile. It would have to be enough. I picked them out and dropped the rest. When the skinwalker grew bored with charging at Tanu and B'Ba and turned back to me, I was ready.

The ugly thing and I ran toward each other, but at the last minute, when it lunged to grab me, I ducked. It rolled over the top of me and stumbled to the ground. I jumped on its back and slammed the empowered pebbles against its skin.

The skinwalker screeched and thrashed. I held on, pressing those stones into its skin. If I let go, it would regain its energy. I needed to keep holding on as it shrank. My muscles ached with the fight of grasping the beast. I thought of my uncle and my best friend and everyone before them who had lost their lives to this devil, and I clamped onto it with every ounce of strength I could muster.

The skinwalker continued shrinking and shriveling, and then the earth beneath us rumbled.

"Don't let go, Akedia!" Morra cried. "This is it—hold on!"

What *it* was I couldn't know, but my instincts told me she was right. Something was happening. I hadn't been able to hold the stone to its skin for this long the first time, but now I understood its power. The earthquake became more fierce until it was an intense throttle. Still, I held on. The skinwalker thrashed on the ground, grabbing a nearby spear and chucking it with aimless desperation. I kept holding.

Then the ground split open—a quivering break in the earth with a fiery brilliance glowing from its depths. I looked at the weakened skinwalker, which was now smaller than me, and back at the growing rift. Then I picked up the monster and threw it inside.

Its wail echoed in my ears until it plummeted too far to hear its cries. Once the earth had its beast, the ground rumbled. My parents ran to me and held me in their arms as we looked on.

The earth continued to shake until the opening closed completely and all that was left in the place of the fiery gorge was a dark scar of freshly turned soil on the sandy surface.

The depths of the earth had consumed its skinwalker. It was back in the place it had been before it escaped to ravage my village. As the people emerged from their homes and hiding places to surround the scar along the ground, I knew we could never go back to what we had been before.

"Akedia," B'Ba cried as he rushed to hold me. A shaky victorious laugh escaped me as I turned to hug him. But my smile disappeared when I saw his tunic stained with blood seeping from the spear that protruded from his abdomen.

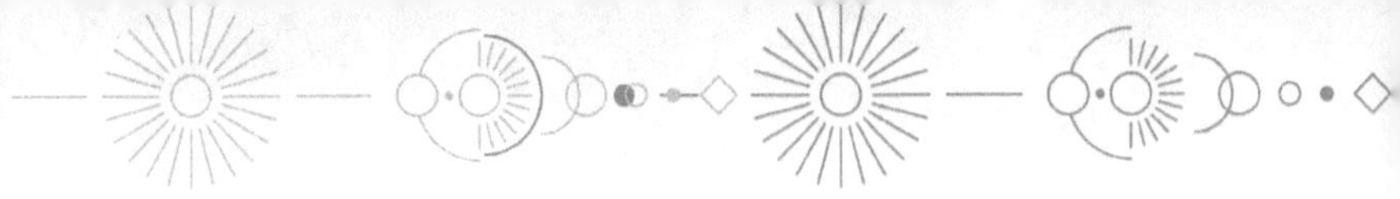

Chapter Twenty-Nine

THE EASTERN STARS

"B'Ba!" I screamed as he removed the spear. His legs buckled, and he fell to his hands and knees, coughing up blood. The dark liquid shimmered where it landed on the sandy soil.

"Armedes!" M'Ma cried. We placed hands on his shoulders until he collapsed and rolled onto his back. With redness gleaming on his dry lips and dirt caked between the lines on his sun-weathered face, B'Ba's glossy eyes searched the sky above. He grasped both of our hands.

I barked orders at the gathering crowd. "Someone, bring linens to staunch the blood! Bring alcohol! *Hurry!*"

"Akedia," B'Ba whispered, tearing his gaze from the departing clouds. "Akedia, listen..." When he coughed, more blood spewed from his mouth. M'Ma wailed.

I frowned and angrily shook my head despite the tears that streamed down my face. "B'Ba, we can fix this. *We can fix this!*"

He pressed a warm, leathery palm to my cheek. "My girl. Look at me."

The tears poured endlessly now as I shook my head again. I didn't want to look at him.

"*Look at me*, Akedia."

Finally, my eyes met his. He coughed but gave me his fatherly smile—the one that always told me everything would be ok. But how could he smile that smile when he was dying? Nothing would ever be ok again.

His large thumb wiped away another tear from my cheek. "You were not made for an ordinary life—your gifts are too great. Remember, your qualm is not with the sun god but with the people who distorted Him."

"How can you say that, B'Ba?" My voice cracked as I cried between angry words. "He's sitting here, letting you die, doing nothing. He is not real, B'Ba. If He were, He wouldn't let this happen. Waikenu—all the gods—they're *stories*, B'Ba."

I exchanged a glance with my mother, whose jaw had dropped with shock, and quickly looked away.

B'Ba smiled again. "One day, all that will be left of us will be our stories. That doesn't make us any less real."

His loving gaze turned to my mother, and he spoke to her in a language I couldn't understand. She sobbed and pressed her forehead to his, whispering more words that were foreign to me. There was so much I didn't know about my parents and how the skinwalker's reign had changed the life they knew before—a life they never spoke of.

When she sat upright, B'Ba looked at me and squeezed my hand. "Akedia, you will find your truth. And it might change as you do. There is nothing wrong with that. But on all your pathways, remember always to follow the light."

"*B'Ba*," I cried through another broken sob. "I don't want to spend the rest of my life missing you. It's too soon for that. *Please*, you have to fight."

"Look up, Akedia," he whispered. I noticed the brilliant purples and pinks shooting across the sky as the light faded. A single star shone. "You don't have to miss me if you know where to find me. Wherever you wander, look toward the eastern stars, and there I'll be."

"B'Ba..."

"Promise me, Akedia—" He coughed again, a deep wet sound as blood filled his lungs. "Promise me... you'll look for me there."

As his glistening eyes searched my face, I knew it was more than a simple request to stargaze. I also knew that no matter how many different ways I believed—or didn't believe—in one lifetime, there would always be a place for B'Ba to live on in some way.

"I promise."

M'Ma and I collapsed over him, our heads resting on his chest where we lay in the desert sands, the dry wind whipping around us in our grief. We stayed that way, tears streaming in endless rivers until B'Ba took his final breath and Waikenu's light went dark to make room for a star-studded sky.

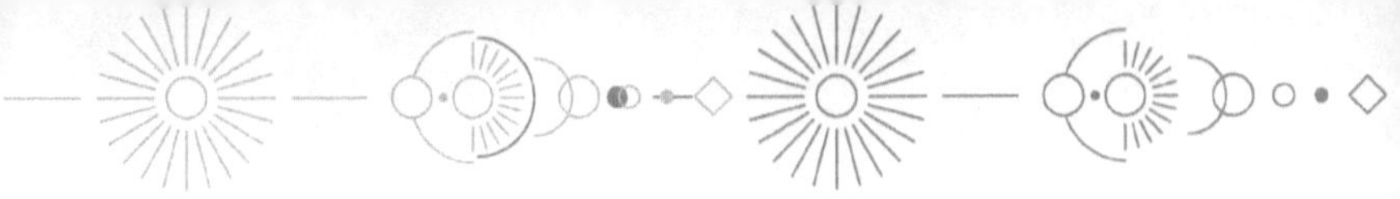

CHAPTER THIRTY

A BURIAL FOR MANY

A warm hand touched my shoulder, reminding me that I hadn't moved in a long while as I lay there curled over my father's body. I sat up and wiped my face, not caring that I had likely smeared dirt into the tears and left muddy trails on my cheeks.

"Akedia," Tanu said, his voice gentle and low. "How can I help? What should we do for his afterlife?"

What would B'Ba have wanted? To be prepared for his walk through the Field of Grains into the land of eternal peace, where the goat was friends with the coyote and trees were giant and bountiful?

M'Ma decided before I could. "We will have the embalmers clean and treat his body as prayers are said over him." She squeezed my hand. "When he is ready in ten days, we will lay him to rest."

I nodded, and Tanu waved for help from another man. I kissed B'Ba's forehead before they lifted his body together and marched him away with my mother leading them to the embalmer's temple.

The people of Bahmisi approached me where I sat in the dirt as the wind wailed in the vast openness. The collective grief hung over us all in a defeated silence. We had been tricked, deceived. The worst part was we had let our loved ones die in the process.

One woman's sob was the first to break the quiet. I turned to see Olana, Lileena's mother, weeping as she wilted to the ground. Her son, Athalo, ran to her side and wrapped comforting arms around her shoulders. I slowly stood and joined him in hugging the woman I considered a second mother. Lileena's loss would leave a scar on all our hearts. There was nothing to say to Olana. There was nothing I could do other than hold her in my arms, squeezing her hard as she convulsed with sorrow. The enlightenment she once believed her daughter had received through sacrifice had been nothing more than death as far as we could see it, and for the first time since watching her walk to the altar, we both could publicly grieve the loss.

Waikenu, if you are real in ways I don't understand, if you can hear me, bring comfort to this woman.

And me.

Another tear slid down the side of my nose as I fiercely pressed my lips to Olana's cheek before standing to look at my people. "We will honor them."

Once more I looked to the crowd as they seemed to wait for answers and spoke with more certainty. "When we bury my father, we will also have a burial for everyone lost."

In ten days' time, B'Ba was ready for his journey in the afterlife, though I had a feeling the fixings and prayers had been more for my mother's sake. And that was fine, I realized, for her to find comfort in that. I suppose it brought me some comfort too.

Before the ten days ended, I had led a team with wagons drawn by donkeys to the cave where the skinwalker kept the bodies. We moved every bone into town and placed them on funeral litters the carpenters had worked double time to construct. We never had the need before to bury so many at once.

On the night of the burial, the sky was black and dotted with brilliant stars. A warm glow from many torchlights followed the litters of skeletons in a line to the Sands of Muertin—our sacred burial lands beyond the village. M'Ma, Olana, and I walked behind the litter carrying B'Ba and Lileena's remains, along with others—some who were indiscernible. I hoped Uncle Peko was somewhere on the litter with B'Ba, but there was no way to know.

High Priest Vikton walked behind the masses with his head bent and eyes swollen and red. When we arrived at the place of the dead, everyone placed their litter on the ground and gathered for a prayer. Normally, they would have looked to the high priest, but instead, they looked to me. I couldn't stand the attention, and I knew it was not deserved. They needed someone who was faithful—someone who understood their love of the gods and how best they could heal and move forward.

I grasped M'Ma's hand as I spoke to the crowd. "My mother knows each of you, and she knew the dead when they lived. M'Ma, would you please offer us some words?"

She looked at me, eyes widening with uncertainty at first, but I nodded a quiet encouragement. She nodded back and cleared her throat as those gathered became silent to listen. Watching M'Ma stand before the crowd felt right in a way I couldn't explain. Vikton looked up briefly and then down at his feet once more, as though his only wish was to become invisible.

"What can we say in the aftermath of such a devastating tragedy?" she began, her voice small at first but growing in confidence. "We... *I*... could not see what was right in front of us. And we allowed a demon to prey on our village." My mother's eyes searched the crowd and landed on Vikton. "What can be said for this, High Priest? Will those of the temple be held accountable?"

This high priest, who always had something to say, was silent for a long moment. When he finally spoke, the man I'd grown up thinking was part god looked like the shattered remains of a mortal man with dark circles under his eyes.

"When I began to suspect Nevario was a skinwalker and sought out information from other temples, it was already too late," Vikton said. "Too many were lost. The only person who was able to defeat him was this young lady here." My heart raced as he pointed to me and a sea of eyes fell upon me. Tanu rubbed a supportive hand on my back. "Please, Akedia. Tell us what gave you such wisdom."

I turned to squeeze Tanu's hand and then looked at the staring faces of my people. Many had spat on me when first I'd returned. They had locked away my parents and refused to challenge the murders of dozens of loved ones. I could have felt angry and bitter. I could have jeered at them just the same before walking away. But as I looked at them, all I could see was the heartbroken lostness I'd felt since the day I decided I would not become an offering. The only difference between them and me was my world had burst at the seams a little bit sooner.

"We will bury our loved ones and know that, whether or not it was Waikenu's will, they died happy to serve their people," I said, glancing at Olana, whose face shimmered with the constant flow of tears. "You asked me what gave me the wisdom to expose the skinwalker, High Priest Vikton, but it wasn't wisdom—it was the search for it. And I think we've paid dearly for believing we already had all the answers." I looked around and realized I was no longer afraid to speak my truth to these people, and yet I no longer needed to. I felt everything burn inside me like a strength

I had never known. "Let us place our loved ones in the sands."

The burial dancers performed a solemn march with faces painted like ghouls to help guide the dead into the afterlife as the gravediggers opened a plot of land large enough to fill with the remains of many bodies. Torches flickered in the night, and the steady thump from the drums resonated in my heart. M'Ma, Olana, Athalo, and I placed B'Ba and Lileena in the grave.

"Goodbye, B'Ba," I whispered through a choked sob.

Then I turned to hold the bony hand that wore the bracelet one last time.

"Goodbye, dear sister." Tanu held my shoulders and reached around to kiss my cheek as we stood back and watched people with shovels cover the bodies with sand and earth.

A piece of who I used to be disappeared beneath the piling dirt along with those who had lost their lives for their beliefs.

Chapter Thirty-One

Healing

The next morning, M'Ma made breakfast as I stared at the ceiling in my bedroom, not sure what to feel as I counted the cracks in the clay above my head. Someone knocked, and M'Ma entered before I could answer.

"You slept late this morning," she said.

I sat upright when she found a seat on the edge of my bed. Comfort sank into my heart as her delicate hands smoothed over my hair the way they had since I was little.

"Oh, M'Ma," I cried, allowing myself to collapse in her arms.

"My girl. What an extraordinary adventure you have been on."

I looked up at her. "You and B'Ba have told me since I was a child that Waikenu is real—that He pulls the sun across the sky, giving us food and life. Are you not disappointed with your faithless daughter?"

M'Ma clutched my chin. "My dear child, we are but simple humans, searching for answers. You are not the first to question, and you will not be the last."

I hugged her tightly, then pulled back to look at her. "Uncle Peko was onto something before he was sacrificed."

"I think you're right. He tried to tell your father and me something the night they took him away, but I wouldn't listen. At the time, it made me sick to think he had possibly turned wicked." My mother looked at her hands and shook her head. "But what makes you say that? What did you find on your travels?"

"The counter-curse, M'Ma. It made Uncle's stone become... powerful," I said. "And then some of the pebbles I found were able to contract the same magic."

She nodded, thinking. "They must have been of the same mineral. Many magical elements can only adhere to other certain types of elements. I'm sure he was getting close to figuring it all out, but he ran out of time, so he left you with a clue when he realized no one would listen." M'Ma playfully nudged my shoulder. "Mage Matka says she was wrong about you. She told me this morning that what you did took a great deal of power."

I smiled briefly. "What use to her is a faithless priestess?"

We were both silent for a long while, and then she kissed my cheek.

"The young man, your friend, Tanu, calls," she said. "I invited him in for breakfast. He's waiting in the dining room."

"Thanks, M'Ma," I whispered.

Tanu's black eyes captured mine the minute I walked into the dining room, where he sat at the table. The neighbors were kind enough to offer him a place to sleep each night, since our home couldn't accommodate a guest. After the kiss she'd witnessed, M'Ma didn't want him under our roof either.

"Hi," I muttered, suddenly wishing my mother wasn't there at all for the first time since I'd gotten her back.

He stared for a half-second longer then shook his head as though he'd just remembered something. "Pharaoh found us. I found him drinking from the river this morning... near where we met."

"That's wonderful news, Tanu. Did the gray return as well?"

He shook his head. "Someone probably found her and decided to keep her. Pharaoh cannot be caught."

"Well, I'm glad you have your horse back," I replied, and we stared at one another, smiling like fools until M'Ma startled us by clearing her throat.

"I invited your other friend to breakfast as well," she said just as someone knocked on the door.

When Morra entered, her face was pale and shimmering with a fine layer of sweat. We all jumped to our feet.

"Morra, what's wrong?" I asked, running to her side to support her weight.

She leaned on me and showed me her arm. Dark bluish color now covered her once olive-toned arm.

M'Ma ushered her to my room.

"This way, Morra," she said. "Let us see what we can do for you."

Morra shivered as she lay under the blankets, more sweat pouring from her skin. I ran to get a washcloth and a bowl of fresh water, then returned to wipe it over her forehead.

"M'Ma," I said, urgently. "Morra was cursed. She has a condition that only stringer can help. Do we know anyone who has the plant?"

M'Ma tapped Tanu's arm. "Go to the market and find the herbalist's cart. Ask quietly if he has stringer. It's unlikely, but he might."

Tanu nodded and fled from my home. M'Ma rooted around our apothecary shelves to find something that would at the very least relieve the pain. She poured different tinctures down Morra's throat. The concoctions helped her sleep, but the blue-blackness under her skin would not recede as it did when she took stringer.

"What should we do, M'Ma?" I whispered. "How can she go on living her life like this?"

M'Ma frowned, staring at Morra's arm, and then her eyes snapped to me. "Stringer was banned here long ago, when Stiliki the fisherman got too much in his blood. Do you remember the night they brought him to me, thinking I could heal him? You were young, Akedia, and it frightened you very much. You hid in the pantry for hours." I remembered now. The man had shouted wicked things like a monster was living inside him, making me realize the ugly feeling I had connected to the tonic and Morra's marks. "The substance is a compound of the desert lotus flower and makasna, another powerful herb found in the high mountains. When used properly, makasna cleans the blood..." She thought for another moment. "We need someone with strong magic."

Tanu returned empty-handed, as expected, unable to find a soul with stringer in Bahmisi. For a people held captive under the fear of their sun god, an illegal substance was not likely to be found among them, but M'Ma offered another idea.

"Bring us the high priest." We frowned at her. The man had become a recluse since my mother had unofficially taken his role of leading the people. But she shooed Tanu back out the door with directions to his home. "Just bring him here. I'll explain later."

When Tanu returned with High Priest Vikton, I found myself stunned at his lowly appearance. He was unable to stand tall as he once had. His beard grew unkempt and scraggly around his thin face. He no longer wore the head cloth and kept his thinning hair in a low bun.

I remembered the day he came to our home to tell my family I would be the next offering. I realized now he was only relaying the message of the skinwalker who had poisoned his thoughts to control him, but it was still bizarre to see him less god-like in my presence.

"How can I help?" he muttered.

M'Ma took his hand and gave it an encouraging shake. "High Priest, you may feel horrible about what has happened. But you must know we still need you, even if it's in a different form now." M'Ma explained the curse that had poisoned Morra's blood. "You are still the most powerful crafter of magic in this village. Can you heal this woman?"

The high priest frowned and sat on the bed, pressing a hand to Morra's forehead and staring at her for a long moment. Her eyes weakly looked up before they closed again.

"I will try."

For the next hour, we ran around at his beck and call, crushing herbs and boiling water, preparing rags and cooking tonics. I wasn't sure how he knew the recipes and methods without a single glance in a magic book, but that was probably how he became the high priest in the first place, before the skinwalker infected our lives.

Finally, amidst the steam and the haziness of cooking, Vikton's concoction was ready. He dipped his fingers into the bowl and slathered the paste-like substance over her arms, where the infection had always been the worst. With his eyes closed, he began chanting a song for healing that grandmothers were known to sing to sick children in the village. His voice was so rich and beautiful. I realized I had heard it often in temple ceremonies, but I'd never heard it full of such emotion before.

We watched as Morra writhed with pain, and I clutched Tanu's hand, feeling sick that I couldn't help her. He kissed the top of my head and wrapped me in his arms.

Soon a greenish glow emanated around her. The high priest kept chanting. Then Tanu chanted a low hum in the background, keeping in tune with Vikton's voice without necessarily knowing the words as their voices merged in a heartbreaking harmony and the light around Morra grew. The more they chanted, the more the light grew and the more Morra thrashed.

"Open the windows!" the high priest shouted between chants. M'Ma obliged, and the draft sucked the curtains outdoors.

Morra continued to writhe. I wanted to scream for them to stop—it didn't appear to be doing anything but hurting her—until she opened her mouth, and a black cloud escaped from her lips, swirling into the air above her and flashing like lightning. Morra's mouth remained open as an endless stream of darkness rose from her body like a storm right inside our home. The cloud then funneled toward the window, forming a tornado as it escaped. More black clouds poured from her lips. I thought it would never leave her, but at last it ended; her eyes rolled to the back of her head, and she wilted from the ordeal.

The high priest's forehead beaded with sweat as he lifted her sleeves to expose the natural color of her skin. "Whoever poisoned her with that magic used a heavy dose. But it is gone. Let her rest now."

He walked to the door as everyone fussed about giving Morra the proper amount of blankets. I followed him out.

"Vikton," I called. He turned to me, and we stood outside my family home in the dusty alleyway. Someone else might have thanked him for helping Morra, but those words didn't come to me. "You failed us. You failed everyone."

How could I want to slap him and spit at his feet and fall into his arms sobbing all at once?

"I know, child," he whispered. He turned to leave, but I stopped him.

"I know it won't be easy to turn things around after what has happened." I waited. Anger and heartbreak still fueled too many of my words, which gave me reason enough to limit them.

He nodded. "I know, Akedia. I was your leader. I should have sniffed out the evil that had penetrated our lands years ago. I should have sought counsel from other priests in other temples before following blindly. That was my responsibility to you and this village." A tear glistened in his eye, but he blinked it away. "I waited too long to listen to my own doubt. And even then, I didn't listen to my instincts. I justified the cave of bodies I found after I bumped into you with the goat. I was convinced it was all an evil mirage to turn me away from the faith. Nevario then said *you* had crafted that mirage, which was why we needed to offer you to the sun god immediately. He said you were turning wicked."

I rolled my eyes.

Vikton continued. "I kept visiting the cave to make sense of it. Even though I could smell the rot and touch the bones, I wanted so badly to believe it was all an illusion. Did you know I went all the way to Kuniki to seek information?"

"Yes," I muttered. When his eyes widened, I shrugged. "We saw you in the temple library. I was afraid you would capture me if you caught sight of me."

He turned his head to the side and smiled. "Clever." His grin faded. "When I was unable to find the information I needed, I came home and still thought maybe I was wrong. By then Nevario had discovered you and was bringing you home. I was ready to torture you. I fought so hard to ignore the truth, just because it was ugly."

I decided to do something I would never have dreamed of doing before. I placed my hand on the holy man's arm as though he was just an ordinary person.

"Today, we are broken. Tomorrow, we will be better for it." I boldly held my hand in place, hoping the gesture wasn't offensive somehow. I'd grown up looking at this man as an all-powerful god, and here I was offering comfort.

He looked down at my hand on his arm and then placed his own hand over mine. "Thank you, child. If this village will still have me, I will try to do right by everyone."

I smiled. "I think we need you more than ever right now."

"I have come to learn everything about Tanu and Mor-ra and their crimes," said the high priest, and for a half second, my throat tightened. "I've already sent word to the high priests beyond our realm to notify them of the misunderstanding. Their names will be cleared once my birds arrive at their destinations with their messages."

It probably wasn't the most proper thing to do, but I couldn't ignore the overwhelming sense of gratitude. I flung my arms around his neck and gave him a hug. He only chuckled and awkwardly patted my back.

"Thank you, High Priest. Thank you."

"You are welcome," he said, turning to leave.

"I just have one question..."

He stopped and faced me. "Yes?"

"When we were on the run, Nevario, or the skinwalker, found me in the jungle. When his men fell, he ran away instead of attacking me. Now, I understood why he never killed me in front of witnesses. But why do you think he never took the chance when we were alone in the jungle?"

The high priest frowned and rubbed his chin. "How peculiar... And a very good question since he was out to silence you. Why did his men fall?"

"They were darted by the Mialinis—people we met in the jungle."

A grin spread over his face. "There's your answer. Those cannibals follow an old mage named Huma—"

"Yes, I met her."

"Huma can see through a skinwalker's disguise. And the Mialinis would have exposed him. He probably saw those darts and headed for the hills as fast as possible." He placed a hand on my shoulder. "You were very brave to do what you've done."

I nodded and watched him walk away, overcome by the latest of my revelations. My high priest, knower of all things worth knowing, was indeed just a man who was now embarking on a journey similar to my own. Perhaps Bahmisi would stick to its faith and find another way to worship the sun god. Maybe it would become a village of thinkers, who could sit for hours and weigh the heavy questions of the world.

I looked at my shadow, which was almost nonexistent. The sun was at its highest, most powerful point in the day, and I smiled.

Waikenu was possibly real. Or He was possibly not a He at all—perhaps there were other reasons unknown for the ways of the sun's movement. Or maybe there was something else out there beyond my understanding that made me and all of humankind what it was, and I would not know the answer in this lifetime or the next. For the first time since losing my religion, that was fine with me. I was at peace with not knowing, happy to speculate, and excited to learn. What I had learned so far was that I didn't need to believe, or even disbelieve, to be counted as whole. To be whole, all I needed was to search for light when the world had gone dark.

I ran inside to find Tanu at the kitchen table, waiting for me to return. "I want to travel, Tanu. I want to find other *sun gods* and beliefs and learn what people are like beyond the sands. I want to see everything."

He laughed, eyes twinkling at me. "*Everything?*"

I nodded and smiled back at him. "Everything. And I want you to come with me. I can't think of a better guide than the one I've had."

He looked at my mother, waiting for a reply. She wrapped me in her arms.

"I have taught her many things from life and from her school books. But she outgrows me. I cannot think of a better education than that of true experience," she said.

Then she let me go and hugged Tanu. "Bring her back to me in one piece. I couldn't bear another loss."

My bare feet danced into the center of town as singers bellowed fiercely and the drum beats resonated in my wild heart. The sun was going to set soon, and the village of Bahmisi was alive with a celebration unlike any it had had before. This day, we rejoiced in our freedom from the skinwalker, while remembering those who were lost.

Other dancers with painted skin and jingling jewelry swirled around me, and even Tanu joined the madness. Watching him laugh during the rush of movement made my heart happy.

The village of Bahmisi wouldn't bring a new offering to the sacrifice altar, but we danced to unhinge something inside us—a new identity, a chance to heal. Tanu and I had plans to leave in the morning, but that night was something I couldn't miss.

Known for being the best dancer, M'Ma showed off in the center as the people whooped and cheered at her stunts. My attention drifted to the outskirts of the madness to Morra and the high priest. He held her elbow in support as she walked with him, the two lost in conversation. They were both still recovering from the wounds that had come before. Together they could heal.

"Can you dance like your mother?" Tanu's voice pulled me away from watching Morra and the high priest.

I grinned and lifted the hem of my flowing skirt. "I was holding back before."

We became lost in the movement and music, swirling around other dancers but constantly reconnecting. I glanced at the sky and saw the glow of the approaching sunset, so I grabbed Tanu's hand.

"Follow me." I led him away from the festivities and along a path I'd traveled many times to watch my goats.

We climbed to the top of the hill and saw the village and the river below, with the open desert beyond. The sun sank into that wide-open horizon as colors lit up the sky. B'Ba was right. Sunset was a spiritual time of the day. Even if Waikenu was not who I always believed Him to be, seeing the day end in majesty made me remember that it was through human beings, in their community, that I had realized the counter-curse to evil. Even if they had welcomed that evil into their hearts, the answer to defeat it was also there.

"Well, my fearless voyager," Tanu said, kissing my cheek. I turned to face him with a broad grin. His light brown skin and black eyes looked like perfection in the golden glow of sunset, and it took my breath away. "You said you wanted to see everything. Where should we begin?"

I watched the sun fade from the desert sky as night blanketed all that lay before us and hot pink and orange formed a living piece of art before our eyes. In that last glimmer peeking over the horizon, I found my answer—the map that would see us to the ends of the earth and back again.

"Let us follow the light."

The End.

A Note from Alythia

I began writing THE RUNAWAY OFFERING in 2017, two years after signing with my literary agent, Moe Ferrara of BooksEnds Literary Agency. We shopped it around to editors, who offered oftentimes conflicting feedback, before ultimately tabling the project. The process took years, and it broke my heart because this was a book directly from my heart.

I was raised in the Greek Orthodox church and, in part, by my maternal grandparents while my single mother was at work. I remember my grandfather—my papou—sitting in his office every day, typing stories on his loud typewriter. I would find out later that they were the bittersweet accounts of leaving his war-torn village in Greece. I would also find out later that, sometimes, the click-click-clack of keys produced an angry letter to the church, criticizing how it had become a business and not what Jesus ever intended. In his youth, he had considered becoming a priest, but he couldn't ignore the contradictions.

I wish I'd known that sooner, before he was gone and became one of the eastern stars, as he said he would. Because even though I believed in something greater than us all, the doubt I had in my youth made me feel deeply alone. That doubt was magnified when I was a pregnant teen, in line to take holy communion as I sought out ways to find comfort and community during an incredibly scary time. In front of the entire congregation, the priest told me I couldn't receive the body and blood of Christ because I was pregnant out of wedlock at 19. Jesus, I thought, wouldn't have turned me away, and yet the church had. Was that truly a reflection of Him?

Along my belief journey, I met and spoke with many people from various religious backgrounds who, like me, were exploring doubt and seeking truth. While there are plenty of funny memes or commentary online about deconstructing from organized religion, one thing the humor doesn't always capture is the intense feeling of loss when you stop believing what you were told. As we entered into the pandemic, several of my friends from churches that were heavily steeped in the political identity rhetoric stepped away, leaving behind lifetimes of tradition and family members who didn't understand. The grief as they shared their stories with me was palpable. We agreed we still believed in *something*, just not... like that.

I returned to this book years later, thinking I would find something that would make me cringe or roll my eyes, as writers are apt to loathe their old work. Instead, I found myself crying and realizing that even if it didn't fit into a tidy publishing box—even if I only sold one copy—I needed to publish it. With Moe's blessing, I decided to become a hybrid author and produce this particular series independently. (We are currently working on projects that will be pitched to trade pubs.) Because even if it touches one reader who might be feeling alone, the investment of time and money will be worth it to me. Much like its very theme, THE RUNAWAY OFFERING would not fit into a traditional box, and it was never meant to.

As for my papou, after the anger faded and the end of his life neared, at his request, my mother took him back to the church where he sat in the front row, listening to the ancient chants, staring at gilded icons, and weeping like a child. It was as though he realized his sun god never stopped letting the light shine while he was away.

THE RUNAWAY OFFERING is book one of a planned series. Please consider leaving a review!

Subscribe for updates at https://runawayoffering.com/subscribe.

Connect with me on social media:

Instagram (@alythiaconner)

Tiktok (@alythiaconner)

Facebook (@alythiaconner)